Goddess Bound

Healer Series Book Six

Sharilyn Skye

This book is a work of fiction. Names, characters, places, and incidents are the product of the author's imagination. Any resemblance to actual events or persons living or dead is coincidental.

Dark Horse Publishing

Morgantown, WV

To Mark, my original fan. Thanks for always pushing and cheering. Someday, we'll race down the Bypass to the Bypass again with only our parking lights to see by.

Special thanks to Heather for her mad skills and ability to ignore my steely glares when she points out my mistakes.

~

Riding slowly through the woods, I noticed the way light played off the river that could be seen through the brush, the way a red tail's wings brushed the trees above, and how chipmunks darted right and left to avoid my horse's hooves. All the times I had dashed down these trails in the name of relaxation, I had missed this.

In the rush to get away from the chaos of life, I forgot that peace can be found anywhere; you just need to look for it.

~Sharilyn Skye, *Finding Peace in Times of Chaos,* original publication date 2005 in Stories Of Strength.

Chapter 1

I dropped the box on the floor of our bedroom and blew from my eyes the errant strand of long auburn hair that had escaped from the fat ponytail lying down my back. I looked around the bedroom that would be mine now. For a decade, my home had been the one constant in the shifting sands of my life. But now I was moving on and moving in.

The Governor of the Eastern Region of Vampires, President of the American Vampire Association, Oldest Fae hybrid in the world, and the Great Goddess's own son dropped a box next to mine. He kissed my cheek, surveying our new space.

The walls were painted in shades of gray. White trim and wide crown molding made it look sharp and clean. The carpet was thick, plush, and the lightest shade of gray possible as to not be white.

I had warned Aedan that between the horse shit on my shoes and the blood often speckling his clothing that such a light color was a bad idea. He had informed me that I would take my shoes off before coming inside.

I agreed.

I had informed him that there was going to be a washer in the garage and that he would strip off his bloody clothes and put them in it before coming inside.

He agreed.

See? Compromise.

The sleek, modern, black platform bed that I had chosen was covered in a dark gray, custom-made comforter with a large scarlet heron stitched onto the front. The color of the heron matched the light-proof curtains covering the floor-to-ceiling windows making up the corners of the room. The infinity windows made it seem like we were suspended in air and whatever beauty nature offered.

His and her walk-in closets, complete with separate dressing areas, stood waiting to be filled. Aedan's would fill much faster than mine, although he was trying to change that. He snuck clothes in for me at an alarming rate.

There was no luxury that these rooms did not contain. The bathroom was larger than my former bedroom, and Aedan had the oversized tub built custom for me. The shower had more jets and steam than was reasonable, and, in truth, we could stay in these rooms forever and never need the rest of the monstrosity surrounding them.

The kitchen was also custom and contained more appliances and counter space than one human living with one vampire could ever need. It was double the size of the one in his former quarters and was a testament to high gloss, expensive tastes, and stainless steel.

It had been featured in Architectural Digest magazine; actually, the entire house was. Southern Living did a twenty-page spread on the place as well, and LarAedan was now a hashtag that trended more often than it should. We were famous, or perhaps infamous was a better word.

Aedan's house had been torched and burnt to the ground just a few months ago, and the graceful beast that grew from the ashes was a marvel. The mix of Old Charleston and modern lines made it stunning. Our suite was massive, much larger than my old place across the field; we had an entire floor to ourselves. Aedan's contractor, Guy, and his crews worked night and day to finish our home in just a few short months.

Yes. Our home.

I had agreed to bind with Aedan for a year and a day, as in the ways of old. He had asked for marriage, and I almost jumped on a boat and sailed to China when he brought it up. In the end, his mother came up with the compromise of a year and a day handfasting that made us both happy.

We could decide after the original agreement expired on how to move forward, and I was comfortable with that. We didn't fight about much, but when we did, it was epic, often involving shouting and wild magic followed by fantastic makeup sex. I had no complaints about that part. But old habits die hard, and I was terrified of making a lifetime commitment, especially when our lifetimes could be extremely long. Painfully long. Like, long as hell long.

Hence the year and a day solution. Because of the looming war with my grandmother, recent unrest among the supernatural community, and the chaos of our lives, we hadn't set a date for the actual ceremony. But my ability to avoid it entirely was quickly vanishing.

"I think that is it," he said, looking around the room at the stacks of boxes we had amassed on the floor. He pulled me to him, bruising my lips with his. "The first night in our new home," he added with a soft sigh.

I sank onto a chair in the reading area because, according to Aedan, we needed one of those; the living room wasn't enough. Neither was the office, apparently.

Through the open doors and windows in the house, I could hear laughter. The comfortable feel of the new place threaded through my bones, and the sounds of moving furniture and the unpacking of belongings drifted in the air.

"It'll take us all night and probably a few more to get settled, but yeah, it's great. I can't believe how beautiful it is and how fast Guy got it done." A hot cross breeze blew, ruffling my sweaty hair.

July is one of the hottest months pretty much everywhere, and Maryland is no exception. Yet we had the windows and French doors open anyway to disperse the smell of new carpet and paint. Huge paddle ceiling fans over the reading area and the bed moved the air even more, making the heat bearable; it felt like home.

Speaking of home, I hadn't been to my beach house in Pawleys Island for months, and it was beginning to wear on me. My mom and dads had been there multiple times. Keelin and her mates had been there. Jeremy and Sarah had gone back once following Aedan's return, but me? I had not been.

The clinic had been so busy that I had to hire an assistant. She worked with me three or four days a week, checking patients in, getting vital signs, and managing office-type things. She was the daughter of a local Lycanthrope and a nursing student. Bethany had saved my ass lately, and I was grateful. Bethany had been to my beach house for vacation; she deserved it, but it still rankled.

"Anamcara?" Aedan moved to stand by me, the concern on his face growing with each minute that passed.

Forcing my attention outward, I finally responded, "Hey, sorry, babe. I just got lost in my head for a minute." Shaking off the last of my thoughts, I turned my gaze to him.

"What were you thinking?" he asked.

Oh, Gods, the dreaded 'what are you thinking about question.' I didn't want to answer but knew I needed to. "I don't want to say; it will make me sound like an ass."

"As you frequently sound like an ass, go ahead. You can tell me anything, please." He sank in front of me, his gorgeous multifaceted whiskey-colored eyes meeting mine.

Taking a deep breath, I started, "I'm excited about this place, I am, but it's been so long since I had a break. Since we had a break, Aedan. We've been working so hard, and I just miss, uh, the beach," I paused, leaving out the word 'home.' As much as I loved my life and loved being where I was, South Carolina would always be home to me.

"I see," he said, his eyes softening. "And you thought I would be angry about that?"

"I don't know. Yes? No? You've worked so hard to get this place ready. I don't want to seem ungrateful." I looked at him with what I hoped came across as cute and hopeful but probably just looked like I was constipated.

"Let us go." He scooped me up from the chair, tossing me over his shoulder like a suit jacket. Ignoring my curses and attempts to hit him, he carried me down the stairs, across the expansive and tastefully magnificent foyer, and out through the kitchen. In the garage, he unceremoniously dumped me onto the front seat of his brand new, blacked-out, two-million-dollar McLaren P1. He had dubbed this one his midlife crisis purchase. Still, he had a thing for McLaren's, so that might not be true. He added the P1 to the stable of new or collectible cars he bought over a lifetime and kept in storage downtown. He had moved most of them to the massive garage under the new house, making it look and feel like an exotic car storage facility. I love cars and had never seen over half the ones gleaming under soft LED lighting.

I struggled with the concept of Aedan having a midlife crisis at all. How does a two-thousand-year-old vampire faerie hybrid define midlife? Better yet, how do they define a crisis? I wasn't sure, but as the gull-wing doors of the sexy, multi-million-dollar vehicle dropped closed, I thought maybe it wasn't far off.

He had changed in subtle ways these past few months. His face was more often than not covered in the dark scruff of a burgeoning beard. He had let the top of his hair grow shaggy but kept the sides short; he looked like a bad boy skateboarder. After he came home from his abduction and torture, he had cut his long hair in a severe, almost military fade; now, it had grown enough to look like the wild creature he is.

"What are you doing?" I asked, turning to stare at him as he manhandled me.

"We are leaving." He flipped up the cover on the ignition and pressed the button, opening the garage door.

"What do you mean? We can't leave. We haven't even unpacked. The house is wrecked." I turned at him, angry now.

"Call Bethany and tell her to take a few days off. Call Noah and tell him you're going to shunt patients his way. Call everyone and tell them we are leaving and to fuck off. I do not care." Nonplussed, he backed out of the garage, shifting the car into gear and leaving rubber streaks on his newly poured concrete.

"Aedan, what the hell?" I squeaked; I'll admit it. I'm not too proud to squeak. I didn't have a purse and only had my cell phone because it was in my back pocket when I got tossed like a sack of potatoes over Aedan's six-foot four-plus inch shoulder.

He grinned at me, taking the driveway as fast as it would allow. "Alexa, call the airport."

"Alexa? When the hell did you get Alexa?" Just when I thought the old man was in a routine, he threw me; maybe it was a midlife crisis.

Ignoring me, Aedan spoke calmly to a man named Joe, asking him to 'ready the jet.'

What the hell?

Joe, no doubt, thought he was an accessory to kidnapping if he heard me screaming in the background.

"Stop shouting, Mo Chroi," Aedan said when he disconnected the call. He reached across the seat, taking my hand and bringing it to his lips. "You are right; we have not had a break. We have not been anywhere together, ever. Let us remedy that. We have nine homes on four continents. Where would you like to go?"

"We can't just go, Aedan."

"It's too late; we already went." I looked over at him. The red highlights in his short, molasses-colored hair caught the light coming through the windows, warming his face despite the illegal level of tint on them. As the smile graced his lips, I stopped protesting. He looked happy and free at that moment.

I liked it.

"I want to go to the beach- my beach, but we can't, so you pick." I settled into my seat, relaxing against the butter-soft black leather.

"Why can we not go there?" he asked, keeping his eyes on the road but his attention on me.

"The spell. My parents even strengthened it."

He tilted his head back and roared, laughing louder than I had ever heard. "You believed that nonsense?" He gripped my hand, rubbing his thumb over the pad of my palm.

"I mean, yeah, they said they were going to." I cocked my head at him, trying to understand his laughter.

"What do you recall about that first day with them together and the first time they headed down to your beach house?"

"Um."

"Do you remember the way they looked at one another?"

"Well…"

"Building that magic would have taken them the better part of a day to complete. I assure you; they did not waste time replenishing it. Besides, I asked them to remove it." He downshifted, revving the engine as he eased onto Route 140.

"You what?" I asked, my voice dropping. I was unsure how I felt about what he said.

"I asked them to remove it, and they agreed. We are engaged, and the truth about the supernatural is out in the open; there is no longer a need to hide. You love the beach, and I love you. I may not love sand in my swim trunks, but I will love nothing more than to watch you swim in the surf. I want to spend time with you in your true home and see the ocean reflected in your eyes." He kept his eyes glued to the road, ignoring me carefully as he spoke.

"Oh." For just a minute, I had been angry, only one, but he was right. I didn't need cover spells and camouflage anymore. We could be together, in the open, wherever we wanted; there was no point in the spell over Pawleys Island anymore.

"You're right, this time, but don't get used to it, and next time, please run it by me. I feel like both of us should make any big decisions."

"And this is why I love you; you will keep me in line. You are correct; I apologize. We should have discussed it." He kissed my fingers again, returning his attention to the road but not releasing my hand.

I settled deeper into the leather seats of his sweet new ride. I would never buy something like this for myself, but I would enjoy someone else's ridiculously expensive whip. Grania was teaching me street slang. Funny, that.

Scenery flew by, and in no time, we were at the private airstrip at BWI. Aedan's Jet was fueled and waiting; our bags were grabbed, and we were escorted onto it. The door whisked closed behind us in a soft whoosh.

I had never been on Aedan's plane; I felt like the First Lady as I walked through the body of the thing. It was incredible.

I was seated, buckled, a glass of Grey Goose in my hand, and in the air within five minutes, I could see the draw. Never had I dreamed my life would be like this. Who would? Some days I forgot that I was a Faerie Princess in truth.

"How long can we stay?" I asked after we were settled.

"As long as you wish."

"Now, you know that's not true." I sipped my vodka and watched him.

"It is true. Grania is more than capable of keeping our affairs in order while we are gone, thanks to you. We are both available by phone and can be back home within two hours if necessary. We can stay as long as you wish."

"My patients."

"Are fine," Aedan interrupted. "Noah will care for them. They survived before you arrived on the scene. Mostly, anyway."

I launched a neck support pillow at him.

"That's not funny." I shot him a glare, even though it was kind of funny; I wasn't admitting it. And he was right, but I wouldn't tell him that.

The plane leveled out, and Aedan got up from the seat beside me, moving comfortably about the cabin, sending texts, and sipping something expensive. I unbuckled my seatbelt and went exploring.

The Gulfstream G650 had twelve single seats that swiveled and two large couches that faced one another. The interior was done in cream, silver, and black and was sleek and modern. There was a small kitchen and a large wet bar, and an even larger bathroom was at the end of the aisle leading to a bedroom. The plane had a bedroom. I wondered if that was normal or if that was some creepy, vampire sex thing. Oh, wait…This was my creepy vampire; I narrowed my eyes and turned to Aedan.

"What's with the bedroom, babe?"

"I often travel overseas, and I used to require much more rest than I do of late." Aedan's voice whispered in my ear, right in my ear. He had been across the cabin just a second ago. I jumped, then punched him on the arm. Hard.

The bed stretched out before us; cream covers pristine and just begging to get messed up.

I started to tug him forward.

He nipped up my neck, drawing blood, then licked the wound closed without taking any while my drenched panties cried to be removed.

"We will begin our descent into Myrtle Beach soon, Anamcara; the flight is short. As much as I would love to christen our jet, we do not have time." His breath in my hair raised goosebumps- the good kind. A shiver went down my spine, and I cursed him inwardly.

"I'm sure the jet has already been christened, babe." I laughed, knowing he liked my new nickname, although he claimed not to.

"And I am equally certain that it has not," he answered.

"Humph."

"A car awaits that will take us directly to your beach house." His lips teased my earlobe, and I melted, electric sizzling straight to my lady parts.

"It will be our beach house, I guess," my voice cracked and filled with need. I couldn't remember the last time we had sex. It was over a week ago, to be sure, maybe two? It's a wonder I hadn't died. That is the true testament to how busy we've been.

"Yes, I suppose that is true, Mo Chroi." He took my hand and pulled me down the hall and back into the main cabin.

He did not signal his flight attendant, choosing instead to pour another drink for us himself. He also handed me a bottle of chilled water from the fridge.

"Thanks," I said, heading to the couch. I wanted to curl up with him as we landed, so I settled, tucking my legs under my hip. He sat beside me, just as one soft bell chimed. The attendant did not check to see if our seatbelts were fastened.

"You need to hydrate. It is sweltering and humid in Pawleys Island today. There is also a chance of severe weather later that might make swimming difficult and force us to stay in." He turned his whiskey eyes to my green ones. His were filled with need and soaking in desire, like mine.

"I see." I could barely make the words come. Goddess, did I need him. How had we let it get so bad? I drank my water before tossing back my Grey Goose.

The jet tilted down slowly, and within minutes I felt the landing gear glide into place. We banked sharply out over the ocean as we made the turn to land. Whitecaps dotted the deep blue of the sea, and the curved shoreline of the Grand Strand reached out to me, drawing me in. My breath caught in my throat, and I felt tears burn the backs of my eyes; I did so love this place. I was glad my parents removed the spell. I loved Aedan, too. It would be fun to see him in my seat of power- my home.

We leveled out and came at the runway, touching down with barely a bump. Aedan's pilot was good, not that I was surprised. The flight attendant came then, opening doors and handing Aedan a stack of papers that looked like business crap. I bet he had to shuffle a thousand things to come away with me; I felt a pang of guilt.

We walked down the steps, and the white-hot South Carolina sun bounced off the tarmac, smacking me in the face. Aedan stepped just a bit faster but otherwise did not react. An escort took us through a covered walkway and into the airport only to walk us right back outside in just a few moments, opening up the backdoor to a long black limo.

Tourists gawked, wondering who they were gawking at, and I imagined that snapshots of us with the hashtag LarAedan would trend on Insta later. I didn't understand the fascination the public had with us, but it was part of our life, and I ignored it when I could.

The driver held the door, and we slid into the air-conditioned, dark interior before he raised the glass and drove off.

"Did you fly your limo down?" I asked, sliding over to the window so I could watch the scenery.

"No, I did not fly my limo down." He smirked at me from the seat across from mine. "Samuel sent a driver and the car. He also left a car at the house for us to use."

Samuel Allston represented the Southern contingent of vampires and was also a good friend of Aedan's and mine. He and his wife, Kimani, had separated for a short time. That separation was highlighted by a kidnapping, a birth, and a reunion. Such is my life.

I had gotten to help out with that, and now there was the most adorable brown-eyed baby girl named after me. I hoped we had time to run down and see her; I'd love to catch up with them all.

Samuel could put on a spread, too. He was a hereditary vampire and loved rubbing it in anyone's face that he could still eat.

Traffic was heavy in Myrtle Beach; it was even heavier on the bypass, and the Bypass to the Bypass was pretty bad, too. When I was a teenager, you could drive on The Bypass forever and never run into another car. At night, my best friend and I used to drag race with nothing but our parking lights on because we thought it was cool; we never got caught. Now there were cars everywhere, and it took us triple the time that it should have to get where we were going. As much as I missed the beach, I didn't miss this aspect of it.

Once we passed Surfside, the roads opened up, and the rest of the trip flew by. Soon, we turned off Highway 17 and onto the Causeway before making the final few turns to the beach house.

Chapter 2

Elegant and slightly weathered, as any proper beach house should be, it stood like a beacon in the hot summer sun. Large French doors opened to larger balconies, and curtains blew in the breeze invitingly. The house faced slightly south and embraced the ocean entirely. I had forgotten how lovely it was.

Samuel's driver opened the rear door, handing me out, and I took a minute just to feel. My eyes closed at the pure pleasure of breathing in ocean air, and an overwhelming peace settled deep into my bones. Despite the concrete of the driveway, power whispered through me, and my soul settled into perfect equilibrium. This place was mine, uniquely mine, and spell or no, it could never be taken from me.

The limo drove away, leaving us standing in the warm South Carolina breeze.

Aedan watched it all, a soft smile on his face. He said nothing, just waited patiently for me to get my shit together. The house hadn't changed much, it was well maintained, and the landscaping was impeccable. A small sign that read Too Ra Loo Ra Lara hung on the house, naming it. I wondered who had come up with that. It wasn't actual Irish, but I loved it anyway; it was perfect. Even the sign didn't make Aedan break his silence. Nothing, not even the white Audi R8 convertible that sat sheltered and snug under the house, made him speak. I took a minute to stare at Samuel's loaner car; these vampires are ridiculous.

Inside, the house was airy and beautiful, the early afternoon sun slanted through the windows, and the sweet, salty scent of the ocean breezed into the house, making it comfortable.

The decor had changed so much. Gone was the tropical tourist trap of corals and turquoise in favor of soft yellows and blended whites. The Brazilian Pecan hardwood floor gleamed in the sunlight providing contrast to the light colors above. Ceiling fans hummed, and my heart melted; I sank onto the couch, letting it all wash through me.

"Go swim. Go walk, whatever you wish, Liomsa, and allow me to make you something. I had the house stocked with everything we did not bring, and there is nothing we lack. The weather is going to turn; you should enjoy yourself before it does." He ran his thumb down my cheek and into the curve of my smile.

"You were busy on our flight; I feel bad about forcing you away. I know you don't want to hear it, but I'm going to say it anyway- thank you." I rose, kissing his cheek, and made my way up the stairs to the grand bedroom that I had stayed in for only a short time.

French doors opened out onto the balcony, and the ceiling fan whirred over the king-sized bed in the center of the room. It faced the open doors, allowing for a marvelous view of the water beyond.

The hardwood carried up the stairs but was softened by a plush white area rug with a swirling yellow design that accented the yellow and white quilt on the large rice planter bed. It was graceful, feminine, and entirely Southern. The bed was huge. Much bigger than the one that had previously been here. I wondered if all five of my parents had something to do with that. I bet they all fit in it. I didn't want to think about that.

The closet and drawers were filled with clothes that would fit us both. For such a sudden appearance, the place was well stocked indeed, and it made me wonder just a bit.

In the bathroom, I freshened up and slipped into the little black bikini that awaited me, grabbed a towel, and walked downstairs and out onto the sand. I didn't make it to the water before I sank to my knees, unable to take another step.

I pulled power in from the ground beneath me and let it flow through my body and back out. Every ache, every pain, every ribbon of stress vanished deep into the earth. I hadn't felt like this in so long that I couldn't remember; I almost cried.

I could feel her below me, whatever she is: the earth, the Goddess, the mother- something. She turned her eyes to me as she always did when I channeled her through my body, and a deeply satisfied rumble flowed through my mind. When the coursing energy was clean and stable, I pushed the extra back into the ground and stood, feeling better than I had in months.

Turning my head back to the house, I found Aedan had come to the deck and was watching. His mouth was open and slack, and his hands frozen in mid-task. The bond between us was open, and I felt his underlying sense of amazement as he watched me. I scoffed at him and walked to the water, my skin softly glowing. In three strides, I was beyond the waves and under their soft crash. I swam, using my legs like a tail instead of kicking the way my mother taught me. I had since learned a mermaid had taught her, so it all made sense now.

When I crested over a larger wave and dove under the other side, I felt the last puzzle piece fall, and peace settled into the marrow of my bones. Goddess, how I loved this place. I almost hoped Dani showed up so I could share it with her, the way she had shared her lake with me. I kind of hoped, but kind of not. As much as I loved the people we shared our lives with, I loved Aedan more and looked forward to having him to myself for a bit.

But the Goddess had taken a drop of my blood when I visited Talamh na Sithe. Since then, she had begun popping in to see her son, interrupting a few moments a mother never should. She didn't seem to care, but it mortified me. Nothing like your soon-to-be mother-in-law chilling out while watching you fuck her son silly.

She would smile and laugh while I dove under the covers, trying to die quickly. Aedan just chuckled and threw pillows at her until she disappeared the way she came, mumbling about how we should hurry up and give her grandchildren. I hated to disappoint her because I didn't think that was possible, but who am I to contradict a Goddess?

Maybe she shouldn't pop in since I hoped there would be lots of sexy moments in the near future.

I floated onto my back and watched the sun begin to settle behind the roof of the beach house. The sky was bright orange and pink, and I couldn't remember a lovelier beginning to a sunset. I could have slept like an otter out here on the waves, but Aedan's shadow moving around the kitchen reminded me of dinner; my stomach growled at the thought of what he might be making. I took a moment to pull some more power from the water and push the extra back out. It felt so good that it was hard not to keep doing it. Swimming to land, I showered, then toweled off before walking the steps slowly, taking in the feel of everything around me.

With the ceiling fans running, the temperature inside had cooled despite the use of the stove. The table was set beautifully, and Aedan served rare filet mignon sliced on top of greens, adding a blue cheese vinaigrette dressing before calling it done. A glass of Grey Goose on ice sat beside my plate, and a glass of bourbon was in his hand.

He had changed into shorts and a tight black tee-shirt, making me stop and stare, my mouth open and watering. I had never seen him in anything so casual. He dressed up so often that I forgot what he looked like wearing something simple. I liked it a lot.

Running his nose down my neck, he said, "Every time I think I have never seen you look more beautiful, you show me how wrong I am. I have never been so glad to be somewhere in my existence. Thank you for letting me bring you here."

"I didn't let you bring me anywhere; you stole me." I tilted my neck to the side, giving him full access. Sex isn't the only thing I'd been missing. My hemoglobin was probably at record levels as he hadn't fed from me since the last time we'd made love. It had been a rough little bit. He growled low into the hollow of my neck, sending a delicious shiver down my spine.

"Eat, then we will swim together before bed, Anamcara," he said, watching me through heavy eyes, and I thought I might not make it to that swim.

We ate, or I did. He sipped his bourbon, never taking his eyes off my face. The intensity of his gaze shot straight to my core, igniting a fire I hoped he was prepared to extinguish. When I finished, he poured me another vodka, reached for my hand, and led me to the door.

We sat side by side on the sand nearest the shoreline, watching the light of the half-full moon rise above the waves. The tide was out, and the ocean flat. Little waves rolled in, barely making a sound as they crashed, then receded back into the sea. When our drinks were gone, we walked out into the warm water.

Neither of us needed light to see, but the glow from neighboring houses and the moon highlighted everything around us. Shirtless and in swim trunks, Aedan was amazing. His nipples pebbled as the water slid around us, and my breath caught in my chest.

"If you don't stop thinking about my body, we won't make it to the bedroom, Mo Chroi." We had stopped walking out into the darkness. The water came above my chest now, but I could still touch my toes.

"I should shield better," I said, giving him a salty smile and a wink before diving under and away from him.

He grabbed my feet before I could outswim him, and we both sputtered to the surface, sweeping water from our faces. "You should never shield, not from me. It amazes me that you find me intriguing. The depth of your desire calms my soul." He surrounded me with his arms, dipping his lips to mine.

"Oh, yeah?" I said, sliding my arms down his back and cupping the hard swell of his ass in my hands.

"Yes." We kissed, our tongues knowing where to go and how to blend into each other perfectly.

"Then, your soul should be very calm right now," I whispered into his hair.

He nipped down my jawline before easing his fangs into my neck in the slow sexy way that drives me nuts; I almost came from it. Not that he used vampire mind tricks or compulsion with me, he never did. I simply loved the feel of him: teeth, tongue, fingers, soul, all of him brought me pleasure. His fangs were no different; I melted into him, sliding my tongue up his neck and opening it with a line of power. I sipped from him as he drank from me, filling himself. I could feel the hard length of him pressed against my hip, and I reached for him, only to have him push my hand away.

I felt his fangs retract and his tongue lick the neat holes they left. Scooping me up, ignoring my hard slaps at his arms, he carried me so fast the scenery blurred. Needless to say, we skipped the shower.

Upstairs, wet clothes left a trail to the oversized bed. The ceiling fan caused goosebumps to rise on my arms, and his head between my legs caused my back to arch. He licked the salt from my skin with soft growls and purrs. "It seems I have forgotten in the last few weeks that you are mine to do with as I please. I have missed this," he said, whispering into the heart of me.

"I'm yours, am I?" I smiled at the top of his head. My smile fell when his tongue parted my lips and drove in.

"Are you not?" he asked, leaving me panting, pushing my hips to him so he would continue, my need so raw I was willing to beg for release.

"I'm yours, Aedan, most definitely." My head fell back when his tongue entered me again.

Two fingers slid in as his teeth nipped up my thigh, piercing the skin above the big vein in my groin. He took one sip, licking the wounds before moving to the other side. He kissed up my thigh again, repeating the process. With his fingers smoothing over that spot deep inside of me and his fangs piercing me, I came. Arching into him, unable to control myself, I panted his name. The feel of his fangs in me carrying the orgasm further. My legs shook from the effort of keeping them bent until I gave up, letting them flop to the sides.

Aedan crawled up my body, stopping at my breasts. He licked and pulled each one into his mouth, using soft laps and gentle nips to drag me from the haze of orgasm. My legs came up, trapping him. He sank his fangs into the soft tissue at the top of my breast, making me cry out. He had never bitten me there before. After licking the holes closed, he moved to the next one, doing the same. The feel of his long fangs in the soft, sensitive tissue had me panting with need. Need to feel all of him. Speechless, I arched myself up, feeling the tip of him just there. I begged, unashamed at my need for him.

He kissed a line to my lips then parted them with his tongue. I tasted blood, salt, and my most intimate places. Taking my wrists into one large hand, he stretched me tight, running his other hand down my ribs and making me take his weight. The feeling of losing freedom was amazing.

Despite Cook's efforts, I never gained an ounce. Not since Daniel attacked me and that small bit of humanity died had I gained weight. Had I known that was going to happen, I would have taken time to plump up. I didn't like being so thin, but I was getting used to it.

Aedan's hands ran over my ribs and traced the spaces between them as he kissed me. My body trembled with every touch, and I whined into his mouth.

"Tell me what you want, wicked faerie." His lips found my earlobe, his teeth scraping it.

"I want you," I panted.

"You have me." He sank his fangs in again, taking one small sip before pulling them out, causing me to moan into his mouth.

"I want you in me." The words came out in a gasp.

"I have been in you multiple times, Anamcara. My tongue, my fangs."

"Fuck me, Aedan. Please," I begged. I could feel how wet I was. I was clenching around nothing, and it was killing me.

"Such language," He thrust into me in one stroke, causing me to moan.

My breath came hard and fast against his chest. I was so full of him. It was almost too much. I felt myself grip him and release in spasms. Every shield I have dropped, and my skin glowed brighter than the moon above. Growling into my neck, he did fuck me then. Hard. The bed was sturdy, and for once, it didn't break. I should thank my parents but probably wouldn't. Because you know, gross.

Releasing my arms, he pushed above me, taking his weight onto them so he could thrust into me harder. He found that spot and angled to make me cry out his name again. The Orgasm, capital O, tore from me, leaving me limp and unable to counter him. He thrust once more, threw his head back, and roared into the night. I'd never heard such a noise from him before. Letting his head fall to his chest, he stilled as the last spasms filled me. Finally, he lowered himself to lay beside me. I would have moved to accommodate him, but I died for a minute- maybe two.

"Do you think it will always be like this?" I hadn't meant to ask the question out loud, just pose it to myself, but he answered anyway.

"I think that we are both passionate people," he said, pulling me to him. "We will bump heads from time to time, as we do now, but we will stay friends as well as lovers. I will never want you less than I do right now. The rest will come. I have waited too long to find you to let pettiness get in the way of what we are." He kissed my hair and pulled his arms from me.

With a groan, he rolled from the bed, struggling to stand. It was such a human mannerism that I smiled. When I first met him, he was stiff and formal, his actions belying his youthful appearance. Lately, he had adopted more human ways. It was cute. If he would learn to use contractions, he could pass for a twenty-something. Thirty at most. It made me feel like a cougar. Rawr. He said I changed him, and maybe I had. Something had, that's for sure.

We showered together. After, I slipped on a light nightshirt, pulled the curtains, and went to bed. Aedan sat in the chair next to me, clicking away on his tablet. Although neither one of us had a break in months, I knew he didn't have time to be here. He seemed content to work in his black boxer briefs, though, and with the soft sound of his clicking, I fell asleep within moments.

I awoke when the sun rose. I turned to find Aedan already gone. His side of the bed was rumpled, so he had rested at some point. The smell of coffee pulled me into a state of deep desire.

When I met Aedan, he couldn't make a drinkable pot of coffee to save his life. Now he had mastered coffee from any device, including Cook's French press. I rolled out of bed and poured myself onto the floor. I brushed my teeth and threw my ratty hair into a long tail before following the rich scent of coffee coming from the kitchen.

Aedan stood, bare chested and wearing a pair of loose pajama bottoms, watching some national news network. Coming up behind him, I wrapped my arms around his chest.

"Good morning," I said.

"Good morning to you as well," he answered. "Join me on the deck?" He poured a second cup of coffee and led the way outside.

The sun glinted off the waves, and birds cried, looking for their breakfast. The tide was coming in. Unlike the night before, when the ocean had been calm and peaceful, today it was something wilder. Waves crashed on the shoreline and into each other, making beautiful music. Aedan was right. A storm was brewing, but then, isn't that always the case?

Aedan put up the patio umbrella and sat underneath the shade. The sun didn't burn him to ash, but without a strong SPF, it did burn him like it did any good Irish boy. I sat where the sun could shine on my face, not caring about sunburn. Closing my eyes, I let it warm me inside and out. I felt Aedan's eyes on me. I stretched over and put my feet in his lap. His cool hands immediately found my arches, and I groaned.

Even though I wasn't a bedside nurse anymore, I was still on my feet most of the day. His strong hands pressed out the knots and found the sore spots, and I smiled, remembering that this was how it all started. A foot rub, a really good foot rub, had sucked me in from the beginning.

"This is how it all started," he said, mirroring my thoughts. "That was the night I knew I was lost to you."

"We had just met, so that can't be true," I said, squinting an eye at him. He stilled for a beat before his expert hands again began to knead.

"I saw you in the neighborhood many times. I was just too shy to introduce myself." His hand came up to my calf, pressing into the muscle there.

I belly laughed at that, opening my eyes to take in his expression.

"I doubt you have ever been shy a day in your life, Aedan." I lay my head back again, baring my neck and letting my ponytail hang down.

"What would you like to do today?" he asked, reaching for the other calf.

"This," I said.

"Then, this is what we will do."

"Except I want to see Samuel and Kimani, but I'm not sure I can move that far." I leaned up and grasped his hand in mine.

"Then we shall invite them to dinner. I have no doubt they would love to see this place- and you."

"We can order out, Chinese or something." I sipped my coffee and watched him watch me.

"I will cook. Samuel will take great pleasure in eating the fruits of my labor while I watch; I have no doubt." One side of his mouth cocked up in a smirk. Being a hereditary vampire, he did enjoy eating in front of his turned cousins.

"It's your vacation, too. You don't have to do that," I said as I sat up, pulling my feet from him to reach over and grab his hand.

"That is exactly why I want to do it. I enjoy cooking, especially for you. It will make me happy. I never meant for us to get so caught up in work that I neglected our relationship," he said, watching me carefully.

"We both need to be better. The house being done will help, Aedan. And if it makes you happy to cook, well then, cook away. Speaking of which, I'm going to grab a smoothie. Can I get you another coffee?" I rose from the chair, grabbing his cup and mine, and went to refill them.

Looking out the kitchen window and into the waves beyond, I wanted nothing more than to forget all about my responsibilities and stay here forever. Just me. Just Aedan. Sighing, I took his cup out to him.

Meeting his eyes, I placed a chaste kiss on his lips. "I love you," I whispered.

He stilled in the way only a vampire can. "I love you, too," he said, his eyes growing concerned. "Are you okay?" he asked.

"I'm fine. Something about being here just has me more…something. I don't know. It's weird."

"I can drink your emotions from the surface of your mind." He sat his coffee down and pulled me onto his lap. "I have missed you."

"I've missed you too. Let's never do that again. It's got me all weird and stuff."

"Deal," he laughed, kissing me deeply.

We left our coffees on the table and went inside to make love again. And again. We were reconnecting after weeks of work and frustration in a way we needed badly. I couldn't get enough of him, and the more he gave, the more I needed. We fed each other in ways that made me realize just how empty the last few weeks had been.

In the end, I lay next to him, my body so pleasantly sore that I would need to heal it before I could take him again. Silent tears ran down my face, and an overwhelming amount of emotions raced through me. I let them; I had no choice. They would not be denied. Aedan ran his hands over my body, whispering in Irish until I got myself under control.

So much had happened. So many things. I wasn't the person I was when Aedan first walked across the field between our homes that cold December night. Why I broke down at that moment, I'll never understand. Perhaps this was the first time I actually stopped to be. Maybe it was time. It had been coming for a while.

For all this Faerie Healer crap, I was still a woman. A woman who had lost much but gained more. Those emotions rolled through me, and I cried in Aedan's arms. When he turned me to my back one more time, I found I wasn't as sore as I thought I was and welcomed him home.

Chapter 3

I awoke a short time later, curled around Aedan. His eyes were closed, and his chest rose and fell softly. He didn't need to breathe, and I wondered about the change. We had shared a lot of blood in the last few hours; it could be as simple as that.

His eyelashes kissed the curve of his cheek, and I knew he was asleep. The dawn hadn't taken him since I became his Source. Even though we hadn't shared blood in a while, the effects didn't wear off that we noticed.

Only after he was drained of his blood by those determined to end his reign as King of Vampires did he return to his pre-Lara self. Once home, we remedied that, after a time anyway.

He said as long as I was willing, he would never drink from another again. I laughed at that because one never knows what circumstances may arise, and I wouldn't begrudge him nutrition. His hands, though? Well, they had better stay in his pockets.

A smile grew on my face, and I wondered again where these strange emotions were coming from: I didn't understand them. I watched Aedan sleep and knew I was never letting him go.

Leaning over, I brushed my lips to his and rose on silent feet, grabbing a shirt before slipping out of the open balcony door. Morning had faded into afternoon, and the yellow sky spoke volumes. There was a hurricane out there; I could smell it. Gone was the calm ocean. It was replaced by a tempest fit for Hemmingway, or more accurately, Poe.

Whitecaps rose and fell, and waves crashed into the shore violently. Wind blew from the southeast, entering the house head-on, making the curtains dance in the breeze. Placing my hands on the railing, I breathed deeply, encouraging the storm to come. My hair whipped around my face, stinging the places it hit. I tilted my head back and pulled the storm's power into my lungs. I loved hurricanes, always have. Always will.

This house had withstood hurricane Hugo, the Cat Five beast that had ripped through the area in the nineties, so I didn't worry. It would be fine. Smiling, I turned from the railing to find Aedan leaning up on one arm, watching me with predatory eyes.

Muscles carved his chest and arms, and whiskey-colored eyes, faceted like mine, glittered at me. I walked to him, closing the French doors. I missed the wind immediately as my tangled hair settled.

Need rose through me again, and I wondered if the storm was triggering my emotions. I took a step toward him and was interrupted.

"A Leanbh? See, I'm learning! I come to your living room instead of your bedroom!" The sweet, accented words of Aedan's mom rose to greet us.

I laid my head back and laughed out loud.

"Coming, Dani!" I said, with a laugh, grabbing a robe with a shake of my head.

Aedan fell back onto the bed, glaring at the ceiling. It must be hard to have a Goddess for a mother.

In the kitchen, I used the instant hot water feature on my sink to put coffee in the French press. Lately, Aedan had begun making my coffee, and I scowled a little over having to do it myself. I was, indeed, becoming a spoiled Faerie Princess.

Steaming cup in hand, I turned to face The Goddess of Life and Maker of All Things, genuinely glad she was here, despite her penchant for interrupting sexy time.

"Your power surrounds this place, daughter. It is magnificent," she said, watching me with an odd expression on her face. "When I retire, and you take my place, perhaps you will allow me to vacation here."

I laughed, snorting coffee out of my nose and all over the counter between us. "Um. Dani, Ma'am. Ain't happening. I'm a Healer, not a Goddess; that's your job. I doubt you have a retirement plan." I hurried to wipe the mess from my face.

"Call me Mom, or Mother, dear. For now, that you are marrying my son, I am your Mother in all ways," she said, with a knowing twinkle in her eyes.

"Oh, God," I said, almost passing out.

"Goddess, dear. Mom to you." She smiled pleasantly, her jeans and yellow tee shirt making her look like a naughty teenager. She was up to something. She had taken to dressing in modern western fashions and walking around like an average person. She's a freaking Goddess; she shouldn't be allowed to do that.

"Mother, you are causing Lara to hyperventilate. Would you be so kind as to dial it back a bit?" Aedan said from the stairs.

"And you?" she accused, turning to him and making his steps falter. "Why is my grandbaby not in her womb?" Her angry glare pinned him in place, and, through the bond we shared, I felt his desire to turn tail and run. The Original Gangsta, the two-thousand-year-old Fae-Vampire hybrid, was scared of his mommy.

I didn't blame him.

I shrank in my skin, trying to be smaller.

"Mother," he sighed. "I do not think such a thing is possible." His glance up the stairs gave away his desire to run.

"All things are possible, my dearest. All Things. Don't forget that," she said, smiling sweetly.

"Oh, God," I said, thinking I needed to add a shot of vodka to my coffee. Now was so not the time to get pregnant. If there ever was a time for such a thing. I had never planned on having children.

"Goddess, dear- mother to you. Stop forgetting." Dani turned to me, and I thought that all of the benevolence must be an act. The gleeful smile on her face when discussing grandchildren made her look downright scary. I needed to get on the pill.

"I didn't come to talk about my future grandsons and granddaughters," she said, making me more lightheaded and dizzier. She used the word 'and,' not the word 'or.' The distinction is important, as it implies multiple grandchildren.

Turning, I grabbed the bottle of Grey Goose from the counter and poured a generous amount into my coffee, gulping it down. I mean, if the Goddess of Life insists on grandchildren, how can I get around that? Maybe there was a loophole. I needed a lawyer.

"Mother," Aedan said, straightening his spine and continuing down the stairs. "You are frightening my mate; what did you come to discuss?" He had thrown on black, silk pajama bottoms before coming downstairs but left his chiseled chest bare.

My eyes got stuck on the sexy curves of his muscles, causing a line of drool to drip from the corner of my mouth. Of course, the Goddess and her son noticed where my attention got snagged; a cocky smile graced Aedan's lips, and an 'I told- you so' look plastered itself on Dani's face. I glanced at the door to the deck beyond, wondering if I could make it outside and down the beach before one of them caught me.

I took another gulp of my drink and dropped my eyes to the floor.

"Ah, yes, business," she said, her face turning somber. "Conditions in Talamh na Sithe are deteriorating. After Aramea's initial temper tantrum, things settled. Now that your allies left, she is on another tear. There may be nothing to save if she isn't stopped soon."

"I'm not saying you need to go today or even next week," she added at my crestfallen look. "But battle plans need to be made. I spoke with Airmed and told her much the same," she finished.

Closing my eyes, I leaned against the counter. She was right. Aedan had been home for a while now, and his affairs were settled. Our house was done, and the Eight and their mates were tucked in and comfortable in various locations around us. Life had calmed down, and I was enjoying it. Maybe it was selfish, but I didn't want to go to war.

Life is balance: not all good and not all bad. Things had been great for us since Aedan's return; it was time to add some balance, apparently.

"It will be okay," she said, "There are so many layers to this plan that it will come to fruition before your eyes."

"I know, Dani." I sighed, turning to look out the window and to the surf beyond.

All the power, all the gifts, all the everything she gave us led to the moment when the fight to take back Talamh na Sithe started. I hadn't asked for this; none of it; neither had my mom, but none of us had a choice. Dani wove the threads of this thing before I was born, and my conception was just another one of her layers.

When I went to Talamh na Sithe to try to find a way to bring Aedan home, she told me that Gods were not omniscient. She claimed they could only influence behaviors and not direct them.

I don't believe her.

The intricacies involved in the centuries of planning are too deep and varied to be left to chance. Dani knows how this will end. She set it up from the beginning. Maybe she lost control of her People all those millennia ago when Aedan was changed, but she got it back. Her chess pieces are aligned, and now she waits for the final checkmate.

I just hoped we weren't the pawns.

I do believe she had no clue about Aedan's punishment-somehow, she missed that. But for an immortal being who has lived countless lives, she has to be an expert in the long game. Undoubtedly even better at it than her son. I certainly never want to play against her.

It's not that I think she is deceitful or has nefarious intentions, not at all. She wants what she wants, and she intends to get it. She is a Goddess, after all. She loves Aedan and will do anything for him; that much is clear. How can I fault her for that?

"Mother, we have friends coming over for dinner tonight. Stay and eat with us," Aedan said, moving to stand beside me.

"Great idea, babe." I turned back to them, smiling. Mother-in-law problems. Everyone has them.

"I don't want to impose," she started but was interrupted immediately.

"It is no imposition, I assure you," Aedan said.

"None at all," I added. "You wanted to spend some time here; it'll be fun." I meant it; I did. I would've loved to have Aedan to myself, but I understood that's not how our life is.

"I will put out something light while you dress, Anamcara. Then you and Dani can walk on the beach while I prepare for our guests," he said, placing a light kiss on my head.

"Call me Dani again, son, and I will take a rod to you. You are not too big: you will never be too big." She leveled him with a look, and I knew that despite their complicated history that they would be okay. Aedan looked away first, and I grinned on the inside-never the outside. Between the two of us, Aedan had no chance of ever going off the rails and running amok again.

I ran upstairs and changed into the white bikini I found in my drawer. I wondered if Aedan had specified one be white when he had the place stocked. I had one like it in our rooms in the city, and it had quickly become his favorite. He'd ripped it off of me more than once, and I always found it replaced. We tended to be hard on each other's clothing.

I slipped a pair of shorts and a soft tee shirt on before skipping down the stairs. Aedan and Dani had their heads together, and conversation stopped when they heard me coming.

"Hey, y'all," I complained. "No more plots, please. This is a plot-free zone." I glared at them, narrowing my eyes as I bounded down the last two steps. They both looked away first, so what does that say about me? I did not miss the look of concern on Aedan's face over whatever they had been discussing; he looked away, not meeting my eyes.

"Ah, daughter, let's walk while my son gets ready for this party," Dani said, stepping neatly away from his side.

"I feel like we should help," I worried, not wanting to help and feeling guilty about it.

"Mother out, Liomsa, you too; you ladies have a nice walk. I will work much more quickly without you underfoot. The Allston's will be here soon, so go while you can." Aedan walked to me, placing another quick kiss on my head. His eyes paled just a bit when he peeked down my shirt and saw the white bikini beneath; I smirked at him as I walked away.

Chapter 4

I hadn't watched the news, so I had no idea where the hurricane was tracking, but I could feel it. Dani and I walked onto the sand, and her eyes pinned to the southeast like a compass. "Of course, you would visit your power base when a storm approaches. That is why I feel your power so strongly," she said, smiling at me.

"I didn't even know the storm was coming," I answered, walking into the breeze.

The wind was stiff, and little grains of sand blasted into my bare legs. I knew from experience the skin would be red later and require extra moisturizer. It wasn't uncomfortable, just noticeable. The sun shone still, reflecting off the sand as the storm wasn't close enough to allow the first bands to block it. The ocean was wild, though, as a hurricane will affect the coast days in advance of its arrival.

"You are the storm, Lara. From the beginning, you were the perfect storm. I knew that mixing your fathers' magics would create something special. I could not have known just how special you would be," she said, walking beside me. She changed her outfit with a thought and now wore shorts and a bikini top; we could have been sisters.

"I couldn't have known when I wove a child from the threads of life and magic that you would be the perfect mate for my son. His only true mate. I thought him dead then. Sometimes I think about how things came together and am stunned but so grateful. I went from having very little in my life to having a family. Even I cannot know which flowers will bloom and which will not. I only cast the seeds," she finished. She closed her eyes and tilted her face to catch the late day sun.

Damn Goddesses. She must have caught my train of thought earlier- mother-in-law problems: mine is omniscient, almost anyway.

"Tuffy came to me during a storm," I started. "I remember the night he was born. I've always loved hurricanes for that reason." I stopped, picking up a perfect conch shell. The great thing about the tides during rough seas is the things they dredge up.

"Yes, he did. I couldn't find a way to give him to you, so he had to be reborn. Let me tell you, he was not happy about that," she said, turning her head my way. Her lovely silver hair getting caught in the wind.

"He wasn't happy about a lot of things." I barked a laugh, remembering that night so clearly. He had kicked his way into the world, and no one but me could do anything with him. "It explains so much, actually. He always was a true redhead; if he can't be with me, I'm glad he's with you."

"Me, too," she answered. "He sends his love."

"In his way."

"Of course," she laughed. "You've made Coi very happy; I'm glad for that," she said, changing the subject.

"He's made me happy too. What were you two conspiring about?" I asked, cutting my eyes to her and hoping to catch some expression that would clue me in.

She sighed, turning to me. "Wedding plans and future plans, my child. You were made for great things; Coi must understand that."

"I see." I walked in silence, pondering the fact that my life would never be my own. For the first time, I understood that. I might have snatches of peace and snippets of choice, but it would never wholly be mine. Not unless I learned to say no. I wanted and believed in free will; I just had to find a way to enforce my right to it.

We were almost to the Point: that place where the inlet meets the ocean. It is my favorite spot on earth. Usually, there was a wide expanse of beach separating the two, but during a storm, the beach was known to disappear under the surge from it.

My best friend and I had once gotten trapped on a skinny strip of sand during a storm-fed tide. Caught between the water and land, we had made a fire and the best of it, never worrying in our teenaged minds about how dangerous the situation actually was. I guess with a Goddess watching over me, we hadn't needed to.

"I'm going to swim," Dani said, turning from me with a brilliant smile.

"That's not the best idea, uh, mother," I warned.

She tilted her head up and laughed out loud at the suggestion that she could not handle the wild ocean. "Magic," she winked, dropping her shorts to reveal her sleek purple bikini bottoms. What else did I expect?

Laughing, she ran to the surf, diving over, around, under, and through any challenge it presented.

She had a point.

I ran to join her.

I have always considered the ocean my mother. So, what does the ocean consider the Goddess that made her?

We squealed and laughed, thumbing our noses at convention and played like dolphins in the tempestuous surf. I don't recommend trying this at home. The waves were high and the current swift. I swam underneath the choppy surface, infusing my limbs with strength and weaving my way magically through rip currents and swift-running undertows.

I had never done this before. I mean, sure, I have swum in a hurricane touched sea, but not like this. It was fun- exhausting but fun.

Too soon, the current carried us back to the beach house, where we stumbled from the white-churned waters, laughing and coughing up seawater as we went. I stiffened and elbowed Dani when I saw Aedan on the deck, staring furiously at us with his arms crossed. Scrubbing his face with his hands, he turned and went inside. The impeccably dressed Allstons stood beside him, their faces a mix of shock and awe.

"Oops," I said. "We got caught," I whispered to Dani, waving enthusiastically at Samuel. He shook his head and followed Aedan inside. Kimani doubled over, clutching her belly as she laughed, and Gennie covered her smile with her hand.

"Well, then we shall fix it," Dani laughed, waving her hand in front of us, causing an opaque glimmer.

We stepped out dressed neatly in matching white capri pants. Dani had woven herself a lavender cashmere sweater with cap sleeves and dressed me in a red camisole with lace straps.

My hair was artfully done in soft beach waves, and hers was perfectly dry and straight. Her silver locks had soft lavender highlights that matched her eyes. Sun kissed our cheeks with nature's makeup. Kimani's expression turned serious, and Gennie's mouth dropped open.

"There. Much better," Dani said, heading toward the house.

I followed The Great Goddess of All Things, including Makeovers, into the house wearing strappy kitten heels.

"Go change while I…pour drinks…" Aedan turned to us, finding our attire perfect. Dani smirked, and I tried to cover my smile by looking innocently away. He pinched the bridge of his nose, glancing at the heavens. He should know no help would come from that direction. His God was looking adorable in lavender and white as she introduced herself to his friends.

"Mother, do you think it was wise to swim in the ocean mere hours before a hurricane is going to strike?" he asked, narrowing his eyes on us.

"Was the water rough, daughter? I didn't notice," she said, turning to me while causing Aedan to sigh deeply. "I am Dani," she said, extending her hand to Samuel.

"Uh," he said. Which was awesome because I have never known him to be speechless.

"Mother! Lara!" Aedan yelled, making me jump.

"Son, two Goddesses swimming in a hurricane is nothing. Mind your manners; you have guests." She shook Samuel's hand then turned to the others. I grabbed my Grey Goose from Aedan and leaned against the countertop, studiously ignoring him.

The place looked and smelled great. We had been gone for longer than planned, and in our absence, Aedan had cleaned up, lit candles, and made dinner. The beach house looked fantastic, lit with their soft glow. The French doors were open, and the soft sheers blew in the breeze. The sound of waves crashing sounded in harmony with classical music of some sort that played in the background.

"Aedan, this is beautiful, thank you," I said, turning to him. I stood on my tiptoes and brushed his lips with mine. He stilled against me, and his body softened as his fury over our antics faded.

"It is my pleasure, Mo Chroi. Mother, I am not sure your introduction was concise enough," he said, turning to our guests.

"It was perfectly sufficient, Coi. It's such a pleasure to meet you. Lilith did a marvelous job- such a marvel. I'm only jealous that I didn't think of it first. You have all the joys of humanity without the downsides," she laughed, grabbing baby Lara from Geenie and rubbing her face on the baby like a cat.

I groaned. "Dani, uh, mother, one isn't supposed to steal children like that. That's the fuel for fairy tales."

"It's fine; she's obviously smitten," Geenie said with a soft laugh.

Dani glowed softly, and you could see her pure heart. She loved children. Giving up Aedan must have been horrific for her.

"She is Perfect," The Goddess proclaimed. She squeezed the poor kid within inches of her life, but all little Lara did was laugh and tangle her hands in Dani's long, silver hair. "Son, I simply must have one of these. You were my last child; it only fits that you give me grandchildren. Immediately. I demand it as my due."

Groans of sympathy went up from around the table. We've all been there, I suppose. Well, not me. I'd never been in this situation before; I sipped my vodka and watched with rapt attention.

"Kimani, you may not know this, but my mother is the Great Goddess of All Things. In truth. I apologize for the kidnapping of your child, and the embarrassment Mother brings. She means well," he finished taking a deep drink from his highball of whiskey.

A wine glass dropped, and the room got silent. I caught the Allstons casting furtive glances at one another.

"So, it's true?" Samuel asked. "I thought she was maybe just original Tuatha de Danann or an ancient line."

"I am The Original Tuatha de Danann, yes, and Coi's mother," Dani laughed, twirling the baby and creating butterflies out of thin air in our living room. The butterflies landed on the baby, making her laugh even harder. "You will call me Nana, little one. Would you like a pony? I can get you one," she cooed at Baby Lara, making the child clasp her face and cover it with sloppy kisses.

I rolled my eyes. Dani whipped around to face me, and I picked some lint off of my shirt.

"How's dinner coming, babe?" I asked, moving to pour another Grey Goose and refill Samuel, Kimani, and Geenie's wine. The twins had stayed behind as all adults were boring at their age.

"It is ready; we should eat."

We closed the doors and ate inside as the wind was picking up. We could still hear the crash of the waves over our conversation, and I vowed to turn the television on later and learn the scope of the storm stalking the coastline.

Aedan first served a spinach and strawberry salad with a balsamic vinaigrette dressing followed by shrimp and gruyère cheese grits with bacon and mushrooms. Shrimp and grits is a traditional southern dish, but he took it to another level with his interpretation. Everything was amazing. Kimani brought sweet potato pie, and we devoured that as well.

Conversation and wine flowed freely. Geenie was still breastfeeding, and after her two glass limit, she was done for the night, but the rest of us indulged; we laughed and talked. Despite her initial Mom'ish behavior, Dani fit in well and eventually sat the baby down.

I wasn't sure if Baby Lara was advanced or it was normal for kids her age to crawl, but she was everywhere. We took turns chasing her, and I think even Dani got exhausted by the sweet, chubby, brown-eyed baby.

Geenie put her down in one of the spare rooms, where she slept quietly through the laughter and loud conversation. Evening turned into night and night into early morning. Dani got tipsy and casually magicked our dishes away. I thought that maybe a tipsy Goddess could be dangerous, so we switched her drinks to water. She dipped her finger in and changed it to a liquid the color of honey, and Aedan groaned out loud; I felt almost bad for him.

Almost.

It was hysterical to see them together, and we laughed from behind our hands, hoping not to be caught. It was a near-perfect evening. The only way it could've been better was if Paul, Grania, and my parents had been there. It was a great time.

Dani popped out first. I mean, just literally popped out. There one minute, gone the next; then I saw Geenie yawn and knew the night was over.

"Dinner was terrific, Governor. I don't think I have had a better meal in Charleston. You missed your calling," Samuel said, rising to his feet.

"There is more than enough space, Samuel; please stay.

"Kimani does not wish to leave two teenaged boys alone for long, with only the staff for supervision. The storm is coming; we'd best be home when it lands," he said as they headed to the door, and I thought it was a wise move. The boys are good-looking, and his staff has shady morals. Especially the one that Aedan snacked on during one of our misunderstandings. I felt myself get warm and tamped the anger down.

Aedan's smirk let me know he knew my thoughts. I punched his arm and trailed the Allstons to the door. "We would love it if you stayed," I repeated.

Samuel moved me into a hug. "I know, and I thank you, but we have meetings tomorrow; it would be better to be at home. With the storm, we shouldn't take the chance of getting stranded. Another time."

"Okay," I said, squeezing him.

After they left, peace settled over the house. We walked the steps to our room filled with inner light from a rare comfortable night where our only responsibility was to be with friends. It was a nice change.

Chapter 5

I felt the pull of the storm awaken me. Aedan lay naked and sprawled across the massive bed in our room. Our room. Funny how two little words can change everything. We never talked about the fact that the first time I made love in this room, it wasn't with him. We had moved past that particular misunderstanding.

The dropping barometric pressure pulled my soul like a magnet. I untangled myself from Aedan's chiseled limbs, letting my eyes travel their lines in appreciation. Goddess, he was beautiful, laying in the perfect surrender of deep sleep. Never had there been a more perfect man- not for me, anyway.

I rose, grabbing the light sheer robe that looked suspiciously like the one I seduced him with that first time. I draped it over my body and belted it before taking the stairs to the deck off of the kitchen. The sun would be rising soon, but that eerie darkness that screams storm covered the dawn, obliterating the sun's rays like they didn't exist.

Unable to stop myself, I opened the door and stepped out into the wind. It swept my hair straight back, causing it to lash my face and leave angry welts. Gods, this storm was powerful.

As long as I lived here, I had never left during a storm. In the beginning, it wasn't my choice; my parents had never thought of leaving. They never worried, and we didn't evacuate, despite the warnings. After they left, I still chose to stay. I never questioned or thought twice about it. I had never lived in a beach house during a big storm, though, and by the feel of it, this was a big storm.

I didn't turn on the radio and obsessively listen to the details: I wanted to feel them. And feel them I did. Through my connection with the earth, I could feel the power grow and the pressure drop as that monster drew nearer.

Hypnotized, I walked to the sand and strolled the few feet to the edge of the twisting, vicious surf as it boiled towards my house. It would stand. I knew that. I would use my power to keep it up if I had to. Though it survived Hurricane Hugo, so the bones underneath the gracefully weathered exterior were strong.

My robe slashed around my body, leaving me naked to the skies above, and I didn't care. The dark power of the storm cycled through me and back into the ground below.

It was terrifying.

It was beautiful.

I leaned my head toward the sky, and the robe was ripped from my body by the sheer force of the winds, and still, I stood, letting that power grip me.

Strong arms wrapped around my middle and tore me from the sand. I wailed, kicking and flailing against Aedan as he carried me to the steps and into the house. "Let it go, Anamcara. Let the storm go where it will- do not drag it to you. Let your connection go. It's sending your mind to dark places."

I heard his words and fought them. The power felt fantastic, and I wanted only to give myself over to it. I needed to experience it all. Taking the stairs two at a time with me in his arms, he tossed me on the bed and followed me down. I did not miss the dark look of lust and near madness on his face as he buried his face in my hair, inhaling the sharp scent of sea and storm from my skin.

I met his mad eyes with mine, and my lips crashed into his, drawing blood when they caught on his descended fangs. I fought to let the power go, but it didn't want to leave. It fought back. Just like that first time in the field where I used my power as a conduit to hide evidence, the land did not want to let me go. I wondered if it could suck me down and make me Gaia.

Without preamble, Aedan sank his fangs into my neck. Striking with the precision of a cobra. I came immediately from the sensation of his fangs and the earth's power. But the power receded, leaving only him. Just him. The link broke, and I caught the breath I was holding.

Leaning into him as he drank, I let my hands trail down his hard body, tracing the lines of his muscles and reveling in their strength. He could free me from that devastating cycle of power, and that's why he was God to me. God to my Goddess.

I flipped him over and sank onto his hardness, enjoying the feel of him stretching me. His groan was primal. Wind whipped around the house, causing her strong bones to creak. My blood made his lips glisten red, and I kissed it from him, enjoying the taste of me before I opened his vein and drank him down. His eyes closed, and the groan deepened to a snarl. He tried to pull me away, but I refused. Storm strengthened limbs held him down, and though my connection with the land had broken, the darkness remained.

Using fingers and tongue, I traced every muscle as he bucked against me, fighting for control. But tonight, control was mine. Sliding down his body, I took him into my mouth, all the way to the base. Sucking the sweet tang of myself off while digging my nails into his hips so deep, I felt blood flow. I fucked him with my mouth, and I took him as far as I could, enjoying the soft gag when it came.

He fought me then. Oh, did he fight me, and it was delicious. We had never played this hard, and I liked it. He grabbed my hair and tried to force me off of him, and I dug deeper into his flesh, sinking my nails in until skin met skin, and they were buried deep.

When he finally figured out that he wasn't winning. At least not tonight. He took my hair in his hands and smashed my face onto him, sucking in his breathe at each soft gag I made. He pushed past it, not caring. I didn't care either. He might think he had all the power, but when your lips are wrapped around a man's shaft, the power lies with you. Never forget that.

With my slobber as a lubricant, I rammed my thumb into his ass and massaged his prostate. He let out a howl that vied with the sound of the wind battering our home, then came down my throat. Swearing, he flipped me over when the last spasms calmed. His pale gold eyes warned me of what was in his heart, and he sank between my thighs to bite the tender flesh at the crux of my groin. I bucked off the bed and into him. Rearing his head back, he struck the other side so fast I didn't see him move, and he drank so much it dribbled from his mouth.

He never wasted my blood.

Crawling up my body like a slow-moving spider, I noted that his control was gone. Just gone. His eyes were almost white, and I didn't care one bit. He surged between my thighs, going balls deep in one thrust, making me scream from the stretch.

He used one broad palm to pin me by the throat while he fucked me hard enough to break a bed not made for this. His wild eyes held mine the whole time. With his free arm, he grabbed one leg and hiked it over his shoulder. The pressure was intense. Too intense, and I fell apart beneath him.

Those few moments when I had control of him fled like tourists in lousy weather. And once again, he broke me, only to build me back up with the sharp snap of his hips. I cried his name until I lost my voice and lay under his onslaught of pleasure, limp.

As his eyes darkened to their beautiful whiskey depths, he tossed his head back and cried my name as he came in the deepest part of me.

It was glorious.

The storm's power left me, and I was boneless and spread like a starfish beneath him. I held his eyes as he kissed the lines of my face and the curve of my collarbone before leaving me.

He came back with a hot towel and a smirk, using the former to clean our mess from my body and the latter to make me grin.

Tossing the towel in the corner and knowing I couldn't move if I tried, he arranged himself around me. Pulling a light sheet over us, we watched as the storm grew closer, and rain began to pelt our skylight.

I awoke sometime later. My last thoughts had been that I would miss the storm, but I was wrong. Wind lashed our house, and it creaked and groaned with every blast. It also swayed. The softness in the sway worried me. I eased from the bed, not wanting to wake Aedan, and went to make coffee. The wide French doors that opened onto the large deck beyond showed the scene in all its terrifying beauty.

Water surrounded us. The storm surge had covered the land underneath the house, and waves crashed beyond where my property ended, battering the road beyond. It wasn't deep, but it was present. High waves rolled up the stilts holding the structure aloft, making it sway. Palms bent horizontally to the ground, and objects flew by at alarming speeds.

I moved to put coffee in the French press.

When it was done, I sat at the table and watched the storm with clinical fascination. I wasn't afraid. Worst case scenario, the house would crash into the tempest of the sea below, and I would use my power to save us. We would survive. I didn't doubt that.

Aedan joined me, and I moved to pour him a cup of strong black coffee. His eyes were a bit wide when they took in our surroundings. "First time?" I asked, cocking my lips into a half-smirk.

"Actually, yes. Somehow, I missed the few hurricanes that came Baltimore's way. I have seen tropical storms, but nothing like this." His eyes darted to the doors again. It was cute.

"The house will stand; I won't let it fall." I chuckled, stepping into his arms. I dragged my lips over his chest, and he stiffened.

"I know."

"There's still power, at least for now; I'm going to grab a shower while I can." Pulling from him, I went upstairs, smiling to myself as his eyes followed me with predatory intent.

I wondered if we would ever get enough of each other. Would forever be enough to calm this wildness between us? I didn't think so.

I turned the water on sear your skin off hot, and stepped in, enjoying the sting of it on my back. With each destructive storm, the south learns. Most power and water lines were now buried deep beyond the reach of the storms that rocked the coast from time to time. We would eventually lose power; I was sure of that. A transformer would blow somewhere, and that would be that. The water would still be there, but it wouldn't be drinkable for a while. The pantries were stocked with food staples and jugs of water. After Hugo, all Die Hards kept at least a two-week supply of food and water. Although with Hugo, the power had been out and the water undrinkable for many more weeks than two. Two weeks was plenty of time for FEMA and the national guard to show up with extra supplies, though, so two weeks turned into the gold standard.

Had I been thinking, I would have a backup generator on hand, but so many things had happened after I bought the place that I hadn't had the time or forethought for that. Next time. I smiled as I washed.

I did love a good storm.

The house swayed gently. The wind seemed to settle a bit; I wondered if the eye was coming. I had no idea what the track of the storm was, but I had a feeling we were at the center of it, like always.

I smelled bacon and hurried to dress. This may be the last hot meal I had for a while, and I wanted to enjoy it as I watched the waters rise. The right side of the storm as it approaches land is the deadliest. The winds are higher, and the rain bands heavier. Storm surge is worse there, too, causing the most significant destruction. I wondered which side we sat on. It didn't matter; I wouldn't have left anyway. Idle curiosity had me wondering, that's all.

I dressed in loose-fitting comfy clothes. We weren't going anywhere. After dusting my face with powder and my lips with tinted gloss, I followed my nose to the kitchen. Aedan sat, scanning his phone. He didn't look up, and worry lines etched his face.

"It is a category 4 storm: a strong four. Landfall is just slightly south of here, but it may track north. We could be in the center of this, Lara."

He rarely used my name. Almost never. He was worried. Actually worried. The thought stilled my heart. I'd never known

Aedan to worry about much. He must be worried about me. A hurricane is something he couldn't control, and it had him on edge.

"Do you trust me?" I asked.

"You know that I do."

"It will be fine. I promise." Grinning, I sat across from him. I didn't want him to know I felt excitement at the thought of being on the right side of the storm. I also felt a twinge of fear, but I would never admit that.

"The storm's name is Daniel," he added.

I threw my head back and laughed so hard tears slipped from my eyes. "Of course, it is."

That's what had him worried. A storm named after one of the biggest betrayers he knew.

I sipped my coffee, watching him over the rim.

"Okay, you win."

Laying the coffee down, I closed my eyes and starting weaving a safety net using the power from the storm. I took the power of the wind, rain, and surge, weaving into a pattern I laced over the house from roof to footer. I took my time and made it stronger than the hurricane that inched our way.

When I opened my eyes, I found Aedan watching me with barely contained…something. I knew he didn't want me for my power, but he wasn't refusing it either. The look on his face was practically covetous.

The house stopped swaying. Water could envelop this place, and it would still stand. It would be a stationary submarine if the storm surge crested the roof. I hadn't been worried before, but I was damn near nonchalant about it now.

My skin glowed the color of moonlight, and my hair moved without the benefit of a breeze. Aedan pulled me from my chair, holding my arm behind my back. Faster than I could follow, my cheek was against the wall, and he was buried deep inside me before I could so much as protest.

I wasn't the only one made darker by the energy surrounding us. I was going to need another shower. He reached around, ripping over the core of me with his freakishly fast fingers until I shattered on him, screaming his name. He followed behind with a grunt, filling me forcefully.

Keeping my arm pinned between us, he leaned in and sank his fangs into the meat of my shoulder. Not to drink, but to claim.

"Do not heal that, little fae. I want to see your radiant skin marred by my fangs. Do you understand?" he asked, his voice dark and threatening.

"Yes," I choked out, blinking fast from the onslaught of emotion.

"Take your clothes off; today, you will be naked for me."

Oh, God.

I gushed my desire onto him with a groan. I liked him like this: wild, out of control, demanding, and dangerous. Just like the storm battering us from the outside, his feelings for me battered my insides. Dark and light; love and obsession- there must be balance. Today, it seemed, he would balance the scales.

My eyes never leaving his, I stripped, dropping the clothes to the floor.

"Eat." His whiskey-colored eyes roamed my body, taking in the way my auburn hair curled around my hips and how my nipples peaked under his stare.

I ate as he paced behind me, antsy with feelings I didn't understand.

Three times he ripped into that spot he wanted to claim, my body refusing to stay marked. Each time he tore my flesh, I screamed from the shock of it but got wetter and needed him more. Eventually, I found a way to block my innate healing ability, and the marks stayed. With a sense of intense satisfaction, he moved to sit across from me. Picking up his phone, he scrolled through the headlines as if I was not sitting naked in front of him.

Eventually, he set the phone down and scented the air. He looked like an animal doing it, and I felt a twinge of worry. His eyes bled a shade paler, and he flared his nostrils again.

"Run, little Fae," he growled. His eyes bled a shade paler still.

"Aedan?" I stuttered, watching his eyes.

"Run!"

I shot from my seat and ran to the stairs, taking them two at a time. Sometimes I forget what he is; how could I? Gods, the power rolling off of him rivaled mine- rivaled Dani's. Since his return from being nearly drained to death, his control had been absolute. Once he regained it, that is. It had not slipped. Not once. Now I wondered if it had been too much. He needed something, and as always, I would give it.

I slammed the door to our room shut, locking it and throwing a bit of power into the lock. I knew he wouldn't hurt me. I knew that. I just didn't understand his mood.

The door blasted from its hinges and flew to the side. He stalked toward me as I backed into the corner, thinking that would save me from whatever this was.

"You like a bit of uncertainty," he growled, crushing me into the wall before I saw him move. "You like a bit of danger, don't you? Does it ground you? Does it fill a need within you?" he murmured into my hair, making me soaked. I trembled against him, unable to form words. "You like a bit of raw power. Is that it?" he asked. "I am stronger than the storm. Never forget that, Lara Hennessey." My body slumped against him.

"You are mine," he said, breathing me in.

"Yes," I answered, my voice shaky.

"You. Are. Mine." It wasn't a question. "You will never let the darkness take you again. Do you understand? You will never bow to the power running through you. You are mine, and with me, you will stay. Do. You. Understand." His possessive growl sent another rush of adrenaline through my veins.

"Yes." Before I finished the word, he had pressed me to my knees and rubbed himself against my lips.

"Open," he ordered.

I opened my mouth and took him in.

I got it then. I had scared him. More than once. Aedan does not respond well to fear, and his reaction to it is always strong. My dark dance with the storm on the beach worried him, then the added fear over my nonchalance about the hurricane tipped the scales. I stood naked under the onslaught of the earth's power, and he hated that. He worried about it. He is unused to me being the dark one- it is usually him. His fear led him to claim me, to remind me that I was his. Possession is powerful, and that need rode him hard.

I understood it then; I did. I understood that he wasn't trying to control me but trying to make me control myself in much the same way I tried to help him regain control after he returned from his abduction. Then, I had used manipulation and gentle seduction to snap him back to reality; he was doing the same, just in a less gentle way.

Dani had warned me about taking too much of the Earth's power. She had. I hadn't heard. She said I needed to stay myself and to stay grounded. In the early morning hours at the edge of the hurricane named after my worst enemy, I almost lost myself. This was my reminder that there was always someone out there bigger than me, someone badder. I had needed it more than I knew.

Aedan set about proving that fact as he destroyed my mouth with his hips, not even giving me the option of gagging on him. I could barely breathe and loved it. I reached down to relieve the pressure between my thighs, and Aedan pulled himself from my mouth, slapping my cheek with his hardness.

"You will come when you deserve to. You are mine, mine to care for; do not make me punish you further." When I dropped my hand, he thrust into my mouth, and I suppressed a chuckle. He played a dangerous game here. I fucking loved this. Control sucked; this was way better.

The thing about power is no one wants it all the time. Control? Same deal. The strongest woman craves someone worthy of ceding control to, at least some of the time. A shiver went down my spine as I took him down my throat. He moaned, his legs shook, and I think he caught the hint that this might not be the punishment he intended it to be.

Gripping my hair, he pulled me to my feet with it and practically dragged me to the bed. He bent me over and teased the tight, puckered hole he seldom used. Using my arousal and my slobber, he coated himself before pushing into me with one stroke.

I howled at the intrusion, stiffening my body around him. It hurt. He always prepped me but not this time. The burn was intense as he thrust into me again and again without giving me time to adjust. He was bigger. He was badder. He was worthy and able to keep my power in check; he was just what I needed.

I relaxed into him, biting back a scream as he continued to dispense his version of punishment.

"I need to come," I whispered. "Please," I begged.

"No. You do not deserve it. You will never again lose yourself to darkness. Say it." He increased his speed, using all the speed a vampire has, and ripped me apart in the best way.

"I won't, Aedan." I cried, unable to stop the sob that trickled out. "Please," I whimpered.

"Promise me," he demanded, placing his hand on the small of my back and slamming deeper past the point of any resistance.

"Aedan." I breathed his name like a prayer. I couldn't promise that. Would I try? Of course. But I couldn't promise to stand on the edge of a storm and not be excited by the prospect of the power it represented. That's why I needed him. He needed to be there to pull me back. He knew that; I knew that. He was just making a point.

"Please," I begged him again. My legs shook from the effort it took to hold us up. The pressure between my thighs was intense, and stars danced across my field of vision. I felt the orgasm coming, whether he wanted it or not.

He emptied across my back, taking away the stimulation. I fell forward onto the bed with a sob forcing my thighs together to try to ease the throb.

"No. Keep them open," he said. "I will restrain you if necessary. Do not move."

I lay on my stomach with his seed cooling on my back and my legs spread wide. He stared down at me for a long time while my hot tears threatened to fall. I got it. I did. Although, I didn't think he needed to demean me to make his point.

"I have never seen anything more beautiful than you at this moment," he whispered in a voice filled with awe.

Oh.

"Come," he said gently.

I rose to shaky feet, letting him guide me to the shower. I couldn't heal the soreness in my ass without risking healing the mark he placed at the place where shoulder meets neck. His favorite spot. It would always be his now, just like me. He sat me down on the closed toilet while he turned on all of the shower heads in the oversized space.

When the water heated, he took my hand and pulled me in. I stood shivering and silent while he washed me tenderly.

I wasn't confused- not really. Love isn't a word; it isn't even a feeling: it's a spectrum. Sometimes hot, sometimes cold, sometimes angry, and sometimes peaceful, love is ever present. Like the air we breathe and the blood that flows through our veins- it is eternal.

He washed every part of me with slow reverence. Soaping and conditioning my hair while I stood on the verge of a breakdown. He saved me. Again. Had I lost myself last night, I would've been gone. Just gone. Sucked into the power that is the universe. How I knew that I can't say, but I did.

"I love you, Aedan. Thank you." Tears fell hotter than the water surrounding us, and I let them.

"There, Anamcara, let it out. I will never let you go. I will prove that however you need, whenever you need it, Liomsa. Is breá liom tú," he finished, his Irish lilt heavy with emotion.

He dropped to his knees behind me, parting the cheeks of my ass and placing soft kisses down it until he reached my core. Tilting against him to give him access, I felt the sharp thrill of his tongue slowly caressing my lips from this angle. He rolled the flat of it forward and back, again and again, until I came, desperately gripping the walls of the shower to keep myself from falling.

The orgasm wasn't soft or peaceful; it ripped from me like another punishment from being delayed too long. Hot liquid seeped from me, and he took it all in. Over and over, I crested and fell, crested and fell, until I couldn't stand, and he had to support me with his arms. When the last orgasm faded, he scooped me up and carried me to the bed, sitting me down and going back for a towel.

He dried me slowly from hair to feet, placing soft kisses along the way. We were spent. Sated. He dressed me in soft yoga pants and a light tee, brushing his fingers over the marks his fangs had left. "I apologize," he started.

"No, Aedan. Never apologize for loving me." I grabbed his hand and rose on unsteady feet.

Downstairs we sat at the table again, peace surrounding us; the spectrum of love shifted as the balance was restored. Outside calm reigned, as the eye was entirely over us.

The odd thing about hurricanes is how beautiful it is in the eye of the thing. Large flocks of birds are known to fly in the safety of the eye as it travels. When the eye makes landfall, the birds will then seek shelter, but as long as the eye holds, they are safe. There is a stillness not seen in nature in the middle of the worst nature can give, and it is beautiful. Funny how beauty can be found anywhere, even in the dichotomy of something so wicked as a category five beast. It could last minutes or an hour, depending on how fast this thing was moving, but until that eyewall passed, you would find peace in the chaos of the storm.

The sun peeked through the eerie yellow haze that signaled the end was nowhere near. The winds had settled to a swift breeze, and as much as I longed to go outside and feel the eye for myself, I did not. I sat and sipped my coffee, watching the yellow fade to gray as the eyewall approached. You could see it, moving in from the southeast, a violent wall of wind and rain. I braced myself for the strike.

And strike it did.

For the next twelve hours, fierce winds assaulted the house, waves crashed over the lower balcony, and we retreated upstairs. I knew the magic would hold, but the sight of the water submerging the railings over and over finally rattled me.

It's one thing to weather the storm in a house set back from the coastline and entirely another to ride it out oceanfront. As much as I love hurricanes, I may never do it again. From our bed, we watched through the windows as the right side of the hurricane roared across our home. We lost power when the transformer down the street blew. Internet service was right behind as a nearby tower fell.

We curled together against our headboard and watched as the grim grey light faded to the dark of night, and all we could do was hear. Sometime during the night, we slept to the sound of howling winds and wild waves.

When veiled sunlight reached us through the skylight above, I knew it was over. After nearly twenty-four hours, the slow-moving storm moved on, continuing to skate up the South Carolina coast before moving out to sea near the Outer Banks.

Hurricane Daniel killed twenty-four people on the coast and inland, where violent tornados struck. The Santee and Waccamaw Rivers raged, flooding and killing more than the high winds. The storm had jogged north, initially following the same track as Hugo but turning just in time to make landfall in Georgetown. The vast eye covered Pawleys as well, and the devastation was widespread. Very little had survived being on the right side of that storm.

Too Ra Loo Ra Lara did. She was the only structure that stood in a mile radius. She was not unharmed, though. The lower decking had been ripped off, and one of the stilts showed signs of severe stress. We had forgotten to lower the hurricane shutters, and by the time we remembered, it was too late.

I was off my hurricane game.

A tree branch had blown through one of the windows in the guest room, and the room sustained massive water damage. A foot of sand from the beach covered the floor of my carport, carrying into the street beyond. Piles of sand were everywhere, and I knew it would be a long time before we could return to this place and even longer before the area recovered.

We walked hand and hand, taking in the destruction around us. We weren't alone. Oddly, we were not the only Die Hards that rode out that storm. Squat concrete homes had survived as well as a few other beach houses. Some, like ours, were barely touched, and others were leveled. That's the one thing I never understood about this kind of destruction.

We stumbled across an entire house sitting in the middle of the road. Just sitting there with the tea service still on the table. That kind of imperfect destruction was unfathomable to me, and I blamed myself for the storm tracking north. Still, the thing was so big a mile here or there mattered not, and I let it go. Could I have pushed it out to sea? I don't know. Maybe. That I discounted it from the beginning made it worse because, by the time I realized the size of the thing, it was too late. Maybe my hubris caused twenty-four people to lose their lives, but I'll never know. That thought would haunt me forever.

Aedan retrieved Samuel's car from Caro's, where he had stashed it for safety. I walked to the closest passable road, and we drove to the airport, boarded his jet, and flew home.

Chapter 6

The flight was quiet. Aedan kept me within reach of his touch as he caught up on business using his laptop or phone. He let everyone know we were okay. Our friends had been worried sick and grateful for the heads up. My parents were like me, sure we would be fine and nonplussed by the storm.

Aedan was not nonplussed. Some level of worry stayed with him as we made the trek from BWI to Westminster. Only when we were in our drive did his shoulders droop, and he allowed his other hand to drift from my thigh to the wheel.

This thing had scared him. Whether it was the storm, me, or his response to both of those things, I couldn't tell, but only when our new house came into view did he relax. Pressing a button, he opened the garage door from a distance then revved the P1 once, sliding into the space smoothly. I would have dropped the tranny trying to get the sleek speedster up the drive and into the garage safely. I was getting those keys so I could practice.

"I'll hold those for you, babe," I said, making a hard swipe at the keys.

"I think not, Liomsa. Perhaps someday, but I've had enough worry over you for a bit," he said with a soft chuckle. He opened the door to our new home and ushered me in.

The chaos we left was non-existence upon our return. Soft music played from the kitchen, and the lights were dimmed. The place was pristine and still had the faint smell of newness and paint to it.

Laughter echoed down the halls, and I thought about what a difference a few weeks make. During Aedan's absence, my house felt vacant and empty, regardless of how many vampires were camped out. Our new home already felt lived in and loved.

The boxes were gone, and everything was in its place. The decorator had done a fantastic job capturing and blending Aedan's style to mine, not that I thought I had one, but she nailed it. If I'd had unlimited resources and a design magazine, I would have made the same choices. With the chaos of moving in, I didn't notice before just how perfect the design was.

We went with nothing and came back with nothing, so we had nothing to put away. We had left the beach house to the management company and the dirty laundry to the cleaning service. We wouldn't be back for a while anyway.

Soft, white light led us deeper into the home. Lunch was laid out in the kitchen, and I grabbed a plate while Aedan walked the hallways in search of the others.

Six feet of blonde vampire tackled me to the ground, causing the air to vacate my lungs."You're back!" Grania said, flashing her fangs dangerously close to my eyeball.

"I'm back! Get off!" I tried to yell, but it came out as a cough because that bitch is heavy. "Ugh," I whimpered, hoping my plate was intact.

She hopped off and pulled me to my feet, "I missed you, too," I grumbled, turning back to my plate. "How have things been?"

I didn't ask how she did without me nearby. She had done well. Her eyes were bright, and her cheeks flushed. She looked great, and never had I been prouder of her for grabbing her independence and running with it.

"Things were good. Fangs is set to open as soon as you and dad are available to be there; I want to do a grand opening, so pick a date," she started. "Your parents have taken over Jeremy. All of him. They are teaching him to ride and swordfight. They may have mentioned that we are all terrible teachers," she stopped with a laugh.

"I knew I shouldn't have left them unattended," I said, shoving another bite of Cook's gourmet beef wellington into my throat. Chewing slowly, I waited for her to continue.

"The clinic was actually kinda slow. Bethany handled almost everything, and what she didn't, Noah did. It was fine; I promise," she grinned, and the light glinted in her iced-husky blue eyes. "The only issue I had with you being gone was a little nausea from time to time, and I seem to have needed more sleep, but otherwise, I did fine."

"Nausea? I asked. "Are you still eating okay? No problems with that?" I asked.

Grania was my best friend, but she was also bound to me by blood. When Aedan disappeared, she had almost gone crazy. The only way to save her was to bind her to me. Since I'm no vampire, there had been some unusual…consequences to my actions. For one, she got her magic back and had been enjoying the best of both the vampire and fae worlds. Also, she could eat. She peed and pooped like the rest of us. She had gotten her very first period ever; that had been a shock.

"Um, any vomiting?" I asked, casting a sidelong glance at her. I put my fork down; my appetite gone.

"Yeah, every morning, I puke. I can't even brush my damn teeth. It's the craziest thing," she laughed, plucking a piece of beef from my plate.

Fuck.

"Hey, honey. When was your last period?" I turned, facing her head on.

"I mean, you were there. When was that? Like six-eight weeks ago? Thank the Goddess that's over."

I groaned low. "You never got another one?" I asked.

"Uh, no. Why would I? It's a one and done kinda thing, right? I mean, you get it, but you're unique," she nodded her head in affirmation. My chin dropped to my chest, and I let out a long sigh.

She'd never gotten a period in her life and, in her undeath, hadn't paid attention to the harrows of humanity. Binding with me had made her unique, too; she had just forgotten.

"Come on, we need to go to the clinic." I grabbed her arm and headed toward the front door.

"No, no. We don't go that way anymore. You left so fast, we didn't have time to show you some of the more, um, exotic safety features of the house. Digging her heels in, she pulled me to a stop and redirected us through the kitchen.

She opened a door, and we descended a brightly lit staircase that ended in a long stone tunnel.

"There's a tunnel to my house?" I asked, shocked. I had never seen a tunnel in the plans.

"It goes right to the clinic so that you don't have to walk outside if you don't want to. Plus, you don't have to disturb your parents. They are, uh, active folks," she laughed, throwing her head back. Her long blonde hair shimmered.

Gross.

"Okay, lead the way, I guess."

"The passage is heated in the winter, but I'm sure it will stay cool in the summer, too. Aedan had the idea, and Guy went with it."

Aedan's contractor, Guy, probably had an offshore bank account filled with the money Aedan paid him. I had no doubt he 'went for it' when Aedan added changes to his house plans.

It was a great idea so I couldn't complain. Too many times, we had been attacked, kidnapped, and nearly murdered, making the journey between our homes. No more.

She opened the clinic door with a push. Light filtered through a curtain that would protect my patients from a sudden intrusion through the door.

"Have a seat." I flopped into my office chair, enjoying the feel of being back.

"Okay, so are we here because you think I have a virus?" she asked. "I haven't fed from anyone but Paul," she finished, referencing the Vampire Infectious Disease that had plagued the vampire community of late.

"No, sweetie. I don't think you have a virus."

"What then? Do you think your magic is wearing off? Maybe I can't tolerate food anymore. I thought about that. I should quit eating."

"Grania," I said, taking a big breath. "I think you're pregnant."

"The fuck, you say?" She jumped up from her seat across from me. "No way. Impossible."

Only it wasn't. I remembered thinking when she got her period that she might need birth control. Then shit went sideways, and I forgot about it. How I could have, I don't know, but I did. "Sit down," I said.

She sat slowly, watching me like a mouse watches the rattlesnake. "It's my fault. I should've put you on the pill."

"A pill? One pill? Of course, you should've given me a pill."

"It's more than one pill, Grania. You take it every day at the same time." Reaching across the table, I gripped her hand in mine.

"Oh, well, I can't do that. I'm here, there, and everywhere. I can't be pregnant anyway; I'm a vampire," she insisted, crushing my hand in her grip. Her eyes were wide and had bled so much that the blue was barely visible.

"But you're not just a vampire anymore, are you, honey?"

"Fuck."

"Yes, fuck."

"Okay, take a look," she said with a deep breath to prep herself. I did.

Closing my eyes, I focused on her body, weaving my way through her systems. Heart and lungs looked good; intestines looked healthy. And there in her uterus sat a little kidney bean-shaped blob that already had limb buds. Its little heartbeat was fast and sure. It felt like a girl.

"I think it's a girl," I said just in time to watch Grania slump from the chair and faceplant onto the floor.

I cradled her head in my lap while her synapses readjusted, waiting for her to come around. I petted her hair until she rolled over with a groan.

"I don't believe you." Her eyes snapped open, and she rushed to sit up.

"Then pee on a stick; damn. I mean, I am a Faerie Healer; this is kinda my wheelhouse," I grumbled, walking away from her to get the damned pregnancy test.

I kept a supply of them for the humans that filtered through my doors; it made them feel better to see the little plus sign. I could tell them with more certainty, but some folks really needed that symbol.

Fifteen tests later, she finally believed me.

"Now what?" she asked; her manner was subdued.

"Now you have decisions, Grania. I'm sorry, I am; I should have thought about it."

"No, Lara. I'm not a complete idiot. I should've known; I'm old enough to know better. I know what a period means. With all the changes in my body, I knew that this was a possibility. Somewhere in the back of my mind, I knew. You were doing your best to hold Aedan's House together and to find him: this isn't on you. It's just a shock, you know? I mean, Paul is no spring chicken."

"Listen. You have some things to think about. Both of you. And as much as I love you and as much as I would give my life for you. Please don't ask me to unmake that little critter in there. It's your decision, and I believe in choice, but I can't do it."

"Okay," she said. "No. I know. I wouldn't ask you to do that. Can I just sit here a minute? Alone?"

"Sure, sweetie." Rising, I left her alone in the dim light of my clinic and made my way back the way we came.

"Aibhleog mo Chroi where in this monstrosity are you hiding?" Aedan asked through our bond.

"Coming, love," I answered.

"Now that is a nickname I can support." I felt his pleasure brush the edges of my mind and smiled as I made my way home.

Chapter 7

Aedan met me at the door, he had showered and changed, and I was sorry I missed it. "Is everything okay?" he asked. "I sensed your worry."

"Let's go upstairs," I said, not wanting anyone to overhear our conversation.

Our rooms were another shock. Someone had unpacked for us, and it looked amazing. Everything was exactly where I would have put it. Knickknacks, trinkets, pictures, and clothes were put in orderly and logical places. I felt terrible yet grateful for whoever had done it.

I took a minute to walk the room and enjoy the fresh, homey feel of it. With the doors and windows closed, no sound penetrated the silence of the space. Aedan had spent a ton on soundproofing. And given our sex life, it wasn't a bad idea.

I wandered the room, looking at things; he didn't push me for a response. He understood that sometimes it took me a minute to get my thoughts together, especially when it was something important. I thought maybe I should keep the news about Grania's baby to myself as it was hers to tell. Still, there were ramifications to her pregnancy that would affect all of us, including Aedan- especially Aedan. When word got out, vampires worldwide would react in one way or another, and neither way would be good for me.

My position with them was already tenuous. After curing Mikolosi of his vampirism, I was feared more than I had been when I was merely an urban legend. Still, I was respected, too. The decision to make him human again had been theirs; I just carried out their will.

Would they come to me seeking help to conceive their own children? Or, knowing my luck, would they feel like their lifestyle was being threatened and want to eliminate the threat? Neither option would be good.

Grania was a fluke. Somehow, binding her to me with magic and sharing blood with her fixed parts of her while allowing other parts of her to remain a vampire. I didn't know, and I wasn't doing it again.

"Grania is pregnant," I said, finally facing him.

Silence stretched between us as I watched him struggle with a myriad of emotions. "She is what?" he asked, settling on confusion or possibly denial.

"Pregnant."

"That cannot be," he said, holding my eyes. I wouldn't hold his doubt against him. It wasn't a statement about my skills as a Healer or healthcare professional. He was just stunned.

"I have fifteen positive pregnancy tests and my own magic that says it can." I sighed, taking a seat in the reading area of our bedroom.

He stood still in the way only a vampire can. Nothing natural can be so motionless; the closest thing I have ever seen are snakes.

Only snakes will occasionally blink. I'd seen Aedan do it a few times, and it was always unnerving. He held the position for a long time.

Finally, he took a breath he didn't need and slid to me like mercury. "I'm going to be a grandfather?" he asked, sitting beside me and taking my hands.

"No. Hell, no. You are going to be an uncle. A really old uncle. See, I'm too young to be a grandma, and Grania is my best friend, so I'm going to be the super cool aunt. That means you can't be a grandfather."

"I am going to be a grandfather," Aedan whispered the words like a prayer, and I knew I was losing this argument.

"Bub, If we are married and you are the grandfather, and I am the really cool aunt, that implies incest on our part. So, no, you are the stodgy old uncle; she can call you Uncle Aedan. Gramps doesn't sound right anyway," I tried.

He crushed his mouth to mine, cutting my lip with the ferocity of his kiss and his fangs. His joy was palpable. Never had I felt such happiness from him.

"Aedan, wait," I started, pushing him away. "She is shocked; I'm not sure she'll keep the baby. She has a lot to think about." He went still again, watching my face.

Dropping his head to his chest, he sighed, rubbing his hand down his face. "You are right. I apologize. This is a significant development. Huge. I got carried away."

"Don't apologize; she just needs time. This is something she never thought would happen. She might need a minute." I leaned into him and wrapped my arms around his waist.

He dropped his head onto mine. "They will come to you when they find out. All of them. Making our own children helps with the desire to procreate, but it does not take the place of having a child of your blood. You will again be hunted," his voice turned hard, and I knew he would do whatever it took to keep me safe. We both would.

"I know," I said, thinking about my next words carefully. "Do you want children?" I asked, already knowing the answer. His only child had died in the womb of his first love. Killed at the hand of my grandmother. Those deaths had sent him on a thousand-year killing rampage; I damn well knew he had wanted kids.

"It is not possible, Anamcara," he answered without answering.

"Aedan, you know that isn't true. I know you keep from me what my blood and magic have done to you. I don't care. I get it, but I know you hold back. A lot. If my magic and blood can fix Grania to the extent she can conceive, it can fix you too; it probably already has," I said, holding his eyes with mine. "Do you want children?" I asked more firmly, enunciating each word.

This is something couples should discuss. We were already engaged, but it still mattered. I'd never planned on being a mom. But as they keep telling me, my life will be long, and plans change.

"I do," he answered, finally giving voice to both our fears.

He wanted children he thought he could never have, and I didn't want children that I believed that he could, at least not yet.

First chance, I was giving myself a depo shot. Dani already warned me she wanted grandbabies. That in itself told me just how possible it was; if the Goddess of Life and the Maker of All Things says she wants grandchildren, you're probably going to give them to her.

"I'm not saying no. I'm just saying not now. Okay? We have a war to win." Before I could say anything else, he kissed me again, effectively shutting me up.

He kissed my lips, my cheek, and my neck until he got to his favorite spot where it meets the shoulder. He sank his fangs to the gum and pulled a mouthful of blood from me, causing a shiver to go down my back. He didn't need it. He could get by with feeding once a month, but we had both developed an addiction to having his fangs in my body. He took another mouthful, and I shuddered against him. No wonder I was addicted.

He smiled, his face was so filled with joy that I couldn't help but smile back. Twirling me around him once, he set me back on my feet. Just me saying I would consider having a baby with him made him so happy. How could I take that away?

Pulling away, he licked the holes closed and dropped his lips to mine. "You are right, and this is one of the many reasons why I love you," he said, rising and adjusting himself through his pants. "Come; there are a few rooms that were not in the filed plans for the house that I would like to show you.

We left our suite to explore. I had visited the house several times a week when it was being built. Towards the end, I would come every day to answer questions or pick out finishes. I had not seen it finished, though; unpacked and put away, it was gorgeous. Aedan's designer had done a fantastic job. His old house had been opulent, majestic even. It had been done in reds and golds and looked exactly what you would expect from a powerful, insanely rich vampire.

This place was different. No longer compelled to show off his wealth and position, Aedan had picked understated neutrals with pops of color here and there. He meant what he said when he brought me those house plans that initially terrified me. He had found a way to marry our styles, and the house was elegant yet cozy, gigantic yet gentle. It was old Charleston meets the modern world, and I loved it. It screamed old money in the way the other house did not. There was nothing pretentious about it.

We walked through the halls, stopping to talk to those we came across. Aedan went to great lengths to rebuild his House after Aiyana burned it down, literally and figurately. There were dozens of new vampires and humans living with us now; all had been carefully vetted before taking his oath. He had not made any vampires since Daniel as he worried his blood was too powerful, but he had been thinking more and more about trying again.

He really did want children, and my soul ached for him.

He showed me a large room behind the kitchen. Windows opened to the side yard, and an open door showed a half bath. The walls were painted white and a calming shade of blue that was not unlike the ocean. French doors opened to another room that contained a functional office that already smelled like blood, honey, and fall leaves.

"This is your office," Aedan said, "You could put in a medical area for emergencies or a desk to work on your paperwork. It would not take the place of your clinic, but it would allow some of those late nights to be here instead of there."

"Thank you, it's very thoughtful. I wouldn't have thought to make an office space." I turned to him, feeling the big smile spread across my face.

"You did not ask for anything," he said. "You made no changes to the plans and requested nothing for yourself."

"Not true. I asked for one of those instant water heaters and for the laundry room to be in the garage, so we don't track blood through the house."

He belly laughed and wrapped his arms around me. "Yes, I suppose you did ask for that, but you asked for nothing of consequence," he said, his laughter showing in the corners of his eyes. "I smell Italian. It is dinnertime, and you must be hungry," he added after my stomach let loose a fierce growl.

"I could eat." I nodded my head like we both hadn't just heard proof of my hunger,

We were heading toward the kitchen when I heard my mom calling from the front of the house. Aedan rolled his eyes, making me chuckle. I guess he has in-laws too.

"There you are," mom said, hugging me. All five feet of her glared at Aedan from around my side. "You stole our daughter and didn't allow her to notify us before she left." She pulled away, crossing her arms. My four dads stood like a wall behind her, scowling. Their arms were crossed exactly like hers; they looked like a step dancing troop getting ready to bust a move.

"Mom, I had my cell. I texted you from the car before we got to the airport." I hugged her hard, then pushed her away.

"Not good enough," Seal said, pinning Aedan with his deadly glare.

"Dad," I groaned.

"It is a courtesy to notify a child's fathers before removing her from their care," Laith added, his own glare so close to mine that it was eerie.

"Dad," I groaned louder, drawing the word out in two syllables in true southern style. "I'm an adult."

"Were we in Talamh na Sithe, you would be considered a child and under our roof," Lann added, his dark eyes flashing mischief.

"Oh, my God," I mumbled. "We aren't in Talamh na Sithe." Inside I smiled. My parents had missed so much of my life that they enjoyed parenting my grown ass endlessly. "I'm going to eat now; you are welcome to join me."

"This isn't over, young lady, and you," she said, pointing a finger at Aedan. "We'll be finishing this conversation later in the basement."

I laughed out loud then. "Mom, really?" I asked. Aedan was the oldest and strongest of our kind, yet she stood in his kitchen and threatened him. I almost felt bad for him, though. As Aedan didn't know who his father was, I only had a mother-in-law to deal with. Yes, she was the Great Goddess and The Maker of All Things, but she was just one person. Aedan had five people to deal with, all of whom had powerful personalities. It was laughable.

Then I remembered what was in the basement, and my eyebrows scrunched together. There were two underground levels beneath the main floor of the house. One contained rooms for the younger vampires who didn't tolerate the sun. There were community spaces and private baths off these rooms, and the area had quickly filled due to its comfort. Below that was an entire level dedicated to training. Areas for the different types of fighting were separated by glass walls, allowing others to see what was going on but not be affected by the odd arrow going array. There was even an indoor shooting range capable of handling any type of firearm fired there.

I had not seen the finished training rooms yet, but Grania had told me all about them. They were, by far, the most popular common spaces in the house. My mom wanted to take Aedan to the training rooms and try her skill against his sword, most likely. Even more likely was it that this whole angry parent thing was engineered to get Aedan down there and fighting against them. They did love to fight, and fighting Aedan would be leveling up for them.

"Uuuuugh," I groaned again. "I'm eating now." Grabbing another plate, I piled it high with Cook's amazing food. Tonight's special was stuffed shells with giant meatballs, a large salad dripping in a light vinaigrette, and homemade bread that was still warm.

"Your cook already brought a meal over to the house," Saige said. "We've left money on the counter, but he won't take it." He walked over, grabbing a seat next to me.

"He has no need for your money. I pay him well," Aedan said, narrowing his eyes at my family as if to say he has an endless ability to care for us all.

I grabbed another slice of warm bread and looked over at Saige. He had trimmed his silver hair to his shoulders, and his gray eyes shimmered in the light from the overhead fixture. High vaulted ceilings allowed the natural light from the windows to make the space brighter and highlight the beauty of his complexion. He smiled, giving me a wink; then he stole my bread.

My mother moved around the kitchen, opening doors and checking out things. Aedan patiently leaned against the door jamb, impatiently pinching the bridge of his nose as he scanned the scene around him.

The only thing that would make this moment complete would be if his mother showed up. I hunched down, peeking from under my eyelashes, hoping she wouldn't materialize.

"Anamcara, when you finish, join us downstairs." Aedan pecked my cheek, sending a warning growl towards my fathers, causing me to drop my head and shake it. I watched their receding backs with genuine concern. They seemed to be taking this hazing of their daughter's mate a bit far. Although who's to say who had the worst end of this- Aedan or my parents.

I chewed the mouth-watering meatballs thoughtfully and watched them walk toward the stairs. There was an elevator somewhere in the back, but none of them went for it. Shaking my head, I finished my meal, loaded the dishwasher, and cleaned up before I headed down. I was determined to make this entire house my home and not just the suite upstairs. With the sheer size of the place and the dozens of people living here, it might be difficult, but I felt like it was necessary. The house needed a center, and as much as I didn't want to be den mother to a bunch of vampires, Aedan and I needed to fill that role.

I said hello and chatted idly with vampires and their human companions as they passed by, heading downstairs. Word must've gotten out that something was going on in the training center because they all headed that way. Sighing, I hung up my dishtowel and followed them.

I followed the cheers to the training room, entering just in time to see Aedan's sword go flying and the triumphant look on my mother's face. My fathers stood, looking sympathetic to Aedan's plight. I'd heard she was unbeatable with a sword; it seems I heard right.

"Again," he said, his narrow eyes marginally paler than they should be.

He picked up his sword and parried with her again. They moved faster than the eye could truly follow. There were flashes of her red hair and sword tips, then a blur of blades. They were incredible. The ringing of swords clashing silenced conversation as the crowd around them thickened. The observation deck above the floor filled, and the air was filled with excitement.

I went and stood next to Lann, who dropped an arm over my shoulder, dwarfing me. "I almost feel bad for the lad, you know? I've been on the other side of your mother's blade. It is not a fun place to be," he finished with a chuckle. "He disarmed her in the first match, first time I've ever seen that, and he's lasted far longer than I ever did against her. He's a good fighter, Lara. He'll make an excellent mate for you," he said proudly, his Irish accent much thicker than I had ever heard it.

"I'm not really sure compatibility should be judged by how well one holds a sword, dad," I said, snuggling into his side.

"What other way is there, lass?" he asked, genuinely not knowing the answer. They are barbarians, all of them.

Aedan's scent mixed heavily with the smell of cookies that I recognized as my mother's. They struck and countered, then struck again. For the most part, they seemed evenly matched. I knew my mother wouldn't pull her punches and didn't think Aedan would either. The fight went on far longer than I'd ever seen of any sparring match of any kind.

I caught Jeremy's eyes, and they shone with glee over the mock battle. He sat on the edge of his seat, barely restrained by his mother's hand on his shoulder. Alisondro watched the fight with clinical, narrow-eyed assessment. The smell of sweat and the faint scent of blood covered the natural scents of the fighters. When finally they stood apart, breathing heavily, they were drenched.

"Jeremy seems mightily interested in this match," Lann said.

"He does," I whispered, looking over at Jeremy.

"He will be a good swordsman someday. He is positively transfixed."

"Yeah, sure. Good idea; make him a swordsman in the age of heavy artillery and smart bombs, dad," I laughed. He scowled down at me, and I turned away so he couldn't see my big smile.

The applause started slowly, then built to a defending level. I'm sure the vampires in the room never dreamed their leader could be defeated by a woman measuring a tad under five feet tall, for he surely didn't win. At best, the match was a draw. Both of them had smears of blood on their skin and broad smiles on their faces. My mother went to shake Aedan's hand, but he pulled her into a quick hug instead.

"Come, daughter. Your turn," Lann said, pulling me onto the floor. "We must hone your skills."

"Dad, I don't think so." I balked, pulling back from him.

"I do think so." He dragged me like a stubborn child. Aedan gave a broad smile as he walked past us.

Others joined in the various training rooms, and soon Saige was making arrows fly as Jeremy stood beside him, mirroring his stance.

"Take up your blade, little one," he said, and I laughed. No one would presume to call me little one.

"Dad, I'm not little."

"You're little to me. Take up your blade."

Laith sidled next to me, holding the sword he'd made. The look on his face was so sweet that I softened. "Fine," I said, clutching the sword.

Aedan and I had sparred before. If I used magic, I wasn't half bad. I know he took it easy on me, as did Grania anytime we used blades to fight. Swords weren't really her thing anyway; she preferred hand to hand. I could be decent with a sword but just didn't see the point. I had so much magic that if it came down to a swordfight, I was screwed. But I could see how much it meant to them, so I took the damn sword and stood blade to blade with my father, Captain of the Queen's Blades, holding a sword made by my other father, The Queen's Master Swordsmith.

He started slowly, parrying to my left and right, testing my responses. I focused on his blade and the movement it made, just like Aedan taught me.

"Bring your elbow in just a bit and straighten your back," he said, correcting my posture before moving back to point.

We parried more, and I got the feel of it. Aedan had started teaching me the sword under the guise of dancing, and he was right; it is a dance. Thinking I was sneaky, I infused my blade with just a touch of magic. It glowed a soft rose-gold, and Lann smirked at me. I didn't let that stop me from cheating.

I moved with my father in a dance most girls would never learn, and I never dreamed I would have a chance to experience. Aedan and my parents watched as the Master Swordsman taught me everything he could. I'd had some practice, but he showed me the finer points and broke it down in a way I could understand. It was easier to learn as he didn't distract me in the ways Aedan did. By the end of our session, I could have definitely fought my way out of a paper bag should I need to. Should my magic fail, I'd have respectable skill with a backup method of protection.

When we were done, I found most eyes had turned to us, watching the lesson with rapt attention. My parents surrounded me with praise and hugs, and for just a minute, I glimpsed what life could have been like had Aramea not forced them to flee their home. They had given me the best foundation they could, though. Under difficult circumstances and with great personal sacrifice, they had provided the best life they knew how, and for that, I was grateful.

"Thanks, Dad," I said, hugging Lann. "That was great."

He smiled his response, his eyes damp at the corners.

"That was beautiful; your focus was much better with your father." Aedan came to my side, placing a kiss on my sweaty hair.

I slapped his chest. "You make it hard to concentrate sometimes, babe," I said with a laugh.

"I am not a babe," he replied, scowling down at me.

"Oh, but you are a babe, babe." I rolled my eyes and patted his chest as we abandoned the sword room for the benches along the walls.

We watched as others practiced and sparred, fought, and played. Everyone seemed to be having such a good time that I hated to leave. The only people missing were Grania and Paul, and I missed them. I knew they had more significant issues but had hoped they would at least make an appearance.

Eventually, we filtered upstairs with promises to meet again tomorrow. The atmosphere had that pre-hurricane feel to it. We all knew something big was coming but wanted to make the most of the peaceful time we had now.

I hugged my parents at the door, watching them walk across the field to what was once my house. I guess it still was, but I didn't look at it that way. When Aedan asked me to live with him, I imagined us moving back and forth between our houses, splitting time. Now that I had spent a few hours in the house we built together, I knew I never wanted to leave. It was ours, and it already had the feel of both of us.

Holding hands, we walked the stairs to our floor, the grand staircase wide enough that we could go side by side. I took in the foyer from above, smelled the fresh paint mixed with Cook's Italian food, and knew I was home.

Chapter 8

The lights were dimmed when we opened the door to our rooms. I moved into the kitchen, turning on the Keurig so I could make a quick cup of coffee. It had been a long day. From South Carolina to Maryland to the emotional time with my family, I was exhausted. It was early yet, and I knew Aedan had work to do. Coffee never kept me awake anyway.

Aedan had loosened his tie and gone to stand by the windows, "Do you want a cup of coffee?" I asked.

"No, thank you. I am going to shower and make some calls. I will use the office up here, as long as it will not keep you awake."

"Actually, I think I'm going to sit on the balcony and watch the stars for a bit. You won't be keeping me up." I took my coffee and opened wide the French doors, letting in the warm night air.

I settled into an oversized Adirondack chair, curling my legs under me. Lights shined through the windows in the little house across the field, and I imagined my parents moving around happily, just glad to finally be together. I could hear Aedan behind me and the soft sound of his voice on the phone.

My eyes were drifting shut when my phone rang, jerking me awake.

"Hennessey," Agent Johnson said when I answered.

"Yeah," I mumbled, shaking off sleep.

"Sorry it's so late, but I wanted you to know I got a lead on those missing boxes of Aedan's blood you mentioned. I've bumped it up the line because this could be big," she started, her voice nearly crackling with excitement.

"Big, how?" I asked, my gut sinking.

"I was able to trace your friend Ben Devers. Using his debit card purchases, I found that after Aedan went missing, he made a day trip to Morgantown, West Virginia."

"What the hell is in Morgantown, West Virginia, besides a bunch of drunk college students?" I asked. Only I did know. Ben Devers, aka Sheriff Collins, told me that Aiyana made sure a box of Aedan's blood went to some out of the way lab. He said they were experimenting with the blood on humans. He told me this after he shot me in the chest with a Mossberg Tactical shotgun, leaving me a little too distracted to ask the right questions.

I had meant to track down labs the blood could've gone to, but with my schedule of late, I hadn't had time. It seems I had mentioned it on the phone to the helpful FBI agent, and the one thing I didn't want her to go after, she did.

"Excellent question," she said, making me focus on her again. "What's in Morgantown is an old pharmaceutical plant that was converted to a private research lab. Devers made a trip there only hours after Aedan went missing. He used his card at a Sheetz gas station directly across the street; it can't be a coincidence. The higher-ups are looking for an excuse to raid the place. I'll let you know when we go in and what we find. Hopefully, I'll have those answers by the end of this week, next week, at the latest," she finished.

"Good plan," I lied. "Make sure you have your ducks in a row and all the warrants signed, agent. I don't want these fuckers to weasel out of this," I said, knowing there was no way we could let the government get a hold of anything in that lab having to do with Aedan. We needed to get there first.

Agent Johnson gave me all the information we needed to find the place. Old Ben Devers had fibbed a little or at least omitted the fact that he, himself, had dropped the blood off. He could have saved me the trouble of having to hunt this place down, but Agent Johnson handed it to me on a silver platter.

"Good luck, Agent," I said. "Update me when you raid the place." I thanked her and hung up the phone, wishing that I didn't have to have this conversation with Aedan.

I was headed to Aedan's office when a knock pulled me to the door. Aedan's old rooms had keycards, and these were no different. The difference was that there were only two- his and mine. That had been his idea, and it was a good one. He wanted to limit access and increase our privacy, and I was not opposed to that.

Aedan popped out of the little office off of the kitchen and met me at the door; experience has made us twitchy. Hopefully, we would feel safe in our home someday, but for now, we use an abundance of caution. I opened the door slowly; I doubted that whoever knocking would shoot me in the chest, although you never know. It's happened before.

Grania stood with Paul at the top of the stairs. I opened the door wider, ushering them in. They glanced at each other before moving into the cool, quiet.

"Have a seat." Aedan sat with me on the smaller sofa, leaving them the couch facing us. I leaned into his arm and waited for my best friend to speak, only it was Paul who started.

"Aedan, I've come to ask you to turn me," he said, and the air went out of the room. "I know you don't make new vampires anymore, but I've been here for this House. I've been loyal to both you and Grania for years. I know I signed the DNR order and said I didn't want to be turned, but I've changed my mind."

"Why have you changed your mind, Paul? After all these years, why now?" Aedan asked, his voice not giving away his thoughts. I could feel his unease through our bond. He didn't want to make new vampires; he worried he was too potent a Sire.

"Because I'm pregnant," Grania whispered. "I want to keep the baby. I never thought I'd be a mom. I was sixteen when I turned and had never thought about it. And of course, after..." she finished, her voice trailing off with unsaid words. "Dad, please," she finished.

"I want to be a father, Aedan. I've always wanted children, but I wanted Grania more, so the sacrifice was worth it. But now, well, I just want to be there for our baby.

"Grania, why don't you do it?" I asked. "You could turn him. It would be easier since you're always together anyway."

"We thought about that," she said, looking over at Paul. "I'm afraid that my…oddities would cause problems. I'm not even sure I'm vampire enough to do it anymore, and I don't want to take that risk." She was right to be worried.

Whatever I did to her had changed more than just her magical abilities; it changed her genetic structure. But I had changed Aedan too. He couldn't eat and didn't have bodily functions that I knew of, but he was still changed. Parts of him were alive that hadn't been when we met. He kept most of it hidden, but I knew he had more magic than he once did.

"Aedan, you've changed too," I said, turning my face to him.

"I have, Lara. I have, but not to the extent Grania has. I am still far more vampire than Fae. Either the binding or direct use of your magic on her changed what she is. That is not the case with me. You healed the fractures between vampire and Fae, making me more of both. She is more Fae than vampire now. I suspect she could refrain from drinking blood altogether. She simply chooses not to. It does not change the fact that she could. Her pregnancy is proof of that; no Turned vampire can produce natural children."

Did Aedan count as a turned vampire? I didn't think so. He was a magically induced hybrid. I needed to get that shot.

"Okay," I said. "Okay. What now?" I asked.

Paul and Aedan stared at one another across the space between us. Aedan broke first, leaning back and scrubbing his hands over his face.

"You have asked for nothing. Neither of you. You have both bled for this House. I will do it, but not until we return from Talamh na Sithe," he said. Still not opening his eyes. I could feel the heaviness of his thoughts. "After the Turn, you will need me more than I can give until then. But hear this, I will push you to be independent in ways I never did with Grania."

"I would expect nothing less, Sir." I watched as they relaxed into one another now that the bigger question was answered.

"Should I not return from Talamh na Sithe, I will make arrangements for Gregory Cavanaugh to turn you. He is an excellent Sire to his children." Aedan leaned into me.

I laughed out loud. Aedan was coming back from Talamh na Sithe, all right. He wasn't dying on my watch. "Uh, sorry," I said. "Inner dialogue."

Knowing exactly what I was thinking, Grania snickered. Aedan shook his head.

"I want you to know," Aedan said, interrupting the violent thoughts in my head caused by the idea of anyone hurting him. "I am overjoyed at the news that I am going to be a Grandfather.

"Stodgy old uncle," I interrupted.

"I cannot tell you how pleased I am over this development. My Grandson will want for nothing."

"Your super-awesome niece will want for nothing," I said.

"Whatever you need…"

"Cool, Auntie Lara will provide," I finished for him.

Aedan's sigh could be heard in the next county.

"Thanks, Dad." Grania jumped up and wrapped her arms around Aedan, peppering his face with kisses. "It's okay, Lara. Grandmas can be cool too."

She ducked fast enough that the ball of light I threw at her smashed into the TV and not her face. Luckily, I didn't put any real punch in it. I guess our sparring days were over.

"Speaking of Talamh na Sithe, when do we leave?" She asked.

"You're not going," Aedan and I said simultaneously. Almost. Goddess forbid the man use a contraction.

"Of course, I'm going," she said.

"Grania, no." I slid to the edge of the loveseat.

"Is this because I'm pregnant?" she asked, crossing her arms and looking at me angrily.

"No," I said at the same time, Aedan said, "Yes."

"No," I said, kicking him. "I need you to take care of things here."

"What things?" she asked, sharpening her glare.

"You are my Second, daughter," Aedan said, answering the question for me as he caught the train of my thoughts. "The House is too big to be left unsupervised. We cannot afford a repeat of what happened when I was gone for merely a week. We may be gone longer this time. Much longer. Supernatural affairs have not recovered from the turmoil my disappearance caused. Any further decline could signal the end of the advances we have made," he said. I applauded his quick thinking. And he was right.

"You have Fangs to run, this household, all my businesses, and all of the AVA's businesses. You will be quite busy, and I trust no one else with these matters. It will take you and Paul to manage." Damn, he was slick. Good recovery, old man. I thought at him, and I swear he almost strangled my knee with the tightness of his grip.

"Okay, Dad," she conceded. "As long as it's not because I'm pregnant."

"Of course not. I understand the modern woman wants to do it all."

I shook my head. He had been doing so well.

Paul and Grania rose to leave.

"One more thing." I stopped them, and they sat back down.

I told them about my conversation with Agent Johnson and about the missing box of Aedan's blood. I explained my worries about what was being done with it and my fear that it was more than one box.

Devers/Collins warned me that they were testing Aedan's blood and that Aiyana's goal was to create a new race of superbeings. Those hopes would not have died with her. Not a chance.

I even reiterated the concerns the former Sheriff had about those beings not having supervision and lacking the control Aedan had taken millennia to learn. I explained this at length while they listened quietly. And then I laid out my deepest worry. Should those superbeings come under the purview of the government? Well, let's just say I had a crisis of faith when it comes to the trustworthiness of Uncle Sam. "That blood needs to be destroyed," I finished, looking sideways at Aedan. "It needs destroyed as does anything that has resulted from experiments with it."

My statements were met with silence.

"What if there are infants?" Aedan asked, his voice so hushed I had to strain to hear. "Would they be my children? My DNA?"

Oh, my Gods, his need was so great. Pain filtered through our link, and I worried for him. So many things had happened. "Aedan. Sweetie. Think about it. Please. Your power- unchecked. Uncontrolled. In whose hands? It hasn't been long enough for there to be actual babies; technology isn't that advanced. But there may be *something* there," I said. "I think that we need to be the ones to find it. Not the FBI. No one should have access to your blood. Do you remember your reaction to me looking at your blood on a cellular level, Aedan?"

And that was all I needed to say. He got it then. They all did. He went from the joy of being a grandfather to the pain of having a powerful part of himself being used for something potentially nefarious. Part of his bodily structure was out of his control, and that was the point.

"We need to go as soon as possible," Grania said. "And don't say I can't go with you. I am your second, but I am also part of your security team. I'm going. This isn't a war; it's breaking and entering."

Aedan and I looked at each other for a long moment. She was pregnant, not glass.

"We will go tomorrow night," he said, his expression closing down. "Paul will drive. No more than the four of us need know about this." He rose from the loveseat and went to his office; I heard the door click closed.

"You're right, Lara. He knows that," Grania said, sliding into the seat he vacated. "It's just a lot for him," she finished.

"I know, sweetie. I know. Hey, I'm so happy for you. I'm really, really happy." I pulled her to me, crushing her in my grip. She'd be a great mother, and Paul would be a good father. The decision to Turn had to be hard for him. "You should, uh, freeze some of your swimmers in case you want another baby," I added without thinking.

Maybe having lots of great-grandchildren and grandchildren would take Dani and Aedan's minds off my uterus. One could hope.

"That's an excellent idea, Lara. Thanks for the suggestion," Paul said, rising to leave.

Grania glared at me, and I gave her a big smile.

"See y'all tomorrow." I jumped up, hugged Grania, and walked them to the door, closing it behind them when they left.

The silence stretched in their absence, reaching all corners of our rooms. Sighing, I headed toward our bedroom and the big shower beyond. Our first day in the new house had been eventful; a hot shower would go a long way to washing some of it away. My day had started in South Carolina near dawn and ended in Maryland after midnight. Over the last few days, I had been through dinner with my soon-to-be mother-in-law, a category four near category five hurricane, and multiple sparring matches between myself, Aedan, and my parents. I was tired. I closed the doors to the balcony against the chilling night air and went to test the instant part of the water heater.

I turned the water on Carolina Ghost Pepper hot and proceeded to burn away the sweat and grime that travel and sword fighting creates. The shower was fantastic. Jets pounded my tired flesh from every angle, and the waterfall showerhead rained heaven upon my head. I let hot water cascade over me for far longer than any water heater could tolerate. Eventually, I took a seat, adjusting the heads with a push of a button, so they followed me.

I leaned back against the wall, feeling the worry fade. Goddess, I was tired: almost too tired to wash. Closing my eyes, I relaxed into the warm tiles.

Strong hands smoothed my hair, gripping it lightly. The smell of Aedan's shampoo filtered through the steam as he began to wash my hair. I felt the smile creep across my face, unbidden. "I was going to get that," I said.

"You were asleep. You have been in here for over an hour," he said, sliding his hands through the ends of my hair before moving back up to massage my scalp. "I wanted you to smell like me and saw the chance to make it so."

Without opening my eyes, my grin grew wider. "I always smell like you, Aedan. You've invaded every part of me."

The low chuckle he made was all male. "Anamcara, you smell like the sun, salt, and the sea. Always. Tonight, I feel the need to smell my products on your skin." His words ended in a growl, and my smile slipped.

My arms were heavy when I lifted them, proving I had indeed been asleep. With eyes still closed, I traced the lines of his muscles. He stood in front of me with his legs slightly spread so that he could reach the top of my head. Using my fingertips, I traced the hard lines of his arms to his hands, then back up to his shoulders and back down the planes of his chest. When I reached his hips, I placed my palms on him, loving the slide of his skin under them.

He groaned when my hands fell to his thighs and began tracing the muscles there.

"It was my intention to put you to bed. The days have been long; you need to rest."

"Mmmhhmm," was all I could get out. He was right. I was so tired my body wasn't functioning, and everything felt heavy. I dragged my eyes open, staring up at him through my lashes.

He was tired. I could see it in the line of his body and the shadows on his face. But he needed me; I could see that, too. His needs had gone unfulfilled for so long that I didn't know if he would ever feel sated.

"You satiate me every time, mo chroi. Every. Single. Time. You fill the empty spaces and light the darkened corners. Never believe otherwise," he said, soaping his hands and washing me.

Had I spoken out loud?

"Yes, you were speaking out loud," he laughed, tossing his head back.

Goddess, he is beautiful.

His laugh deepened, rolling out of him. "And you still are," he said.

I shut up.

He finished washing me as my eyes drifted closed again. I thought our first night in the house would be different. Maybe a candlelight dinner and some soft lovemaking, but it had been more perfect, really. We'd shared the day with friends and family, finally ending it together.

The shower of water stopped, and Aedan wrapped me in a fluffy towel. On the side of the massive tub, he dried me before scooping me into his arms and carrying me to the bed. Gently he placed me in the middle before climbing next to me and pulling the covers high.

"Davis, close the curtains and turn off the lights," he said, and the lights went dark.

"Who the hell is Davis? I asked, suddenly awake.

"He is our virtual assistant. He can do anything you need. You just ask," Aedan said, pulling me closer, tucking me into his arms.

"Davis," I said. "Make love to me." I gave a soft snicker into the darkness.

A growl ripped from Aedan, and he was between my thighs in an instant, his nose buried in the base of my neck.

I smiled into his hair.

"I will change our virtual assistant's name tomorrow. You will scream no other man's name but mine," he growled.

"Mmmmm, I didn't scream Davis's name. Not yet, anyway."

"And not ever, brat." He pushed into me with a quick snap of his hips, and I groaned his name. "Open your eyes, Anamcara, and see who between your thighs, now and always."

I looked at him, watching as he made me cry his name more than once. His eyes faded to pale yellow multiple times, darkening again in a moment, and I wondered what thoughts triggered those lapses in control.

Sweat dripped down his chest as he ruined my shower in the best possible way. He stayed braced on his arms, never breaking eye contact. There was something incredibly intimate about it, and when I clenched around him again, desperately stilling his hips with my hands to extend the orgasm, he came. Arching into me as I squeezed him over and over, he emptied inside of me with a long grunt that bordered on wild, his eyes never leaving mine.

Chapter 9

I awoke with Aedan still wrapped around me. The man's emotions were so intense I could feel them in his sleep. Love, desire, passion, respect, and awe towards me flowed through his mind. He once said he rarely dreamed, now I wondered if that is one of the things that changed with our bond and shared blood. His fingers twitched on my side like a puppy running in sleep. It was adorable.

The sun had risen and moved beyond the range of the windows, meaning we had slept in, but we'd been up so late that I suppose it's relative.

"Davis," I whispered. "Brew me some coffee," I whispered, easing from Aedan's side.

"Davis now answers to the name Mavis," Aedan growled, dragging me back to him as I squealed. So maybe he wasn't dreaming. He snuggled me like a favorite teddy bear, tucked under his arm and chin.

"Mavis, make me some fucking coffee," I said, adding some snark to it.

"Yes, Mistress," the smooth, disembodied voice answered.

What the?

"Why is she answering me?" I asked, whipping my head towards Aedan.

"I thought you would like that feature."

I wiggled away from him, snatching a pillow and hitting him with it. "You knew darn well that I wouldn't like that," I laughed.

"Mmmmhhmm," he said, mirroring my eloquence from last night. I hit him with the pillow again, and he rolled onto me with a laugh and an arched eyebrow.

"And you call me a brat," I said. He kissed me, pouring all the passion we shared last night into it, leaving me breathless. And speechless.

"Start the shower, and I will bring you coffee." He pulled his lips from mine with a smirk. Cocky bastard. Then he walked away from me naked, the sight of his muscular thighs and hard ass causing a line of drool drip from my lip. Asshole.

"You are still thinking out loud, Anamcara."

Fuck.

Both of us had busy days planned, so we showered quickly. Aedan's calendar was booked with meetings all day. Mavis ran through the list of his appointments, making my eyes pop. He was meeting with both the Senate majority and minority leaders, the newly formed Paranormal Relations Committee in the House, and the Surgeon General to discuss medical advancements for paranormal care.

I ate breakfast in our kitchen, delivered by Cook. The sneaky Brownie knows our routine and feeds me at every opportunity. I appreciate him endlessly because, without him, I would probably die.

Aedan enjoys cooking for me and will randomly do so. Still, most of the time, Cook took care of all the household duties, including cleaning. He may have been the one who put our belongings away while we were at the beach. I haven't seen him since that one time I found him living under my stairs in the old house. Still, he manages to be everywhere, all the time. Brownie magic is wicked good. Aedan and I could use a bit of it ourselves.

Aedan sat across from me, sipping coffee and reading the paper on his tablet while I chugged orange juice and shoved eggs, bacon, and a cream cheese bagel down my throat. The TV was on some channel that talks about stock reports and financial stuff.

I tried to pay attention. I needed to invest the money the AVA and my paying clients paid me and maybe start another IRA. Do Faeries need IRAs? The fae always paid me in jewels, gold, or silver. I needed to get a guy for that.

"Babe?" I asked, looking away from the TV, more confused than I was before I started staring at the numbers. "Do you know anyone I could use for, I don't know, financial planning?" I asked. I had retirement accounts and a small investment account on the side, but the hospital's people managed it. Now that I was no longer employed there, I needed help.

He chuckled low in that sexy way of his, raising his eyes to mine. "I know some people, yes." His multifaceted whiskey eyes twinkled when he spoke.

"I'm sure you know how and probably do it for yourself, but I don't want you to take on any more. Mavis proves you are busy enough. Just put me in touch with someone; I don't have much anyway."

"Have you checked your balances lately?" he asked, glancing at his phone like it was super important. "Your clinic is performing exceptionally well. Not to mention all the gems and precious metals you are hiding in our sock drawer. I had our accounts linked, so you have access to everything of mine as well and can view those balances online. If you used the cards I gave you, you would know this."

"I don't need your money, love," I said, watching his small smile grow wider at the use of that particular nickname.

"Of course, you do not, but we are engaged. What is mine is yours."

"And what's mine is yours," I replied, crossing my arms over my chest.

"We own an investment company, Anamcara. They do an excellent job, as you would expect. Mavis, import contact for Monumental City Investments to Mo Chroi's android device." My phone beeped, and I glared at him.

"Would you like me to take the most recent bag of diamonds and other things to your safe deposit box?" he asked, smirking over the rim of his mug.

"Ummmm. Yes? Please? But they don't open until nine p.m.." His smile widened further, crinkling the corners of his eyes and showing even white teeth.

"You own the damn bank, don't you?"

"We own the damn bank, Anamcara; your name is on everything. We are to be married." He winked at me before turning back to his phone. I knew what he was doing. He was trying to make this out like it wasn't a big deal.

"Fuck," I said, slumping in my seat.

"Having second thoughts?" he asked, narrowing his eyes at me.

"No. No, not about that. It's just a lot. I knew you had resources. I guess I just didn't understand how broad they were."

"Had you read the pack of information Domingo gave you while I was missing, you would have."

"I know. It's just not about the money for me."

"And I appreciate that. I appreciate that you do not need my money. I appreciate that you are wealthy in your own rite without adding a single penny of my resources, as you call them. You will develop investments throughout your long life that will rival mine. You must accept that I love you and accept that I will share all parts of myself with you, as you will share all parts of yourself with me, including money." He rose, coming over to kneel at my chair. Taking my hand, he pulled it to him, fingering the ring he placed on my finger. "This is a promise. I have never been married, and I intend to do it correctly. All that I have and all that I am is yours," he said, his smile beautiful when he looked up at me. After kissing my ring finger, he walked to our room to get a bag of diamonds and jewels from the sock drawer.

When he came back, he kissed the top of my head. "We have sex almost every day, yet our relationship is not about sex. We share each other's blood almost every day, yet our relationship is not about blood. We both have immense power, yet our relationship is not about power. We have more money than we could ever use or need. Let us not make strife about money. Together, we are all things and everything. Let us not forget that. No single element is the crux of our relationship. We are equals in all things, and I would have it no other way."

I jumped up and wrapped my arms around him. He was right, as he often is. I would learn not to find an issue with something that wasn't an issue. "I love you. You're right."

"Say that again so that Mavis can record it for later use," he laughed, hugging me back. "I will see you tonight."

I punched his arm and watched him walk out the door.

I took a minute to just be. Be in our home; be in my skin. It felt good to be still and to feel the peace of our space surrounding me. There was no discord here. How a house could feel like home in such a short amount of time is beyond me, but this place did. It had the soul of a house that had stood for a long time. I wondered if the lives of those lost in the fire had something to do with that. This home needed a name, for it already had a spirit.

I wouldn't open the clinic until noon, so I walked our rooms, acquainting myself with everything I saw and every space I found. Then, I walked the rest of the house, stopping to speak to the rare awake human.

Opening the large French doors to the courtyard, I sat on a bench, listening to the koi pond fountains bubble in the one place that hadn't changed at all. Even in the place where Daniel died and blood had been spilled, there was peace.

Using Goddess magic, I wove an intricate spell over the house. I infused enough power into that spell to protect an entire town, not just a house. It would stand forever, whether we lived in it or not. No fire, no hurricane, no tornado would ever tear it down.

My parents said it took all five of them and many hours to build the spell that protected me in Pawleys Island. It took me just a few minutes to shield the physical structure Aedan and I had built together.

It made me feel good to know that regardless of what happened, our home would stand. Smiling, I walked the field between the old house and the new. I wanted to enjoy the early summer heat that reminded me so much of home. I applauded the tunnel below the ground but wanted to feel the sun on my face, and I dared anyone to touch me as I went.

Chapter 10

I rode Galahad. It was a split-second decision. I was brushing the saddle marks off him and cleaning up the barn when I said to hell with it and jumped on his back. I rode the overgrown trails behind my house since I didn't have enough time to trailer anywhere. He kept his mouth shut and didn't buck me off.

Maybe I would try riding him without a saddle the next time, but he could be cantankerous. Someone else had been riding all the horses, and I was okay with that. I hated for them to stand around doing nothing. I knew my mom loved horses and that my fathers rode well, so I imagined it was them.

I had more land than Aedan and needed the property for the horses, but I wasn't sure what I was going to do with my old house. I had no doubt my parents would move back to Talamh na Sithe when this was over. It's all they talked about.

Grania and Paul were staying in the new house or the city, but they might want a place of their own to raise the baby. I guess we would figure it all out when the dust settled.

Galahad and I ambled along, quietly enjoying the sun. It warmed our skin and lightened our hearts. Back at the barn, I wiped him down and went to open the clinic.

I heard my parents' footsteps above me as they moved around their day. I gave Bethany the day off since she had been working so much lately, but the clinic was busy, busier than usual. I could've used her help. I didn't advertise or let anyone know when I was in, but they seemed to know regardless.

Tonight, we were going to Morgantown to check out the lab. The vials they had would be the first ones drained from him and the most potent. Not that its potency would decrease much over time. But he had taken my blood hours before his disappearance; it could make a difference.

I took care of simple things, mostly giving fluids and healing lacerations. In the medical world, early summer is known as trauma season. After a long winter, folks are ready to go out and hit the road. They play on dirt bikes, boats, ATVs, and cars. They hurt themselves. A lot.

I fixed a few broken bones and patched up a kid who flipped his dirt bike. I never had an empty waiting area, but my magic was getting to the point where I could Heal almost anything without breaking a sweat. In the beginning, it would exhaust me. I would blackout after a complicated healing and often leave myself pulled thin.

I no longer had that problem. The more I used my magic, the easier it became. Some of the Fae women stopped by, wanting their pregnancies checked. Those women were made of steel, and I knew they would carry well. After years of miscarriage, trauma, and infertility, they were overprotective of those babies. I didn't blame them, not even a little bit.

While I was in the bathroom, Cook quietly delivered a plate of warm cookies for my patients and a tray of food for me. No one claimed to see him come and go. After lunch, my parents sat with me, chatting amongst themselves and with my patients. It was almost a party atmosphere.

I loved spending time with them, and they loved being nearby. I would catch their glances and soft smiles as I worked my magic. They were proud. But so was I. They looked so happy. I wondered if my mother would be the next to get pregnant. I supposed she would be the last one. All the others already were. They talked of their missing friend and loss, but they also talked of love, and that made the struggle worthwhile for them. All of it.

Ravena had been the last to come to this plane, and I had told her she was pregnant this evening. She and her mates had cried, clutching at one another. She had three mates and told me the story of how my mother had killed the fourth. She was very proud of that.

She told me of her miscarriage and my mother's famous potions. They had been best friends, and I hoped they found their way back to that. There was a quiet strength in her that mirrored my mother's. I could see how they fit.

Ravena sat with her in a corner while the men chatted, catching up and telling stories. They talked about the future, the war ahead, and life after. They were confident Aramea's days were numbered. I hoped they were right.

By evening, the place had cleared out. I cleaned up, turning off the lights before I left. Grania had not come today. She had a lot on her plate and needed time to adjust. Just because you love the idea of a thing, or wanted it badly, does not mean it doesn't frighten you if you get it. It is natural to fear the changing tides. That pinch of fear is what makes life exciting. You still have to wade through it, though, and that is what she was doing, wading through.

I knew I should walk through the tunnel, but the evening was warm, and the breeze felt nice against my face. I believed our old enemies had been dealt with, and the new ones hadn't surfaced yet. I felt safe. Beyond safe, I felt peaceful. I would take my peace where I found it. '

No reporters jumped out of the bushes. I was not bothered in any way as I walked through the field. I stopped briefly to cycle the earth's power through me, loving the way it felt and enjoying the feel of her peace, washing the stress away. The earth loved it too, and I felt her pleasure. She let go quickly when I severed the link. There was no darkness in her power tonight, just peace. Finally, I walked through the front door.

Jeremy ran by, almost knocking me down. Another boy chased him, and their laughter and loud screams echoed off the fourteen-foot-high ceilings. A small girl came crashing after, and the chase was on. Wooden swords clanked as they stopped to fight in the kitchen. Kicking off my shoes, I walked into the large living room and sank into the couch, watching them with a smile.

This is what home should be. I might have never wanted children, but I loved watching them play. Their joy is palpable and genuine. Their laughter filled the far corners of the new house, making it a home. My life had always been so screwed up that there was no room for children, but maybe that would change. The future was unknown, and I faced a lot of it ahead of me. I hadn't lied when I told Aedan that maybe someday, we could try for a baby.

Jeremy ran by me again, jumping my legs deftly as only a supernatural child could. He showed more signs every day of what he was. He had grown several inches and lost the chubby look of a little boy. His longish hair made him look like a rogue, and I knew he was going to be a heartbreaker.

The other kids crashed after him until Sarah yelled at them from the kitchen, telling them to stop bothering me. They weren't, though. I was just soaking it all in.

Finally, I rose, walking upstairs to change. If we wanted to make it to the lab and give ourselves time to search it without rushing, we would need to leave as soon as Aedan and Grania got home.

I pulled my hair into a long ponytail and slipped on a black shirt and pants. I ate the light dinner Cook left in the silence of our rooms, missing the sound of the children's laughter.

Aedan rushed through the door as I finished, tossing his briefcase, suit jacket, and tie on the couch. He gave me a quick kiss on the head as he rushed to the bedroom to change. I cleaned up the kitchen while I waited, feeling the butterflies build.

There's no telling what we'd find in the lab. I had to hope it wouldn't be much and that their research hadn't gotten very far. It had been months, though, so anything was possible. At the end of the day, I would burn that place to the ground if need be. Every experiment, every note, every sample had to be destroyed. There was no other way. Aedan didn't understand that, but I did. Some things are too powerful to be left unchecked. Even Aedan and I had our checks and balances; whatever was in this lab might not be so lucky.

Dressed in dark clothing, he hurried into the kitchen, snagging the glass of wine I held out for him. "My last meeting ran late. It took a while to compile a list of individuals willing to work with local trauma centers. The Surgeon General is asking them to get some medical training, so they are not overwhelmed by the sights they will see."

"That makes sense," I said, filling my to-go cup with coffee.

"It does. But asking vampires, some of whom are hundreds of years old, to go back to school is asking a lot," he chuckled. "I tried to assure him that vampires are used to blood and crises, but he is still asking for a short course on general medical practices. They would then be 'certified to assist,' he said, making air quotes. He grabbed my hand, pulling me to the door. "We'll take your truck. It'll fit in better than one of the Escalades."

We took the stairs two at a time, ducking into the climate-controlled garage. My truck was running with Paul behind the wheel; I did not like other people driving my truck. They didn't do it right, and being a passenger in my own vehicle was not my speed.

"I'll drive," I said, walking around the truck to find Grania kneeling at my rear bumper. "Uh, whatcha doing?" I asked.

"Not all of our businesses are squeaky clean, Liomsa." Aedan walked over and took my Maryland tags from Grania, putting them on the shelf behind us. "These West Virginia tags are untraceable, but it would behoove us not to get pulled over. Considering the weight of your right foot, it would be better if Paul drove. Besides, I have building schematics to run through before we get there."

I felt my shoulders slump. He was right. The police officers in Westminster knew me by first name, and it wasn't just because I used to work in the local Emergency Department.

Grania straightened, brushing her hands off on her pants. "Voila! And now we look less like government agents and more like locals," she laughed.

They had a point; the black Escalades did look very official. Throw in Maryland tags, and you've got The Men in Black. They say West Virginians are suspicious of authorities; I didn't want to test that.

Aedan and I sat in the back, and Grania slid in front next to Paul. "There are four entrances, five including the loading dock," he started immediately. "We are going to use the entrance next to the loading dock as it faces a school and not the road. There will be no one in the school to report our activity," he stopped, swiping through screens on his tablet.

"There are four exterior security guards," he said, pointing at the map. "Stationed here, here, here, and here. Two patrol and two are stationary at the gates leading to the facility. However, according to camera footage pulled from the lab, the guards are often lax once the last of the staff is gone." He swiped through the tablet again, bringing up footage of the four guards smoking and playing on their phones inside one of the booths.

"The school has an entrance on a side street. If we park there and come through the chain-link fence at the back of the building, then we may be able to get into the lab without discovery. There are two guards inside that make rounds, but as with the others, they seem to be lax at night. Either they do not understand the worth of the experiments the lab is conducting, or they do not care. If any of these men worked for me, they would be fired. Are you sure you should be drinking that much coffee, Anamcara?" he paused to question the fact that I was attacking my gallon of coffee with gusto. "I do not wish to stop as that increases the risk of exposure." He narrowed his eyes at me when I took another long drink.

I laughed at him, tipping my thermos back for another long pull. "Ex-nurse; I got this," I said, patting his knee and eyeing him back.

Scrubbing his hands over his face, he continued. "There are other security measures in place. There are multiple points where key cards are required for entry. During one of my breaks today, I had a master key for this exact system made. I am hopeful this mission will be a surgical strike. In. Out. Done."

"How?" I started only to be interrupted.

"Remember, not all of my endeavors are legal, strictly speaking, most are, but not all. I have shadow companies in place to make sure that my legal activities and close associates stay on the up and up. That type of investigatory reach requires a bit of illegality." He grinned at me with a wink.

"Okay," I said, drawing the word out. "We need to get every scrap of paper, ledgers, or notes related to whatever they are doing with your blood," I added, sharing my thoughts. "It might be easier to just burn the damn place down, Flame Keeper," I teased.

"It might. I do recall that you wield fire very well yourself, Anamcara. You turned my cell to liquid and ash, despite the fact it was mostly steel."

"You saw?" My breath caught in my throat. By the time I burned the storm cellar Aedan had been held in, I thought him long gone.

"You were beautiful in your fury." His eyes paled a shade, and he flashed me another grin.

"Oh." I didn't think he had seen my giant temper tantrum.

"Get a room," Grania snorted.

Aedan glared at the back of her head, causing me to hide my smile behind my hand.

"In the end, fire may be the easiest way. Before the place goes up in flames, we need to see what is inside. A fire could be accidental; the destruction or theft of their experiments would draw unwanted attention. That is assuming these people know my identity and that I am the basis of their work. After looking at the schematics for the building, I believe the most likely area to house these types of experiments is on the third floor. It has the best security with limited access and points of entry. There are also several offices in that area that are separate from the lab at large."

"Agreed," we all said simultaneously.

"Paul, you will stay with the vehicle in case we need to leave rapidly or we are apprehended."

We all chuckled at that. Like any of us would be apprehended. After Aedan's abduction, it was not likely anyone would ever get the drop on one of us again. Besides, I had enough magic to get us out of any trouble a human could cause. Now, anyway.

The drive to Morgantown went fast. When we passed the little farm where Aedan had been held, he went silent, looking through the window at the darkness below. No lights lit the sprawling house, and I wondered if Devers had abandoned it or if he had been caught by his former group. I never heard what happened to him, and I guessed I never would. He'd been so sure they would kill him for his betrayal.

Soon, we began our descent into the quaint city nestled at the base of the mountains, and the dark of the countryside faded as more and more lights popped up. Grania was right. We blended in with the trucks and other four-by-fours dominating the road. No one would notice the red Chevy one-ton pickup with West Virginia tags on it. Even if the whole thing blew up and questions were asked, no one would recall anything out of the ordinary.

In no time, we were pulling up at the school, headlights off. Paul let the truck glide to a stop before popping it into neutral, never touching the brakes. Aedan, Grania, and I eased out. My dome lights had been turned off, and there was nothing to signal our presence but the soft snick of closing truck doors.

"I deactivated the cameras a mile out. At a glance, they are working, but there will be no recordings," Aedan said, his voice low. Had I not possessed excellent hearing, I may have missed it. Grania nodded her head in approval of his actions.

This sneaky side of Aedan was sexy; I liked it. I guess after a few lifetimes, you pick up on this stuff; I just never thought of him as anything other than Mr. Clean. Yeah, he was dangerous. For sure, he was a predator. But this lawless side? Hot. He caught my gooey look and grinned, making light from the sliver of moon glint off of his white teeth.

Moving through the dark like ninjas, we crept to the razor wire-topped chain link fence. I felt the sting of iron the closer we got and wondered, not for the first time, if these people knew exactly who they were dealing with. By the tightening around the eyes around me, I knew the others felt it too. But after being poisoned by iron during Daniel's attack, something had changed for me. I recovered from what should have been a fatal dose of iron poisoning with my magic stronger, not weaker. Cold iron didn't affect me anymore. I felt it, sure, but it did not drain my power.

Electricity coursed through the fence, causing the wire to snap and pop. Without a thought, I unmade a section large enough to pass through. I didn't sever the fence completely as I didn't want the electricity to stop running. There could be an alarm that sounded if the connection was broken, and we didn't need any type of alarms.

I wove a spell of darkness around us, placing a glamor so that should anyone be looking, they would see nothing but the night. We reached the edge of the building, waiting as the guard made his rounds and disappeared around the corner. He didn't notice our trio sneak toward the door.

Aedan used his hijacked master key to open the door next to the loading dock, then we slipped inside. He placed his finger to his lips, pushing us behind a stack of pallets.

One of the interior guards rounded through the hall in front of us, whistling quietly as he went. Once he was gone, we stepped out from behind the pallets and walked through the first floor of the building, looking for anything that shouldn't be there.

The first floor was nothing but offices. There was an area for patients that looked set up for legitimate research and patient care. The area itself was secured only with regular office-type doors and standard locks.

"Six hearts are beating on the upper levels and two more further down on this one," Aedan whispered. "The two on this level are likely guards as their office is near the front on this floor," he finished. He continued moving like water flows down the hall to the staircase.

I stopped. Mouth agape, I stared after him. Even after his most recent reminder of what he is, I had forgotten again. For all his manners, grace, and civility, he is still an old as fuck vampire that had lived half his life as a monster. Of course, he could hear heartbeats. I shook my head as Grania skirted around me, giving me a sec to get my shit together.

"Anamcara, you are projecting your thoughts. Loudly," he chuckled low, the predatory edge of it wrapping around my soul, causing my heart rate to increase in a primal way. Goddess, he was hot like this. Scary as hell, but hot. I could tell he liked this walk on the wild side. He must enjoy breaking the monotony that control brings.

He held the door open, waiting patiently for me to get myself together. Flashing him a wild grin, I sped soundlessly to the stairwell. He flashed me a smile showing a hint of long fangs, something he rarely did; he was excited. We took the stairs to the second floor, sliding to the side to peek through the small glass window above the handle. There was a small anteroom, then another solid door. Red eyes gleamed from security pads, and Aedan flicked his Master at the first one. It clicked open, and we shut it quietly behind us as we passed through.

He held up six fingers, pointing at the door ahead of us. I felt the soft brush of him in my mind: I opened myself to him.

"The six heartbeats are behind this door. There is no way to tell what we are walking into. Be ready," he said through our link. Grania nodded her head once to let us know she had heard.

Aedan held up three fingers, tucking one away as he counted down. Swiping his master over the security pad, he shouldered into the second door. Surprise flitted across his face when nothing happened. The master didn't work this door.

That's when I knew we were in the right place.

This particular security pad had been updated recently. We stilled, waiting to see if an alarm sounded or guards came running. The building remained silent. Holding up a finger to pause his next action, I shouldered past him, holding my finger to my lips to urge silence.

I unmade the electrical wiring inside the pad and the locking mechanism in the door with a touch. I tried to do it at the same time so that no alarm would sound, only there was a short chirping sound that died as soon as it began. Knowing there may be a silent alarm, we separated and sped into the lab.

I saw Aedan freeze near the back of the room, going still in the way only a vampire can. Soft pink light filtered through a glass tank along the wall, and then I saw what he saw.

Six huge men were suspended naked in a viscous pink substance. The soft sound of bubbles in the air would have been soothing had it not for the fact that two of the men were chewing pieces off one another as they fought. They instantly healed from the damage they caused. Long fangs scored and ripped flesh from bones in a never-ending fight for a death that would not come.

All six men had their whiskey-colored eyes open, and the wrongness in them glowed through the glass at us. There were no words for this. None. I remembered something else about that first box of blood that would have been drawn from Aedan. It had been heavily mixed with mine. My hand flew to my mouth to cover the choked sob that echoed through the space around us.

"I'll do it," Grania said, stepping up to the glass as if to break it.

"No. Don't. We don't know what will happen if we let them loose. We may not be able to contain them," I said, moving to stand behind her.

Aedan hadn't moved a muscle. Not one. These men weren't the babies he feared we would find; I thanked the Goddess for that. In a way, this was worse, and it was evident from looking at them that there was no way to fix what had been done.

Clipboards hung on the outside of the glass, and I picked one up. Each man's name, age, and medical information were listed along with details on the effects of the DNA they had obtained from Aedan's blood and spliced onto their stem cells. The men hadn't started out in the tanks but had been moved there when it became apparent they couldn't be controlled and were beyond any type of reason. According to the notes, the researcher thought with this special fluid and time, the men would come back to themselves and be the good little warriors they had hoped to build.

No, we could not let the government see this. Not ever. Aedan slipped up beside me, staring wordlessly at the two men as they slowly ripped parts off of the other one, only to have them regenerate in a flash. These things would be immortal.

The other four men were suspended and motionless, far enough apart so they couldn't immediately rip into each other. Still, it wasn't for the lack of trying. Joints went the wrong way, and fingers extended into claws. Vicious teeth gnashed, and dull eyes stared at us. Even the fighters paused, leaning our way as if they scented fresh blood. They were mindless killing machines and nothing like us.

"They aren't ours, Aedan. You can't think that. They twisted our DNA and injected it into volunteers. They are not us. There's no humanity left in them. There's only one thing we can do," I finished, knowing I would fight him with everything I had if he even suggested we save these things.

"I know, Lara," he said, using my name. My heart broke for him. It broke for us. This was an invasion, a violation that I felt to my core.

The root of life had been taken to create these things clawing toward us. While the joining of two people's DNA can be a beautiful thing, this was not, and it cut to the quick. These researchers had stolen something sacred, and it would take everything in me not to hunt them down and kill them even though they had not been involved until after the fact. This wasn't research; it was a crime and a heinous one at that.

I placed my hand on the glass as one of the creatures opened his mouth, showing wide, long fangs. He snapped at me from behind the glass. I thought I would have to touch him to do this, but I found I could look into his eyes and see the threads of his change.

For one moment, just one, I thought I might be able to undo what had been done to him and make him a man again. Mikolosi had survived being changed back, and I thought perhaps these men could too. Then I dove deeper and found that the very marrow of their bones had been corrupted by the changed stem cells. They would never again make normal ones; the DNA would always be twisted. They could not be saved.

Hot tears slid down my face as I pulled the life threads of the nearest man snapping his jaws at me. I pulled until there was no more man, unmaking him into the essential components of life. Ninety-nine percent of the human body is made of oxygen, carbon, hydrogen, nitrogen, calcium, and phosphorus. The other one percent is made up of other elements, and that is what I reduced him to as my tears flowed hot and fast.

He had a life somewhere, a family maybe. They would never know how this ended and would not get closure. Had he signed informed consent? Had they even told him what they were doing? There was no way to know, but there was no going back for him either. Not ever. This type of creature in any hands would be horrific. Good intentions or bad, this could not be fixed. I moved on to the next one.

Aedan stood by my side as I used Goddess Magic to destroy the results of his involuntary genetic donations. I felt his pain through the link between us, but I also felt his resolve; he understood and agreed.

This was something he could never hold against me in the long game. Grania moved through the lab, doing Goddess knew what. I felt her in my periphery, stalking through the place and tearing things apart.

She was pregnant. This had to affect her on a primal level too, but she didn't disagree with my decision. If anything, she wished she could do this for me; I felt that desire through our link as well.

In the end, all six men were turned into the elements that made them. I sagged against Aedan when It was done; the effort to stand cost me more than I had left to give.

He scooped me into his arms. "Is everything in place, daughter?" he asked.

"Yes," she said, her voice breaking as she looked at me. "We are getting out. Just go."

He ran with me out the door, down the stairs, and into the night air. We blew past a security guard before he could register what we were.

"Stop!" he shouted.

Oddly, Aedan stopped. "Do you know what they are doing here?" he asked. I could feel his compulsion. It was so thick it skated across my skin, leaving me weaker. The man had no choice but to answer. We had not used the keycard on the second door upstairs, and the alarm began to sound. Aedan didn't move.

"They are creating genetically modified cancer treatments," the guard answered.

"A fire started in the lab upstairs; you tried to put it out but were unable. You smelled gas earlier in the night but could not find the source. Everything checked out, and nothing unusual happened," Aedan said, the pupils of his whiskey eyes flared wide as he compelled the guard. "Later, you smelled smoke and pulled the fire alarm before running out of the front entrance, taking with you as many of the others as you could."

The man turned to run. Aedan pulled the fire alarm and slammed through the last remaining door between us and freedom. Halfway across the expanse of grass between the building and the hole in the fence, the building blew. It knocked us momentarily to the ground, but Aedan recovered quickly, jerking me back into his arms. The vampires sprinted forward, their speed blinding. I looked over my shoulder, watching as flames kissed the night sky.

"Go, Go, Go," Grania shouted when the doors to my truck slammed shut. Paul slid sideways out of the school parking lot, lights off and engine humming.

Back on the road, Paul slowed. Flipping the lights on and using his turn signal, he made the turn onto the road that would take us past the front of the lab. It was leveled. Fire licked over the ruins and spread onto the grass where dark silhouettes huddled, watching the place burn. If there was evidence left behind, it would incinerate. The fire burned hot and fast. Sirens sounded in the distance, but they were too late. Would the researchers know what happened? Maybe. There would be no burned bones left behind, and that might be suspicious to them, but they may also be grateful. There was no explaining what was going on here to authorities.

"I got the invoices you wanted, dad. I gave them a quick glance. There are no records of shipments leaving here and going anywhere else. There was a lot of other stuff," Grania said, twisting in the front seat to catch his eyes. "They tried werewolf DNA and the blood of a woman who claimed to be Fae, but nothing happened. From what I can tell, your blood was the only time these experiments had been successful," she finished, flinching at her own words.

There was nothing successful about those experiments.

"Thank you," Aedan said, pulling me to him and kissing the top of my head. He didn't correct her misstatement.

We passed a dozen fire trucks and as many police cars. Traffic thickened, but we were able to jump on route 705 and get out of Morgantown before it became impassable. The truck was silent as we curved through the town. Once on the interstate and away from the potholes that seemed to be a thing here, the soft thrum of tires lulled me to restless sleep.

Chapter 11

I awoke in a wash of afternoon light that streamed through our bedroom windows. Aedan was tucked beside me, his back turned but skin touching mine. His chest did not rise and fall, and I wondered if the dawn had taken him like it used to. Lines of exhaustion rode his face, and I could feel his tiredness in my bones. I didn't remember coming home, being placed in pajamas, or going to bed.

I had worked a lot of magic, and it had taken its toll on my body and my psyche. Using power for anything but healing or helping those in need went against everything I believed in. It also went against the oath I took all those years ago when I became a nurse to first do no harm. Knowing a thing is right and being okay with the act are two very different things. I felt that perhaps my soul was a touch darker upon awakening.

Not that there had been any other choice, and that's the funny thing about choice; sometimes there is no good one, but you have to choose anyway.

My skin was sticky with dried sweat and road grime. I turned the shower on hotter than Georgia in July hot and stepped in, sighing as the first burst of water drilled into me. Today was another day. The threat the lab posed had been astronomical, but it was over now.

I dressed quietly in soft pants and a loose cotton tee. I needed to go to the clinic at some point. Bethany would have texted if there were anything she couldn't handle, and she had not, but appearances needed to be made. That girl was getting a raise.

In the kitchen, I poured coffee from the hot French press left sitting on my counter and grabbed an English muffin filled with eggs and sausage before turning on the TV. Cook was too good to me, but it freaked me out more than a little that his food was always hot, fresh, and waiting the moment I wanted it. Funny with my life, such as it is, that is one of the hardest things to fathom. What a difference a year makes.

My cup froze on the way to my mouth when the news channel Aedan had left it on showed live footage from Morgantown. News helicopters circled the giant hole in the ground that smoldered still, and a crowd had gathered outside the gates. I turned the volume up.

"Officials say no one was killed in the blast at Core Lab Group in Morgantown, West Virginia last night. In a news briefing earlier, Morgantown's Fire Chief stated that the cancer research lab experienced a gas leak before the explosion. All the staff working overnight made it out with only minor injuries. Businesses surrounding the lab felt the explosion and suffered minor damage as well. With the blast and subsequent blaze, Morgantown is lucky there were no fatalities." She thrust her microphone at the guard from last night, and he repeated the story Aedan had planted in his mind. The other guards backed him up in a case of follow the leader, and the interview soon ended.

The reporter then switched to taped footage of the blaze that followed the explosion, and any worry I had about evidence or samples left behind vanished. The blazed had taken everything.

"Core Lab Group released a statement saying that their cancer research had been promising, and they were saddened by its loss. They further mentioned that this research had taken a lifetime to achieve, and due to safety and pirating protocols, it was likely lost forever. Shares of Core Labs fell sharply with this release. Back to you, Robin."

I turned the TV off and sat heavily at the kitchen counter, downing the coffee. Maybe there had been legitimate cancer research going on there, maybe not. I could not feel bad about it if there were. I refused to feel bad about any of it. A soft knock at the door caused a long sigh to escape me.

"Come in," I said, hoping whoever was there had supernatural hearing, so I didn't have to raise my voice.

"Hey," Grania said from the doorway. She leaned casually against the frame, her long white-blond hair loose around her shoulders.

"Hey," I answered. "Is everything okay?" I asked.

"That federal agent is here. The one from the warehouse thing. She wants to talk to you. She already grilled the rest of us."

I nodded my head slowly. I had been expecting at least a phone call. We had synced our stories before ever leaving the state, and I knew that they would hold. My truck would have a full tank and be parked where it always was, Maryland plates reattached should she look. There was absolutely no way this could come back on us.

Rising, I filled my coffee and followed Grania down the stairs.

"Good afternoon, Agent Johnson. It's good to see you. What brings you out this way?" I asked, putting on my best nurse smile when I came to the bottom of the stairs. You know, the one meant to be calming and sincere. I had perfected it during my long years at the bedside and used it in my clinic. The smile said, 'trust me,' and people did.

"I wanted to drop by and update you on some new information," she said, scanning the foyer. Her eyes were flat and official, and I knew I wasn't the only one wearing a mask.

"Come in, have a seat. Can I offer you some coffee? I believe there are cupcakes. I'd be happy to show you around if you came to see the house," I said, playing the part of the perfect southern hostess.

"I saw the spread in Architectural Digest," she said, walking into the main living room. Her eyes scanned every detail as the house opened up to her. "It's lovely; your people did a great job."

"Thanks," I said, taking my coffee and curling up on the corner of one of the large sectionals spread across the room. Grania leaned against the fireplace mantle, sipping coffee and looking wary.

"I came to talk to you about that lab in Morgantown," she started, perching on the edge of the sofa across from me.

"Perfect. Did you get your warrants? Please, let me know what you find. Aedan has been so worried about this. No telling what his blood could be used for."

She scanned the parts of the house she could see again. "No televisions?" she asked.

I laughed lightly. Whether or not to put televisions in the common spaces of the house was one of the most vicious arguments Aedan and I had when designing it. I thought that people would gather in those areas to watch them, and he felt that they should be relegated to the private spaces in the home. He thought that people would talk more with each other if there were no TVs. I thought they would hide in the bedrooms and glue themselves to reality TV.

Aedan, of course, had not seen a television until he was older than dirt, whereas the rest of us cut our teeth on TV remotes. Aedan won, but at the end of the day, he'd been right. We spent hours each day in the common rooms talking and sharing stories, but I will never admit this to him.

"There are a few televisions around here, but since we are often on the news, we don't watch them." I leaned back, widening my smile.

"There was an explosion at the lab in Morgantown last night. The place was leveled," she said, gauging my reaction.

I let my eyebrows fly to my hairline, then scrunched them back down in mock confusion. I watched her watch me. "What happened?" I asked, leaning forward to show my interest. I uncurled my legs, planting my feet on the floor.

"That's what we are trying to find out. Cameras weren't recording. The footage should have been uploaded to a secure online vault but was not. The only thing we found was a hole in the electric fence behind the building. No sign of missing metal or broken links, just a gaping hole.

"Do you think they knew you were getting closer?" I asked, meeting her eyes over the rim of my mug. "Maybe trying to cover up something?"

"It's possible. We know the lab's work wasn't entirely legitimate. We were going to hit them hard on a lot of counts. Aedan's blood supposedly being there was simply the icing on the cake."

"It sucks; it would've been nice to make them accountable," I said with a sigh and a shake of my head.

"Just to dot the Ts, where were you last night? And where was Aedan?" she asked.

I laughed, tossing my head back. "Oh, that's a really cool story," I said. "Come here, and I'll show you." I popped from the couch, looking over my shoulder at her.

She quirked her eyebrow but rose to follow.

"If you watch the news or tabloids, then you may have heard that Aedan and I took a trip to South Carolina to spend a few days together alone. Well, lots of stuff happened there, and I won't bore you with those details, but we haven't been back long. Our friends and family wanted to spend last night in our new training area," I explained, leading the way down the wide stairs and into the brightly lit gym.

Humans and fae sparred on the mats as the vampires were sleeping. Still, every sectioned-off area was full. Guns blared from the shooting range at the far end, and the noise level was explosive. As the occupants of the gym noted our arrival, it decreased by a few decibels as their activity stopped.

"We came down after dinner and stayed until the wee hours of the morning. Due to the particulars of the fights showcased, the place was packed." I watched Agent Johnson note the cameras along the walls.

This area was continuously monitored by security. Supernaturals used the space with humans, and we wanted no problems. If it came down to it, the footage from two nights ago had already been labeled with last night's date and time stamps, providing us with an excellent alibi.

"Hey, Boss Lady, excellent job kicking your dad's ass with a sword," one of Aedan's new human guards gave me a high five on his way to the next workout station.

"I don't think I kicked his ass, Brody. That was all my mom," I chuckled. He shrugged his shoulders and kept walking. No one here would offer any information other than what they had been told.

"This place is amazing," Agent Johnson said as she scanned the crowds working out around her.

"Yeah, Aedan is determined that nothing happens to anyone in his House again. He really ramped up his training programs," I said.

"Yes, I have." The man in question wrapped his arms around me, pulling my back to his front. I hadn't heard or felt him approach; he must've been shielding hard. I could usually get through them but didn't try. If he was shielding, that meant he needed privacy, and I understood that.

"Hey, babe," I said.

He closed his eyes and gave a shake of his head.

"I am no babe," he griped.

"Not this again." I smiled up at him, and he kissed my cheek.

"Lara was just telling me what you did last night. Care to elaborate?" she asked, not mentioning what I actually said.

"We worked out with most of my House, Lara's parents, and a few other Fae," he said, turning his stunning, whiskey gaze to the agent.

"Master Aedan, Lara's mom wiped the floor with your ass. When's the rematch?" a passing fae commented as he strolled to the gun range.

"Walk faster, son; I have not fed today." The man sped up, moving away from us as Aedan gave a long-suffering sigh and shook his head. "Children," he said to me. "Feel free to go against her yourself!" he shouted above the din at the retreating fae warrior who shook his head repeatedly.

Agent Johnson chuckled under her breath. "All right," she started. "If anything comes up, I'll let you know."

I escorted the agent upstairs. On the way, she paused at the door to our garage. "I've heard about your collection. Care to show it to me?"

"Not at all, Agent," Aedan said, placing his thumbprint onto the scanner by the door.

The lights automatically came on as we walked into the cool, dry air, and a sharp intake of breath was the only sound she made. We watched as she walked through the vehicles, looking at each one.

My truck sat behind one of Aedan's black Escalades in the same place it had been before we took it to West Virginia. Its high shine glimmered under the soft LED lighting. It had been detailed, and not one bug stain from our trip remained.

We watched as she walked through the vehicles, glancing down at the plates and checking the tires, her sense of duty outweighing her curiosity. "I was a gearhead when I was younger; your collection is impressive, Governor," she said, walking back to us.

"Thank you," he answered simply, leading the way back to the door. We had agreed that this was as far as we would go. Should she ask any further questions, she would be talking to our lawyer, Domingo.

"I appreciate your time. If anything new comes up, I'll let you know. We are assuming that any samples taken from you were destroyed in the explosion. We have video from the surrounding businesses and will be combing through that over the next couple of days. The scientists in charge of the place are under scrutiny, and there is no evidence anything ever left that lab and went to another. Still, if it's out there, we'll find it," she finished, placing her hand on the door.

"We appreciate your efforts," Aedan said, reaching to shake her hand. "I cannot tell you what an invasion of privacy this has been. It is unsettling to think that something so personal could be taken and used in ways I cannot even imagine." He released her hand, and we watched her walk out into the fading sun.

I was grateful then that I had yet to modify my truck in any way that could be identifiable. Should they see it on video footage, it would blend with all the other red, factory-stocked Chevrolets we passed on the road, and there had been dozens of them. The windows were tinted just enough to mask features, and I knew that not one shred of evidence we had ever been in Morgantown existed.

I breathed an internal sigh of relief as I waved goodbye to Agent Johnson.

It was over.

We turned our back to catch Cook, placing dinner on the large island. He froze. I almost never saw him; none of us did. "Gotcha!" I yelled with a loud laugh.

He shook his finger at me and disappeared into a shadow. "You be a naughty lass," he answered, his voice fading to nothing as he slid into whatever hole he came out of.

Sighing, I sat at the table and ate with those who had an appetite for solid food. We laughed and told funny stories as the day turned into night. Coffee turned into wine that turned into liquor, and we shared friendship until dawn.

Chapter 12

I went to the clinic early the next day. My head hurt from the amount of vodka I drank the night before. I didn't find it amusing that I had a hangover. I mean, come on, Faerie Healer...had a hangover. It was humbling. I took two Motrin and powered through.

When I left Aedan, he was still curled around the Fae-shaped dent I made in the bed. He hadn't moved when the bed dipped as I shifted. I wondered if vampires got hangovers. The amount of alcohol we ingested last night was epic.

Not long after Agent Johnson left, my parents had come over. Then Ravena, Finn, Lochlann, and Rory dropped by. After them, it was Keelin and Finley with their mates. Then the vampires woke up and joined us. As if we had sent up a signal, most of our friends followed suit. It wasn't long until the entire main floor of the house was filled with vampires and fae talking and drinking. Well, the pregos didn't drink, but the rest of us sure as hell did.

For the first time, I saw the need for such a large house. It was a pleasant night, and the back French doors were opened to allow people to spill into the courtyard. Food fit for a king arrived on platters, and I hoped Cook was in his glory. He loved to feed people; he fed a houseful last night.

Groups ended up in the training rooms and observation areas. There was sparring, dancing, mingling, and a good time was had by all. Alcohol continued to flow, and the feeling of more than one deal being made with a fae flowed through the air. Turns out the fae were crazy good at business. Despite the lack of amenities in their own land, they were making US dollars hand over fist in just about every category of business around.

I don't even know what time we stumbled into bed. The staff made sure that no one drove and that the many guestrooms were full, and our friends comfortable.

The sun dragged me out of bed early, despite the automatic light-blocking drapes. I could feel the bright yellow ball of light mocking me beyond the glass. Even after a gallon of water and a half-gallon of coffee, I still had a headache.

I sat at my desk in the clinic, reviewing the charts of the patients Bethany saw in my absence. She had done well, and I gave her the day off with pay as a reward. The house above me was silent, my parents likely still out. My mom drank freely last evening, so I knew she wasn't pregnant. She was the last holdout of the group. Maybe if she had a baby, the Goddess and Aedan would shut up about me having one.

A little brother or sister would be fun, but my mom didn't seem to be on that train yet, although she did have a big fight ahead of her. I couldn't blame her for being cautious in the face of so much uncertainty. I explained birth control to all of them when they arrived. Maybe she had decided to err on the side of caution until the issues with Aramea were settled.

I saw my first patient by eleven. Word of mouth traveled, and when folks found out I was in the clinic, they flocked to me. I saw a few cases I would have thought serious when I first came into my powers. A teenager with a gangrenous appendix came with his parents, and I had him fixed and on his way in no time. I set two broken legs and healed a nasty wound from a lawnmower rollover accident.

Lunch and coffee appeared in the afternoon, and I sat watching the TV during one of my rare breaks. The local news carried a story about the lab in Morgantown, and I learned there was an update. The explosion had been caused by a confirmed gas leak. No sign of accelerants had been discovered, and it was all deemed accidental.

Shards of bone had been discovered, but they were linked to the lab animals used in cancer research. I knew better. Aedan had counted the heartbeats, and he never mentioned animals. Knowing how I feel about them, he would have. The more I learned, the surer I was that we had done the right thing. Nothing good would have come from that place and those experiments.

There were stories about Aedan and I taking a vacation and a few fae and shifter stories. But for the most part, all was quiet on the news front.

Noah walked through the door as I shoved the last bite of chocolate cake into my mouth, smearing icing all over my chin. "S'up," I mumbled around creamy buttercream icing.

A wolfish grin crept over his face, which is hysterical, knowing he is a werepanther and not a werewolf. "Looks good," he chuckled.

"Want some?" I asked, waving at the entire cake sitting on the wet bar above the minifridge full of medicines and wine. Thank the Goddess I didn't have to deal with Joint Commission inspections like the hospital. My entire clinic was one giant violation. No hiding the coffee cups around here.

Nodding, he helped himself to a huge piece before taking the seat across from me.

"Everything taken care of with Aedan?" he asked.

"Yeah," I answered, pausing to think about how much detail he needed before deciding he didn't need any, at least not about the lab in Morgantown. "There won't be any fallout from Aedan's abduction."

"Good," he said around a bite of cake.

"How are things with the shifters?" I asked.

As a group, they worried about me. Noah knew that I harbored no ill will or intent towards them, but the general shifter did not. They feared my close association with the vampire community, my magic, and my ability to call them to me. Once upon a time, shifters had been hunted to near extinction by the vampires that vastly outnumbered them. Shifter blood was potent, and a vampire benefited greatly from drinking it.

Under Aedan, it was outlawed unless consensual. During his short 'absence,' vampires had started hunting them again, and the tenuous peace between the species had suffered. Together, Noah and Aedan were working to repair it, but centuries-old fears are hard to assuage.

"It's a long road, but it gets better every day. Now that we are out, it will be that much harder for vampires to go after us like they used to. Every group is on their best behavior- for now. No one wants the darker side of the supernatural community exposed, at least not yet."

I sat, nodding my head. "Have things settled in general?" I asked.

"They are better. Not great, but better. Most of the violence has stopped, but there are a lot of prejudices to overcome. People lost their jobs, some got ran out of communities they'd lived in for decades. Still, more are keeping their identities hidden for fear of the same. It didn't go as smoothly as I would have liked. That the bloodsuckers got better treatment is a sticking point with me." I gave a small laugh and a wide smile.

"Money," I said. "Their success was one hundred percent about the AVA and money," I added.

"You got that right," he said. "It'll get better. As per your request, the shifters are going to take credit for the VID cure. That will help build a bridge between both communities. Your contribution to that cure will be made known, and that will help your position with the shifters. They won't know what you gave; they will just know you helped. The vaccine and the cure will be available to all next week. You did that. Thank you," he finished.

"I didn't do crap but bleed a little, Noah. Nice speech, though," I chuckled at him, going to get another piece of cake because it was delicious and I could, dinner be damned. "You and Aedan did all the work. The lab technicians and scientists are the ones behind this, not me," I added.

He quirked his eyebrow at me, shaking his head with a small smile.

"There is one more thing you should know," I started. "I want you to hear it from me and not on the news, and I'm sure the news will eventually break. It's not like there are secrets in this town." I stopped with a heavy sigh. "Grania is pregnant," I said, feeling like something this significant needed to be shared. There would be fallout from it. Maybe on many levels.

He dropped his head to his chest, rolling his shoulders and stretching his neck from side to side. "That complicates things, doesn't it?" He brought his head up and met my eyes; his were a little bit harder. "The one good thing about vampirism is that they cannot procreate," he made a stab at laughter, but it fell short.

Aedan was one of his best friends, so I knew that he didn't really mean it. "They don't tend to make many bonded children as each one takes time to mature, and not all of them survive the turn. Being able to conceive will give them an edge in the eyes of my people and may create further conflict between the groups."

"Grania is a special case. There won't be any more vampire children, and honestly, Grania is more Fae now than Vampire. Whatever I did to bond her to me changed her on a cellular level. She still drinks blood, but she is more or less fae. I think she drinks out of habit and not necessity." I sat watching him, hoping we didn't have a problem.

Grania was my best friend, and my loyalties would always lie with her and the vampire community. As much as I would help everyone, I hoped the others understood that and didn't threaten me.

He nodded his head up and down, his eyes softer now. "They'll hunt you down, drain you dry, and torture you if they think it will allow them to have biological children."

I threw my head back, laughing at his statement. Power flowed from me accidentally in a way that hadn't happened in months. "Let them try, Noah. Let them try. I'm not helping the vampire community welp a bunch of little vampires. Grania's situation couldn't be helped; I'll not be bonding any more vampires to me, and I pity any that try to force my hand." I wouldn't be forced, never again. From conception, the Goddess had given me the power to protect myself; I just hadn't had access to it until I was forced one too many times. It would never happen again. Never.

Seeing the look on my face and feeling my raw power flood him, Noah stilled, his face narrowing. I pulled my power back and put the lid on it. "Sorry," I said with a faint shrug of my shoulder.

I heard heavy footsteps above me. The feel of wild magic must have awakened my sleeping parents. Four gigantic dads with glowing swords got stuck on the stairs as they tried to push their way through one smallish opening simultaneously. "It's okay, dads," I said, shaking my head at them. They were cute. Really.

One by one, they pushed through and came to stand by me and glare at Noah. "Dads. It's fine. We were just talking; I'm a little hungover and got carried away." Lann's hand came to rest on my shoulder, and his hulking presence filled the room.

Noah shook his head, and a big smile spread across his face. "I forgot for a minute that you aren't the delicate woman you appear to be," he explained. "I'll not worry about you again: much, anyway. Just be careful. It will cause some ripples. I'm assuming Aedan's issues with infertility are also fixed?" he asked.

I answered with a simple gallic shrug I had learned from the others. "Time will tell, I suppose," I answered.

"Okay. Well, good luck in your upcoming battles; I'm assuming you will be leaving soon?" He plucked his cake back up and took another bite.

"Soonish, yes. The sooner, the better, really. Life is in a suspended state until we see this through." The dads at my back stiffened as one before their collective slump. I didn't look at them, but I could feel their readiness to argue, just not in front of others. I smiled at Noah as he finished his cake and rose.

"Call me when you get back," he said as if my coming back was not even a question. We can have coffee and go over the results from the first round of treatments and vaccinations at the official level." He reached to shake my dads' hands, and I heard them grumble but grudgingly accept.

"I look forward to it, Noah," I said, rising to pull him into a hug. "Tell Liam I said Hi."

"I will. Take care, Lara."

When he was gone, my dads sat on chairs scattered around the room.

"You're not going. We forbid it," Laith said, growling at me with clenched fists.

I tossed my head back and laughed so loudly that I had no doubt the neighbors heard it. The neighbors being Aedan with his supernatural hearing. "Dad. I'm going. The only known Faerie Healer is most definitely showing up to the war you plan on waging. I'm not leaving y'all unprotected."

"We are not unprotected!" he shouted, causing smaller feet to pound overhead.

"Dad, I was literally *made* for this. This conflict was my sole purpose in being born. I'm going." I crossed my arms and met him glower for glower.

"I told you, Laith," my mom chuckled from the door. It sounded like a thousand bells. Like Aedan, there was magic in her laugh.

"I thought you were going to wait and allow us to discuss this together?" Aedan said from the tunnel entrance.

"Et Tu, Brute?" I asked, staring down my sneaky sweetie. He glanced down the tunnel, and I thought he might slip away.

"Well, the cat is out of the bag now," Saige grumbled.

"I'm going; period the end. Mom, you know I have to go," I said, looking over Seal's shoulder at her. "It's literally my sole purpose in life."

"It isn't your only purpose, dear," she said, trying to hide her smile and look marginally fierce. "Your life hasn't been only for this purpose, but I agree that you were *initially* created to be a weapon in this war," she said, ducking her head away from her mates.

"Airmed," Laith growled.

"Do not call me that, Laith. You know it's true. You were there for Goddess's sake." Her glare would've cut a lesser man in two.

Laith shut up.

"I can't believe y'all. You planned on ganging up to keep me from going?" I cast an accusatory scowl around the room.

"Not me," my mom said. "I knew better. You would think these idiots would too. They've been dealing with a strong-willed woman long enough to know it wouldn't work," she said, coming to hug me. "In their defense, they just want to protect you," she added, smiling up at them.

Their faces fell in defeat under the force of it, and I wondered if they ever won an argument. The four big, strong, warrior males didn't stand a chance against my tiny mother. I loved it. Aedan narrowed his eyes at me as I watched my parent's exchange.

"I still think the idea of Lara staying home has merit," he argued.

I rolled my eyes to the ceiling and shook my head. "Babe, I have to go. You know that. You're going, my parents are going, The Eight are going, and I'm going. This fight won't be easy. Y'all will need me, and I'm not taking chances with any of you." My southern accent got as deep as it went as it filled with emotion. I pinned Aedan with my biggest smile, mirroring my mom, and his eyes narrowed further. I felt my face fall.

"That will not work with me, Anamcara," he sighed.

"Aedan, I can't stay here. You know that."

He crushed me with his hug. "I know, but I had to try."

"I understand," I said, pulling from him. "I appreciate it; I do. It'll be okay." He searched my face, his showing more concern than I cared to see.

"I don't know about you, but I'm whipped. The clinic was busy, I'm starved, and I still have a hangover. How can a Faerie Healer have a hangover?" I asked with a laugh, trying to dispel the tension in the room and giving voice to my earlier thoughts.

My dads smiled reluctantly, coming over to hug me to them. My mom gave a wink and a slow nod of her head, congratulating me on my mass male manipulation.

"I love you guys, but after last night, I'm going to bed early," I groaned, making them chuckle.

"Goodnight, daughter." My mom saved her hug for last. I wasn't model tall. Still, she had to stretch to reach me. I laid my head on hers, wished her goodnight, and Aedan and I walked hand and hand through the tunnel to home.

We ate dinner in our suite. While I showered, Aedan made seared, blackened Ahi tuna with roasted parmesan brussels sprouts. He even warmed some French bread that was leftover from breakfast. When I came out of the bedroom wearing a light dressing gown Aedan had bought me, dinner was laid on our small table, and the lights were dimmed. A glass of wine sat next to my plate, but I pushed it aside, going for the coffee instead. I still had a light headache despite Motrin; I blamed caffeine withdraw.

Aedan was nowhere to be seen, but I heard the rustling of paper from his office. I sat, tearing into the tuna steak with gusto. I alternated sips of coffee with wine, and halfway through dinner, I began to feel better. Aedan slipped from his office, dropping a kiss on my head as he went to our room. Our suite was quiet, and after the last few days, I appreciated that.

I finished eating, then washed my dishes by hand since we never had enough to run the dishwasher, then I took a fresh cup of coffee into the sitting room in our bedroom to wait for Aedan. He did not disappoint.

He strode from the bathroom, naked except for the few drops of water his towel missed. I sipped my coffee and watched him over the rim. Goddess, he was incredible. "Mavis, dim the lights," I said, grinning when the lights grew softer.

"I have a bit of work to do, mo chroi." Aedan walked past me to the bureau, and I stood, stopping him.

"Hmmm, maybe in a bit. I won't keep you long," I answered, placing a hand on his chest. I thought about all the times he ruined my showers as I herded him to the bed. When his knees hit the mattress, I shoved him back and crawled up his still form, placing kisses as I went.

I nipped at his nipples and kissed a line to his jaw. Placing kisses down his throat, I tasted my way to the other side of his face. His eyes were closed, and his mouth slack as I traced more kisses down his chest while taking his hard length into one of my hands. I marveled at the contradiction between soft and hard as I traced the ridges and veins that pleased me so easily. He lay before me like a buffet of all my favorite things; I have never seen a more perfect man. And I've seen my share of them.

The air left his lungs when my hair skimmed his chest as I moved to place a chaste kiss on the tip of him, but that wasn't what I was after tonight. I bit the area where his thigh meets his body. That sweet dip between those hard, male muscles held my fascination, and I did something I have never done. I opened his femoral vein with my power-infused tongue. Then I sipped from him until he bucked under me, thrashing almost uncontrollably.

I drank until he fought himself to be still for me, then I slid up, kissing him forcefully with blood-covered lips. As I had no fangs, I could never match his efficiency at blood-sucking and tended to spill quite a lot.

Groaning into my mouth, he flipped me and slid in with the same motion. I had intended to take him from above so I could watch his face, but drinking his blood in such an intimate way had sent him beyond the edge of control. I liked it.

He sank his fangs into me, and after several days of not sharing blood, the bond between us refreshed and tightened once again. His thoughts were wild as he tested the strength of our new bed in a way we hadn't yet. I came shuddering against him with his second swallow, and with the tenth, I came again.

Pulling his fangs from me, he licked the wounds closed and braced himself. I watched his face as he slowed his pace. The smile he gave was slow and victorious. I brought my hand to his cheek and held it as we moved together in the perfect dance of bodies and souls, then I wrapped it around his neck and drew him down into a kiss.

Chest to chest, we made love until he shuddered; he brought his mouth to mine and came in the deepest part of me. When the last spasm was done, he rested his forehead on mine. "Is breá liom tú," he said, his breath coming fast. "There is nothing I would not do for you. No task is too great, and no trial too difficult," he said, sharing my breaths as I shared his.

I remembered the days when he breathed only to make humans feel more comfortable. He breathed almost all the time now, and I wondered if this was yet another change in him. "I love you too," I said, winking at him. I had looked up that particular Gaelic saying the first time he used it.

We got up, slowly untangling our bodies and minds. After rinsing off in the shower, I slipped the light nightgown back over my head as he kissed me goodnight and headed to his office. Luxuriating in the feel of soft sheets against warm skin, I snuggled deeper into the mattress. At the same time, I stretched out, taking up most of the bed. For the first time in a long time, I was in bed and asleep hours before dawn.

Chapter 13

When I awoke in the morning, I was well rested but alone. It was the first time in recent memory that Aedan hadn't slept beside me. "Mavis, where is Master Aedan?" I grumbled, wondering where my wayward mate had slept.

No one was more surprised than me when the disembodied voice answered, "Master Aedan is in the first floor office."

"Oh, well. Um. Thanks?" I responded, wondering what the hell.

"Thanks are unnecessary, Mistress," it answered, and I started thinking about Sci-Fi movies with bad endings.

"Oh, Lord, I need some damned coffee for this," I muttered.

"As you wish it, Mistress."

I got up, shambling to the bathroom and eyeing the walls with mistrust. I am all about technology. Let me rephrase that: I am somewhat about technology. Mavis was pushing my comfort level.

I once read a series of books in which the premise was that technology wiped out about three-fourths of the population. I could see that happening. Mavis gave me the creeps. She did, however, make a damn fine cup of coffee.

Cook's was better.

"Nevermind, Mavis," I said. "I want Cook's French press coffee," I pouted a little over the fact that I didn't smell it waiting for me.

"I will contact Master Cook," it said.

"Don't you dare, Mavis," I countered.

"As your AI assistant, it is my job to see to your needs," it said with more snark than an AI assistant should.

"Mavis, if you bother that little gnome, I will smack you," I growled.

"Master Cook is a Brownie, not a gnome, Madame."

"What did you just call me?" I asked, astonished with myself that I was about to bitch slap my AI assistant, whatever the hell that actually is. "Show yourself and let's handle this in person," I said, spinning around and walking straight into Aedan.

He stood with a cup of coffee in one hand and his face in the palm of the other.

"It's her fault; she goaded me," I said, defending myself.

"The Artificial Intelligence Assistant goaded you?" he asked, shaking his head in disbelief.

"Yeah, she got snippy with me too; where is that bitch. We are about to have a Come to Jesus moment." I went to move by him, and he stopped me, placing the coffee in my hand.

"Drink this. Please. Quickly," he added with a low chuckle.

"Do you want some of this smoke?" I demanded, snatching the coffee and taking a giant gulp. It was from the French press, not the Keurig; I was glad that bitch Mavis hadn't made it. She probably would've spit in it.

"That bitch, as you so eloquently put it, is in the mainframe of the computer system that makes this home a smart home," he answered my previous question.

"Well, she's got it coming to her," I said, glowering at him while I sipped hot Costa Rican coffee. I felt my muscles relax as the caffeine hit me. "Speaking of getting it, where were you last night?" I asked, rounding on him.

"I was working out the details of our trip to Talamh na Sithe with Grania and the others," he said, deflating my anger immediately.

"Oh," was all I could say.

"My mother sent word that it is too quiet and that she fears Aramea is massing her forces to make an attack here; I do not want to bring warfare to our doorstep. We must go to her as soon as feasible." He walked by me and went to sit in our sitting area.

"You're right." I sat across from him, cupping my coffee in both hands. "When do we leave?" I asked.

He placed his face in his hands, not answering me for a very long time. I sipped my coffee and waited. "Is there nothing I can say to change your mind?" he asked.

"No." It was a simple answer; it was the only answer.

"Very well. Tomorrow. We leave tomorrow. We need a bit longer to finalize the details." He glanced up at me, his face full of worry. I put my coffee down on the side table and went to him, placing myself between the cage of his knees.

"It will be okay, Aedan," I said, pinning his eyes with mine and willing him to believe me.

"War is never okay, my love." The corners of his eyes crinkled with worry, making him age before my eyes. I know how old he is, but most days, he's just another thirty-something-looking bro, just like a lot of other bros, only hotter. Sometimes he looked younger and sometimes older, but at that moment, I felt the weight of his years.

"We can't outwait her, Aedan. She is nearly immortal. We can't change her mind. Time has made her worse, not better. We can't allow her to come here and wreak havoc on this plane; that would change everything for supernaturals. There is no decision here, not really. No, war is not ideal, but in this situation, it is the only option we have. After everything she has done and everything she has threatened, she has to die. I believe that." I watched acceptance cross his face. He knew I was right.

"As do I. I had simply hoped to convince you to stay here and let us handle it. This conflict started millennia ago; there is no reason for you to engage in it," he pleaded with me one more time.

"There are a thousand reasons, love. I'm going, and it will be okay. The Fae deserve to return to their homeland and live without the shadow of her tyranny hanging over them. As do their children. They like it here, but this is forced exile for them, and they deserve to be able to choose."

His shoulders slumped at my words. Pulling me into a hug, he placed a kiss on the top of my head and breathed in my scent. "You will take no unnecessary chances. None. You are not trained as a warrior and will accept guidance from those who are. You will not place yourself in danger, and you will not fight on the front lines. I would never deign to control your behavior, but in this, I will have my way. Do you understand?" His eyes bled paler as he spoke, and I got it then. He was afraid, probably of many things. He was afraid of Aramea, of going Talamh na Sithe, and of losing me in this fight.

"I understand, and I mostly agree. I am not a primary fighter, but this is the point I'm going to argue: I can't be at the back either. I need to be where the fighting is so that I can help. I need to be able to get my hands on the injured and attempt to mitigate our losses. Besides, if that is where you will be, then that is where I will be. I'll fight you on this." I fisted his hands in mine, shaking them. I would not sit on the sidelines and wait for the outcome to be determined. I was almost as vested in it as the others.

"I cannot focus on fighting if I fear for your safety."

"And I can't focus on staying safe in a hostile land if I am afraid for your safety. If you get injured, I will heal you. If mom or dad are injured, I will heal them. I can't heal them from miles away. I have to be there."

He kissed me fiercely, wrapping his body around mine like it was the last kiss we would ever share. "There will be another strategy session this evening; you need to be there," he said, pulling away from our kiss. "Galahad knows the time has come, and he is ready as well. You need to pack lightly. Whatever can fit in small packs is all we can take; the rest we must procure there. We will go over the details this evening. I have an urgent board meeting to address my upcoming absence that I am already late for." He rose, walking to the bathroom without a backward glance. I knew he was angry, but I also knew he would get over it.

I poured another cup of coffee and walked through the silent house and out the front door. As much as I appreciated the tunnel, it was impossible to use it on such a beautiful day. The sun shone on my face, and birds chirped in the distance.

It was the calm before the storm; I knew that. The horses grazed in the field, sunlight making their sleek coats gleam. Galahad raised his head in acknowledgment when he noticed me. I knew I should go and see them, but I would wait until I tied up loose ends.

In the clinic, I called Bethany to give her another day off with pay. I let her know that I would be gone for an indeterminant amount of time and that she would be in charge. I arranged for her to be paid in my absence and called Noah to let him know it was go time. We talked for a while about nothing. I could tell he worried for me, and I continued to ignore any thoughts that there was danger in my near future.

I saw a few patients, but it wasn't busy. Like that yellow cast to the air that warns of the coming storm, the air was heavy with anticipation and warning. The patients I saw were edgy and off-kilter. They all complained of feeling like something big loomed on the horizon. Being supernaturals or humans that lived with them, they had an excellent sixth sense for danger, and as the day wore on, I began to feel like a fool.

I locked the door behind the last patient and walked to the barn. I had an hour before the meeting, and I wanted to see my horses; I needed to see them. There is something cathartic about the smell of a horse; their scent is incomparable to any other. Sarah and Jeremy had been taking care of them for the last few months, and I found that I missed it. I put their feed out and called them in.

Putting Imp into the crossties first, I brushed him down, going over every inch of the aging paint horse. He still looked good, but there was no denying he was advancing in years. I thought about my life and how much a part of it he had been. That being said, I didn't think I would replace him when he was gone.

Next, I pulled out Foxie and checked her over as well. Sarah and Jeremy were amazing, but being new to horses made it possible they could miss something. The little black mare looked great, not too fat and not too thin. Her coat shined like a mirror, and I knew that she was in good hands with them.

Finally, I dragged the giant Guardian out of his stall and clipped him in the crossties. He snorted at me, and if a horse can roll his eyes, he did.

"You don't have to restrain me; I would've just stood there and let you scratch me," he said, causing me to shake my head at him.

"Sorry, it's a habit," I looked sideways at him but didn't unlatch the tie.

Sighing, he cocked once back hoof to rest it. "So, are you ready for the big dance tomorrow?" he asked.

"I mean, sure. As ready as I can be, I suppose." I ran the brush over him, scratching the spot he loved on his neck. He bobbed his head in acknowledgment.

"Are you going to make me wear a saddle?" he asked.

I chuckled. "I was planning on it, Gally. You can be contrary, and it might be a dogfight. I don't want to have to focus on staying on your back."

"Can you at least not use that fancy crap Aedan bought me?" he asked, turning his head into my stomach and rubbing it on me. "It makes me look like a candy ass."

I melted into him, wrapping my arms around this neck. "I could use T's western saddle. You might like that better anyway. You'll look kinda goofy with it on, but I don't care if you don't." I pulled my fingers through his mane, tugging a few stems of hay free from it.

"Goofy, how? You mentioned you would let me talk to the ladies in Talamh na Sithe. I don't want to look like a jackass for them." He preened a little, stretching his neck down and out.

"I mean, you're a warhorse. Not sure how cool you'll look in a Western saddle, but if I strap some guns to it, the ladies might think you're a bad boy, kinda like an equine Jesse James. In fact, the saddle will make you stand out to them; you'll be mysterious and unique."

"Oooh, I got you. I like that. I can see it now; they'll all flock to me. They will chase me down and ask about my saddle and all the things attached to it. I'll play it coy and be the tall, dark, handsome rake of their dreams. I'll play the strong, silent type; I'll be hit." He shook his long black mane, sending it cascading across his eyes to make him, indeed, look rakish.

"Yeah, Bud. Not sure about the silent part of that equation, but the rest of it sounds spot on." I began brushing the tangles out of his tousled mane, hoping it would be that easy.

"It's a good plan," he said with a definitive snort.

"For getting ladies, yes. But what about the rest of it?" I asked. He hadn't mentioned the upcoming conflict to me at all.

"Eh, it will work out. Aramea is too confident. She hasn't been challenged in a real way in so long that it will make her sloppier than she already is."

"Won't that make her more dangerous?"

"She has always been exceedingly dangerous. You just never recognized it," he said, leveling me with his dark, expressive eyes.

"Right. Well…" I started.

"We have strong warriors, a true Healer, and Dani on our side. We've got this," he bumped me with his head again, nibbling softly at my shirt. "Now, let's get this over with so that I can cozy up to all those hotblooded Fae mares."

I laughed out loud. Males of every species are fairly predictable when it comes to the females of their species. "Okay, Gally. I'll get right on it."

I walked into the meeting late. If it hadn't taken me three tries to find the correct meeting room, I'd have made it sooner. I'm not sure why we needed at least three meeting rooms, but apparently, we did.

No one looked twice at the dirt and horse hair covering my clothes. I brought the distinct smell of barn into the room with me, but wisely, no one mentioned it.

There was a large map displayed on the screen at the end of the room. There were Xs and Os placed here and there, and I really hoped someone besides me paid attention to it. It was labeled 'TnS,' and I assumed Aedan had had it commissioned. It was all Greek to me.

"Anamcara, we were just beginning; you did not miss anything," Aedan said as I found an empty seat. The room was packed.

"Perfect," I said, trying to smile the sarcasm out of my voice at his dark look.

"The staging area will be a property I own in Ireland," he continued, narrowing his eyes at me. "If we walk the old ways, we would need to travel too far to reach the Capital, and the risk of immediate detection goes up. Should we leave from the cottage in Béal an Mhuirthead, we will arrive near the center of the city. We will be closer than the way from Clifden you took, Airmed." Aedan glanced at my parents, who were seated on the opposite side of the room. They nodded their heads tightly.

"Do you have the old ways mapped, then?" Seal asked, his eyes glinting as he looked Aedan square in the face.

"As a former Captain of the Queen's guard myself, I do. The sword was not my only skill. I was destroyed for more than one reason, father-in-law," he said, meeting my dad's eyes. There was danger in the glance they shared. "I was born to be King, though it is a title I no longer want. I had more magic than any other until your daughter. The memory of the old ways is as fresh as it ever was. The home I speak of was my first outside of Talamh na Sithe. I had it for a reason as it was close to the capital by the old ways. I used that particular path daily..." he paused, and his eyes went unfocused. It wasn't long, just pause enough, and I knew what he was thinking. The others didn't notice, but I did. "Aramea would not know of this place; it is safer and will put us in the center of her stronghold where we can take her measure," he finished, his gaze slipping over me briefly. "It's little more than a cottage but will serve its purpose," he finished. "Unless anyone has another idea that doesn't require days of travel through potentially hostile territory."

No one spoke up. My parents looked tense, and I wondered why. Maybe it was because we were finally acting, or maybe it was something else. I watched Aedan from the corner of my eye and saw he was tense as well, but I imagined his reasons were different. We were about to travel to the home he shared with his first love and unborn child. I knew without listening to his thoughts that this was the case.

I wasn't jealous of a dead woman, not at all. I knew he loved me, but I couldn't help but feel a twinge of sadness for him. Our twisted roads had brought us together, and I couldn't regret that. But what would his life had been had Elizabeth not been killed? He would be King now, or maybe his son would. Who is to say? With a sigh, I looked over the crowd, catching the look of concern Aedan cast my way.

"A plane will take us to Knock. The old ways from the Americas to Ireland are not plentiful, and it would be exhausting to travel in this manner," he reiterated, glancing around the room. "The plane will leave from BWI at two AM, arriving in Knock at approximately noon, Irish Standard Time. The Fae contingent recommends this timeline, and I approve, as it gives us the day to rest and prepare before moving in the morning."

There was a shimmer of light as Dani stepped into the room. "Ah, yes! The final planning session. I apologize for my tardiness." She beamed as she walked through the room, finger waving to my mother but taking the seat next to me. "Carry on," she said, with a wave of her hand.

The room was silent for the span of several heartbeats. "Mother, we were just discussing the itinerary for travel to Béal an Mhuirthead. Unless you can provide travel for over one hundred people, the plane leaves at two," Aedan said, waiting for his mother to respond.

Dani looked at me for a long moment, and I knew from her look that we could weave a way to anywhere we liked. "As much as I would like to, I cannot directly involve myself in this conflict. I can provide knowledge, insight and cheer you from the sidelines, but I cannot intervene. My apologies. I have done all that I can through the years to place the pieces on the chessboard, but I can do no more. Understand that this was a long game, Coi, which is something you know well. I believe that the pieces will move in your favor, but I can do no more." With the blink of an eye, the room froze, and time stopped. "Say nothing, Lara. You could do this magic, but it would be unwise for many reasons. A Goddess, like all females, should keep some powers hidden, else all will try to use us." She looked straight ahead, and time resumed again like it had never stopped.

I was caught looking at Dani while she fastidiously ignored me. I looked away. Aedan caught the movement, and his entire face narrowed on the two of us. I didn't meet his eyes as he continued. "Lara and I will leave Westminster around one. Any who want to follow are free to go with us. Are there any questions?" I wondered how my warhorse was going to get to this place in Ireland but kept my mouth shut.

Hands raised like we were in school, and I tuned out as questions were asked about money, logistics, and affairs people were leaving behind. Aedan, Grania, and others answered as best they could. The Great Goddess popped out of the room with promises to see us in Ireland, and I just got more tired.

I hadn't eaten, and my stomach could be heard growling from every corner. More than once, people glanced my way until finally, they stopped asking questions and began to filter out. Aedan hung back, talking to those that surrounded him, requesting his time. I got up and headed upstairs to finish getting ready to leave.

My parents were waiting for me in the hall, looking determined. Sighing, I waved at them to follow; I had food somewhere with my name on it. We passed the kitchen and found it empty, so I took the stairs with them behind me.

Using my fingerprint to gain entrance to our rooms, I ushered my parents in, inhaling the scent of curry as they closed the door behind them. Cook had made Indian food. I hadn't had Indian food in ages and immediately set about correcting that.

"Dinner?" I asked around a mouthful of curry chicken and with a bite of naan.

"No, dear, thank you," my mom said, sitting across from me at the island, silently rolling her eyes and glancing over her shoulder at the large men behind her.

"Do we trust this old Fae, Lara?" Seal said, jumping right into it.

"Which one, dad?" I asked. "You are all technically old Fae." I smiled, enjoying the way he got flustered at my picking.

"Aedan," he said, his stormy features meeting mine.

"Oh," I tried to bite back my surprise and failed.

"It's just that no one knows the old ways like he seems to, Lara. We worry he is leading us into a trap," Laith responded, making me drop my hands and stopping my fork from making it to my mouth.

I growled in anger over the food, not at their suspicions. I had gotten used to Seal and Laith's innate distrust of everyone. They liked Aedan and thought him a suitable mate for me, but it was no surprise that their suspicion had finally reared its head. "Yes, I trust Aedan. Obviously, I trust Aedan. He's a gazillion years old; it would be weird if he weren't informed about the intricacies of Talamh na Sithe. Don't you think?"

"I think it would be unusual, yes," my mom answered at the same time; Seal and Laith said no. The other two men, wisely, said nothing. I imagined what fights looked like in their house, and I was almost glad I had missed most of those.

"Aedan was tortured by Aramea. I won't go into the depths and depravity of the things she did to him, but if anyone has cause to want her gone, it's him," I sighed, weighing how much to say. Most of this was Aedan's private business, but not all. I needed them to understand a fraction of what he lost. "Aramea killed Aedan's first, uh, fiancé and their unborn child. Why? It's a long story, but suffice it to say that I have seen them together, and no way, no how, is he leading us into a trap. He would've ripped her head off in the beginning, but he was letting me come to my own conclusions about her," I said, and I saw the moment three-fifths of my parents dropped any concerns they had about him.

"Does he wish to be King?" my mother asked, leveling me with her bright green gaze. I figured that was the crux of the matter; she worried for her crown. In a fair fight, Aedan would beat her; I believed that.

"No, I do not," Aedan said, closing the door behind him. "I have no desire to return to that place, and, frankly, were it not for the fact that Aramea has threatened Lara on multiple occasions, I would let it burn." He moved to the other end of the island so that we made a rough circle.

The air was heavy with a challenge. I looked back and forth between them all while shoveling the fantastic Indian food into my mouth. Cook needed a raise. Indian food that tasted Indian was hard to pull off.

"I am no threat to your throne, Airmed," Aedan said with finality.

She nodded her head once in response. I wondered why my mother would ever want that job; it seemed like a lot of work for little reward.

"My apologies, Aedan. We need to know we can trust you. This feels like a setup; you must understand that our daughter is our highest priority," Lann surprised me by saying since he was always the supportive one. Our kitchen lights shined on the darkness of his skin and the seriousness of his face. Maybe they had all been worried and just chose to say nothing.

"Apology accepted. There's something I need you to understand as well," Aedan started, and his face narrowed with fierceness. I suddenly worried whether or not my parents would be leaving this room in one piece tonight. "I am in love with Lara. I have searched a hundred more lifetimes than you have lived to find her. I do not want her power, and I do not want your crown. I want nothing other than to retire to some remote place and live out our days, but that is not to be. As the strongest of our kind, we have a responsibility to maintain order for all paranormals. This, in turn, protects the human communities."

"As much as I would like to walk away from the conflict in Talamh na Sithe, I cannot. Aramea will just bring her war to me, and that is unacceptable. Is she setting a trap? Perhaps. There is no way of knowing what plans she has laid or what moves she has made in the absence of those who oppose her."

"As my mother said, this is a long game, and Aramea has been playing it longer than I have. We can only hope we are ready and that the Goddess speaks true." He rose to his full height to stand even with the giant men surrounding the island. "Now, if you will excuse me, I need to shower and pack so that we can arrive at the airport in time for our flight."

I watched him walk away from us; he didn't pause or look back. I piled another spoonful of curry chicken on my plate. "He isn't setting a trap; Y'all know that," I said, downing my coffee and enjoying the mix of flavors. "Sure you don't want some? I asked. "There's a ton."

"No, thank you. Aedan is right. If we don't pack and get our things together, we'll be late. If all goes well, we won't be returning; we will be staying to rebuild." My mom slid her elbows off the counter where they had rested during this conversation and stood straight, coming around the corner to hug me tight. "I am very sorry if we upset Aedan, but your fathers were worried. I feel I can take the measure of a man much more quickly. After all, I did not kill them the first chance I had. Had they been bad men, I would have. Aedan is a good man, Lara. I see that, and so will they," she finished, reaching up to plant a kiss on my cheek.

"We think he is a good man too, honey. We just have to be sure. We don't want to risk you in a fight that isn't yours to begin with," Saige said, scooting my mom aside to sweep me into his arms. He hugged me with my feet hanging off the floor, and I giggled at that, feeling little again.

They moved in for hugs as they left, promising to pack quickly and have the house settled in the hope they wouldn't return for a while. It made me sad to think they'd be staying in Talamh na Sithe, should all go well. I had gotten used to them being right next door, and a new sense of loss settled over me. After so long apart, it was nice being neighbors, even if Aedan likely didn't agree. I washed my dishes and went to find my mate.

He stood at the wall of windows that overlooked the field. My parents walked under the light of the moon, holding hands. My fathers' heads bent toward my mother in conversation. They moved with a lightness the situation did not warrant. Then again, they were together after over thirty years of separation; every step they took might feel carefree.

Moonlight filtered through the glass, framing Aedan in a soft glow. His head moved as he followed their progress. "They don't mean it, you know," I said, moving in behind him to wrap my arms around his muscled waist.

"I know. They are concerned for your safety." Placing his hand over mine, he rubbed a circle over my skin with his thumb. "They might be wrong about me, but they are not wrong about the rest. We have no idea what we are walking into," he finished. "Are you certain I cannot convince you to stay?"

"I'm sure, Aedan," I said.

"Then gather your things. We must go soon." He turned in my arms, surrounding me with the scent of blood, honey, and fall leaves. He wrapped his arms around my back and held me tight, resting his head on top of mine. At my size, not many men could make me feel small, but he always managed.

"Okay. What about Galahad? I assumed we were taking the old ways and that I would be able to ride him." I pulled away enough to look up at his face, suddenly concerned. What good was a warhorse for a Guardian if he couldn't go?

"He made his own arrangements, Anamcara."

"The horse made his own arrangements?" I asked, my voice raising an octave.

"He is more than a horse; try to remember that. His magic is old and was given to him by the Maker of all Things," he said, dropping a kiss on my head.

"Right," I said, moving away from him to grab a pack I bought specifically for this trip. "I still need to get him ready. If left to his own devices, he'll show up missing two shoes and not wearing any tack.

"You can correct all of that with magic when we get there." Aedan gave me a pointed glance, moving to grab his own bag.

"Right again," I mumbled as I shoved everyday sundries into the pack. I could make myself a saddle and some clothes if I had to, but deodorant and toothpaste were a necessity I wasn't willing to leave to magic.

We were traveling lightly, relying on allies in Talamh na Sithe to provide for the bulk of our needs. I tossed underwear and a few extra bras and left it at that. Dropping my pack beside Aedan's, I went into the bathroom and turned the shower on you may never see hot water again hot and stepped under the steaming spray. A soft groan escaped my lips as hot water kneaded muscles I hadn't known were sore.

"I love you, Lara," Aedan said from behind me.

"I know, Aedan."

"I want nothing from you other than for you to return that love," he added, sliding the glass shower door open and stepping in with me.

"I know that too."

"It unnerves me that my motivations are being questioned."

"I would feel the same way. They don't mean it. They are just being parents and trying to make up for not being there all those years." I started to turn and face him, but cold hands on my hips stopped me. His fingers dug in.

"Goddess, I need you," he groaned, Gripping my hips tighter and dragging me toward him.

"You have nothing to prove," I whispered.

"Do I not?" he asked.

"Not to me, Aedan. Not to me."

He released one hand, trailing it down my spine. It was so cold that goosebumps rose beneath it. He hadn't been sleeping. I knew that. He'd been working twenty-four-seven to prep for a war he didn't need to fight. Regardless of what he said, it wasn't his responsibility. He hadn't actually fed lately either. He fooled me with frequent little sips during sex, but the time was long passed for him to drink his fill.

"You need to feed," I said, feeling the brush of him against my core.

"I take from you almost daily, Mo Chroi." He nudged the tip of himself against me again, and I almost came apart. Gods, the things his body does to mine. It was surreal and the most real thing I've ever felt all at the same time.

"You don't take anything, Aedan," I responded, irritated by his turn of phrase. "And you haven't actually fed; you're not fooling me anymore."

"I do not wish to give them another reason to be suspicious. I do not want you for your blood." He rubbed against me once more, and I shuddered in his iron grip, my core clenching desperately around nothing.

"So, you just want me for sex then?" I chuckled darkly. "That's the only thing you haven't mentioned."

He cleaved me in two with one move, causing me to cry out and my orgasm to extend as I clenched around him. He left me panting hard with him sheathed to the base. He ground against me with a growl.

"If you say the word, I will stop," he said, pulling me to him and thrumming his fingers over the heart of me.

I writhed against him, trying to make him move his hips. "Please," I begged.

"Please, stop?" he asked, moving to withdraw from me.

"Please, don't," I whispered, my voice shaking. Without even moving inside of me, he had me on the edge of another orgasm. My legs shook from the need racing through my body.

"I am not sure what you are asking for, Anamcara. Be more clear."

"Please, don't stop, Aedan. Please. All that I have and all that I am, that was the promise: blood, sex, power, love, all of it belongs to you. I'll take it, and I'll give it." He sighed into my neck, and I felt the strain leave him. "There are no lines between us, Aedan. No boundaries. You will take, and I will give. You will give, and I will take. God, please," I begged him harder.

The feeling of constant fullness bordered on uncomfortable. I needed him to slide out and back in again. The burn from the stretch was too much until he flicked his thumb over me one more time. He gripped my chin, pulling it back, and watched me fall apart around him, screaming and begging him for more.

He exploded into me without one movement, and the feeling of fullness tripled. Power leaked from my shields, finally crashing through and enveloping us in rose-gold light. He dropped his shield too, and his silver-blue power danced with mine. I could see the waves of it surrounding us as it expanded like ripples in a pond.

Our power hadn't danced like this since the first time we were together. The scent of the sea mixed with the scent of honey, and I could feel the house notice our lapse in control; I didn't really care. Aedan's power was a perfect match to mine, yin to yang. We complimented each other in ways most didn't understand. Still, as our combined power coated the house, maybe they understood better.

Aedan balanced me, and together we were indeed one thing.

Unbreakable. Inseparable. Undeniable.

I sighed as the feeling of fullness faded. Aedan's heartbeat pounded against my back, and he released the hold he had on my chin. His body slipped from mine in a flood of our combined pleasure. And I mourned the loss of him inside me. Turning in his arms, I nestled my head into the crook of his shoulder.

The feeling of our mixed power ebbed, and time seemed to restart. He brushed the hair from my neck and bit into the spot opposite the one he marked. He pulled long and deep from the vein there, swallowing over and over. My eyes drooped closed at the feel of him taking from me. It is indescribable just how good it feels; it transcends sex and is more fulfilling than the best orgasm.

I went limp in his arms, not from blood loss, but from satisfaction. He drank and drank. I was glad he did because we didn't know what tomorrow would bring, and he needed to be at his best. He pulled from me too soon, licking the holes in my neck closed. We stood for a long time, wrapped together by arms and legs. Finally, we separated. I washed and shaved for what might be the last time in a while.

Aedan stepped out and trimmed his beard to just a tight scruff while I dried and redressed. Funny how these simple actions of life filled me with such peace. Peace before war, it was ironic how simple things seemed at that moment.

Chapter 14

We took the black Escalade to the airport. My parents rode with us and judging by the surreptitious glances they cast our way, our display of power had not gone unnoticed. I tried to remember if they had ever experienced Aedan unleased and couldn't. It may be a good thing that they did. Aedan had power in spades; it would be good for them to understand that he didn't need mine.

Aedan drove the Escalade straight into the hanger. No doubt, the line of vehicles following ours did look a bit like a government procession. Another reason to leave at such an odd hour was to avoid notice and speculation from onlookers and the ever-present paparazzi.

Next to Aedan's Gulfstream stood an enormous plane; my mouth dropped open at the sight of it. When Aedan said he booked a plane, I assumed he meant a JetBlue or something. This was an Airbus 380 private plane. I turned my stunned face to his.

"It belongs to one of my children," he said with a noncommittal shrug. "You will get bugs in your mouth, Mo Chroi."

I closed my mouth.

The others were dropped off, and the line of cars left. Their goal was to win this war and come back to visit, but not to stay. Only two vehicles remained in Aedan's hanger. The two black

Escalades were parked next to the smaller jet as the handful of vampires going with us boarded the larger one.

Aedan and I boarded last, and I had to school my face to keep the surprise from showing. The jet was incredible. Done in cool grays and whites, I knew immediately to whom it belonged. If I hadn't guessed, the tasteful insignia over the front wall of the plane would have given it away.

Seats were scattered in groups around the cabin to make it look casual. Still, this plane reflected every bit the business mogul Gregory Cavanaugh is. Aedan and I took a pair of seats joined together toward the back of the plane. I sank into the soft white leather, and immediately the footrest on the chair reclined, dipping me back into leather scented bliss.

"Oh, Aedan," I purred. "This plane is fantastic. You must thank Gregory for me."

"If you want one, we can buy one, Anamcara. I just do not see the reason to travel with this many people often enough to make it a worthwhile purchase."

I looked over at him and saw the sparkle in his eyes. Then I looked around the plane at the hundred or so folks clustered in groups. "Good point, babe," I whispered with a wink and a smile.

Within moments of us sitting down, the plane was in the air. Flight attendants brought drinks and snacks to those interested. I cupped my Grey Goose loosely, sipping it as I watched those around us watch us from the corner of their eyes. Once the drink was gone, I tipped my head onto Aedan's shoulder, he curled around me protectively, and we were instantly asleep.

The plane's slow descent eased me awake. No sunlight filtered through the light-blocking shades, and my eyes opened slowly into the darkness of the cabin. Aedan lay curled on his side, facing me. His arm draped over my hip since, at some point, I had turned my back to snuggle into him. His chest rose and fell, and I watched those rare movements in fascination. Goddess, I loved him.

He stirred under the weight of my stare, his whiskey-colored eyes opening to meet mine. A soft smile graced his lips as he reached up to caress my cheek. The lines exhaustion had caused on his face eased, and his skin glowed healthy and pink. That part might be from gorging on my blood like a super cute tick, but I was cool with that.

"What are you thinking?" he asked.

"That you're cute," I whispered, leaving out the other bit.

His smile grew, and he shook his head at me. Rich, molasses-colored hair flopped over into his eyes, making him look even cuter.

"We're almost there." I leaned down and stole a kiss while he stretched to his full height in the comfortable seat.

"Are you worried?" he asked, catching my hand in his.

"No," I answered. And I wasn't.

We had a lot of magical heavy hitters with us and even more strong fighters. Laith, Lann, and Saige swore that more fae were waiting for my mom's return and that the scales would balance; I believed them. The whole point of their forced exile from her was so that they could build an army. It was time to see it in action.

Aedan rose, walking through the cabin, checking on the handful of people he brought personally. The plan was that Aedan would take us to Béal an Mhuirthead via the old ways and then come back for his vampires after dark. He'd been cagey about why he brought them, simply stating that all were old enough to function during the day.

I knew they were soldiers and probably children of his. They would make an excellent adjunct to the Fae fighters, especially at night, when they would move light and fast.

I went into the bathroom and took care of my teeth, my hair, and my bladder, in that exact order. By the time I was done, discreet chimes signaling it was time to buckle up sounded. Aedan joined me as the landing gear descended, and together we waited as the plane touched down in the gentlest landing I've ever felt in such a large plane.

The airport was small, just one low building. We taxied towards the front, and the plane glided to a stop. The attendants lowered the stairs, and we grabbed our packs and walked onto the tarmac. The air smelled sweet, and a chilly Irish summer breeze blew. Heads turned as we walked into the airport.

Our arrival had been expedited; money will do that. We met with airport officials, had our papers stamped, and were out the front door in minutes, not hours. It seemed Aedan was as well known in Ireland as he was in the US, and they considered him a favorite son. He may be an original son, for that matter. He laughed with them, speaking Gaelic, as they ushered us through the gate.

The light in his eyes was noticeable, and the lightness of his step plain. He was happy to be home, and that's what this misty, crisp, green island was to him. Home. In the same was Pawleys Island would always be my power base; this wild place was his. I could see pieces of him I had not seen before. Parts of who he might have been had my grandmother not gotten her hands on him shone through, and everyone around saw.

Gripping me by the waist, he swung me around before setting me down with a kiss to the top of my head. "On the way home, we'll drive. I'll show you the beauty of our homeland; maybe we'll spend a few days, Anamcara," he said, his eyes dancing over the scenery around us.

I smiled at his excitement. It wasn't often I saw the millennia-old vampire in such a state. He looked like a twenty-something kid.

"I would like that," I said, grinning up at him in the Irish sun.

As a group, we walked out of the airport proper and into the green landscape beyond.

"By car, it is an hour and a half to Béal an Mhuirthead. I can open the old way and walk us into the yard. I would prefer not to spend any more time traveling. Plus, that will allow me to come back and get the others as soon as the sun begins to fade." He walked forward, and we followed. "Plus, it will allow me to teach you how to do this, Liomsa."

"Okay, sounds fun," I said, taking his hand.

"The old ways are conduits of memory," he started. "They are not actual paths or roads. Certain areas of this country lead to others in Talamh na Sithe. The more people that have walked that particular way, the more stable it is. In America, I have built ways to places by traveling them repeatedly. I can step through the door at the house and be in my office in Baltimore if I choose. As I am the only person to travel them, they are not always stable, so I only do it when I must." He stopped walking, looking out into a field of heather.

The plants bloomed purple as far as the eye could see, and the view was striking. The light, sweet scent that filled the air was more earthy than floral; it was like walking into a poster, it was that beautiful. "I traveled this particular way thousands of times, as did other Fae warriors under my command," he stopped, looking out across the field as he got lost in some old memory. "We will keep the link between us open. I will lead, and you will trail; the others will go between us. This way is very stable, and it will hold without effort. I will give you a picture of the cottage. You will hold it in your mind and believe you will walk out there, and you shall. Hold the thought; it is possible to get lost in the ways if your concentration falters."

"It's that simple?" I asked, squinting my eyes at the summer sun.

"It is." He took my hand, rubbing his thumb in soft circles over it.

"But, can't I just picture anyplace and go there?" I looked up at him, watching as his eyes still roamed the Irish landscape.

"No," he said. "It does not work that way. It takes many intentional trips by someone who has a strong memory of the place to start a new way. It must be traveled over and over again to create a reliable path. The more people that travel the way, the more stable it becomes. We could create ways from one place to the next with effort and time, and someday we should do that, but that is a project for another day," he finished with a gentle smile as he finally met my eyes.

He opened the link between us to its fullest and whispered into my mind, "You could weave a thousand ways with your magic, and they would be as solid as the oldest routes. Most of the ways were started by Goddess magic, and you possess a great deal of that. Perhaps someday we can weave a way between all our homes so that we may spend the day on the beach and the endless summer twilight in Ireland. I would like that, but today is not that day, and it is not a skill to be shared, my love." He continued his slow perusal of things around us so that it wasn't apparent that we were sharing our thoughts. I knew that, like Dani, he was worried people would begin to realize exactly how much power I had. I got the point and shut my mouth.

"Okay, I think I got it."

Aedan started walking, letting my hand go as he went. Keeping the link open, he showed me the cottage, only it was confusing because it looked like a castle. My eyebrows scrunched together as the picture became clearer.

Mist surrounded the grey, stone-walled home. I could see waves beyond and smell the sharp Irish sea in the air. He kept the image in my mind. I watched as he walked into the field of heather and disappeared, one by one, so did everyone else. My parents waited with me, and as the people before us stepped in, they followed. Holding hands, they stepped into the field of purple flowers with occasional dots of white on them and were gone. My mom looked over her shoulder and smiled, and I thought about her history.

She had once fallen off a cliff and gotten lost in this world. A Huntsman, fueled by love and his magic, found her and brought her home. I was born nine months later. I stood alone on the edge of that vast field of heather as it stretched out before me. It waved like an ocean in the breeze while its cloying scent filled my heart with peace.

I was on the edge of something, just as my mother had been the first time that she traveled the ways. Wind caught my hair, ruffling it, and aside from my place in Pawleys Island, I had never felt such peace before. Maybe Aedan was right and that this was my home too. Perhaps, deep in my genetic code, was the memory of this place.

A cord struck in my soul that resonated to my core. Feeling Aedan's concern and his gentle pull on my heart, I stepped into the field of heather, believing I would end up at his side. I lost the image of a cottage that didn't fit the image a cottage should and walked to him instead. For wherever he is, I am home.

From the ocean of heather onto a vast grassy plain, I arrived. Rocks dotted the field, and sparse, tall grass waved in the wind. The muted sound of waves crashing upon rocks hit home in a way no other sound can for me. In the distance sat a castle, it was not tall or sprawling, but it was ancient and made of stone. Three-story drum towers made corners to the structure and were connected by high walls. Fortified wooden doors stood open, and most of those in our group were already heading toward it.

The dwelling itself had small windows and no balconies. It was primitive and beautiful at the same time. That Aedan referred to this place as a cottage was laughable. It was a castle designed for a warrior and a lord; it would withstand a siege for days and keep those inside safe.

Aedan stood at the edge of the sea, and I couldn't tell until I got closer that it was a high cliff and that the sea was a hundred feet or more below. His head was tipped back, and his shoulders low. As I approached, I could see the deep breaths he took as he scented the air; his emotions were as wild and tumultuous as the seas below.

He turned to me, and I saw that his irises had paled. Not much, just enough to let me see the strong emotions that roiled between us through our bond. "I do not often come to this place. I pay for its upkeep and check in when I can; the memories can be overwhelming. The power, the emotion, and the past can be too much. Never had I thought I would find love again, and never did I think I would bring you here. Yet, here we are." He came to me in two strides and picked me up, crashing his lips to mine and cradling me in his arms.

He kissed me like he required it to live, tangling his tongue with mine. His fangs caught my lip, and he pulled at it while it bled, groaning into my mouth. The sound of the sea below and his low moan made me melt.

Power thrummed through him, and white-blue flames surrounded us as he lost control of it. He deepened his kiss, pulling me so close I thought we would become one creature. Flames danced across our arms as I struggled to contain my own power that fought to meet his flame for flame. We were saved from destroying the Irish coastline by a discreet clearing of a throat.

"Do you intend to take our daughter right here on the edge of the sea, Coimeadai Lasair?" Saige said from beyond the wall of flames surrounding us.

Aedan growled low, gripping me almost to the point of pain. I laughed wildly into him, slapping at his chest until I felt him relax; the flames disappeared as he regained his composure. He dropped me to my feet and twirled me to face the water beyond, and I let out a gasp at the beauty spread before me.

I thought Pawleys Island was beautiful, and it is. This? This was magnificent; it awakened something raw and ancient in me that recognized this place. Maybe it was genetic memory. Or perhaps the Goddess placed a strand of herself in me when I was made because I knew this place, and it did, indeed, feel like home.

"Breathe, Anamcara," Aedan said, chuckling in my ear.

"Stop it, Coi," I said, freezing as I spoke that long-lost name of his.

"I like it, cailín álainn. I like it much better than 'babe,'" he laughed. "Come, let me show you our home." He gripped my hand in his and ignored the concerned looks on my parents' faces.

I could feel their worry as they walked beside us. This was a different Aedan. Better yet, this was truly Coimeadai Lasair. Before he became Aedan, he was Coi, and this was the seat of his power then. He was home, and the feel of his magic saturated this place. Not many knew how much power Aedan held. Like Dani, he believed one should play some cards close to the vest.

Here, there was no denying that he was most definitely more powerful than anyone realized. There was no hiding the fact that he still possessed incredibly strong Fae magics. It oozed from his pores and echoed off the stone walls we approached.

Aedan's broad smile grew impossibly wide, and he reached to touch the stones with his hands. Power thrummed again, and I felt as he renewed his bond with the stones. I wondered if he built this place with his bare hands and what being with him in Talamh na Sithe would be like if he was this powerful here.

He always tells me I'm stronger, more powerful. Dani agrees. But in the rare moments his power shines? I doubt it, and I'm good with that.

"I did build this place with my bare hands, Anamcara. I had some help here and there, but I placed almost every stone and designed every curve. I maintained a place in Talamh na Sithe, but this was my true home once I reached the age of independence," he said, picking my thoughts from my head.

We walked through the gate and onto the well-groomed grounds. In some places, the house attached to the fortified turrets, but in others, there were spaces filled with stone beds and hardy landscaping. A wooden door stood open, and we walked inside the towering stone entryway. It stretched to the roof, and a wide staircase curved gently upward.

Colorful banners hung on the walls that bore crests, and though the place was fresh and clean, it had that unlived in feel. In a way, it made me sad because as impressive as this place was, you could tell it was empty, and the hint of sadness in the air was undeniable.

Aedan showed us to the kitchens that, at some point, had been modernized. Every convenience was available, and the clean, modern lines were incredibly similar to those in our new house. I dropped my bag and opened the fridge, grabbing bottled water.

"It's beautiful, Aedan," I said, letting my eyes roam the open space between the kitchen and the great room. People sat on the scattered furniture or meandered around, taking in the sights the house offered.

"Thank you. When this is over, we will visit, and you can change anything you want." He smiled at me over the glass of wine he had poured himself. My parents sipped wine, too; they looked far more relaxed than they had on the moor.

"I don't want to change anything; I just want to see it all."

"That may take more time than we have allowed. On the way home, I promise. However, there are things you will want to change; you just need to find them." He gave a lopsided grin, making himself look rakish and up to no good.

Oh my. I very much liked Aedan in this place, but then, I liked him everywhere.

We gathered in the great room, talking through the afternoon. Some cleaned guns and others swords to pass the time. Dinner was laid in the vast dining room by staff that seemed to appear from thin air, and in this place of ancient magic, I suppose it is possible they did. Aedan swore they were townspeople coming to help their former lord, but it's hard not to wonder. Dinner was fantastic and all local, meaning no pasta or pizza was to be found.

They served Irish stew, boiled bacon and cabbage, and soda bread. Meade flowed like water as we sat around two incredibly long, wooden tables that had to have been built with the house. Fires roared in bookend fireplaces that took up the entire walls, chasing away the dampness and chill. Light from enormous, round chandeliers high above us illuminated the room, keeping the shadows at bay. We laughed and told stories, which, in a diverse group such as this, were incredible.

Aedan ducked out as soon as the sun began to lower and came back with his men. They moved among us, sipping wine and sharing tales, but there was no mistaking what they were- soldiers.

My mom and I sat talking well past the time when the sun should be setting. My dads were off looking at things, and we sat alone by the fire. I hadn't left the main floor to do any exploring yet; I was happy to be spending time with her. As the hours wore on, I could tell that she was both nervous and excited for dawn to come. To us, it was a point in time, but to her? This was a culmination of her whole life's work. She had suffered and bled for what was to come, and she was just ready for it to begin. She had waited a lifetime for this moment.

Eventually, she drifted off to find her mates. There were enough rooms in this place for all to be comfortable, and others trickled off as well. Fun fact about Ireland in the summer, there is a ton of daylight, not necessarily sunshine, but daylight. At the height of summer, the sun doesn't set until around eleven at night only to rise again by six, leaving a mere seven hours of darkness. For one week, there is no darkness at all, just a weird twilight that seems to last forever.

Aedan and I walked the grounds hand in hand until long after the sun would have set at home. He talked about the native plants growing in his gardens and about how some of them were nearly as old as he was. Deep quiet settled over the compound, and he moved to close and bar the gate and front door. We weren't anticipating trouble, but it didn't hurt to be prepared anyway.

He led the way up the stone staircase, pulling me along until we reached the massive doors of the master's quarters. He opened them, ushering me inside. He had grown quiet on the way, closing himself off to me bit by bit. I hid my thoughts and wondered what it was about.

A fire was laid in the hearth, and dim Irish twilight filtered into the room through open windows. The fire was meant to chase the damp away, but if the windows were closed, it would be too hot. The room was devoid of personal effects, but that didn't change the fact that it still felt like Aedan, or maybe Coi. A piece of him never left this place; I could feel that now. Down to the mortar bonding the stones, it was all him.

The bed was oversized, unlike ours at home; you could get lost on it. A dark red duvet and a mountain of pillows covered it. Everything smelled clean and freshly laundered. Tall candles rested on the surfaces, but they were not lit. To the side of the bed was a sitting area. And over one of the couches was a portrait of Elizabeth.

She was beautiful: long blond hair and light green eyes graced a heart-shaped face much more Fae-like than mine. Her bow-shaped lips were stretched into a smug smile. I walked to the portrait, looking up at her. The colors were still so vivid, and I couldn't understand how something so old could look so new. Then I felt it- magic. Aedan wavered behind me, his emotions hidden.

"I never took it down," he said, adding nothing more.

"And you shouldn't, Aedan. Not unless you want to." It doesn't bother me. And it didn't; she was a part of his past that he shouldn't have to erase. She was the lynchpin to everything that came after, and if he wanted to keep her portrait on his wall, then so be it.

"No, I do not want to keep it." He walked to the wall and took the painting down. "My life started anew the first time I saw you. I did love her, but it was the love of a boy, not that of a man. I was a child still enamored with himself and the world. She carried my babe, for that I loved her more, but she is not you. You are the beginning and the end for me, alpha and omega. There is no room for another." He took the painting and placed it backward against the wall. "Things change. I had to grow up before I could understand what love is and is not. It is only you, Liomsa. It will only ever be you." He wrapped his arms around me, pulling me to his chest.

I returned his hug and rubbed lazy circles on his back; he relaxed in stages into me. This had bothered him, I could tell. He could've raced up and taken the painting down without my ever knowing it was there, but he didn't. Maybe he had to see us side by side to come to his final decision. The past can be hard to let go of, but in the end, we must let it go.

"Is there a bathroom in this place, or do I need to run out to the loo?" I asked when he finally relaxed into me.

"There is no loo," he said, pulling away with a wry grin. "Through those doors." He nodded to a door I hadn't seen. It must have been another room at one point, one attached to the master's suite, possibly the mistress suite. I thought that might have been a thing back in the day.

The room was big, and again, it didn't disappoint. Sometime recently, this house had been retrofitted with plumbing and all the best of modern conveniences. It was done in silvers, grays, and whites. Some of the tiles were reflective, and they were all spotless.

"Oh," I whimpered, shucking my clothes with a greedy glance at the giant shower. I turned the water on hot and used the other facilities while it warmed. "This could definitely be a backup house, babe," I said when he walked in to join me.

"I am no babe; I thought we were past this," he growled, stalking toward me with a hard-on and a smile.

"Well, hello there," I grinned, gripping him tightly.

"You need to rest," he tried. He really did try; I applauded his efforts internally, not externally, though, because that would be weird.

"I need you more. I'll rest when I'm dead."

"That is too long of a wait to rest. Tomorrow will be exhausting," he said, bringing his hand to my face and stroking my cheek.

"And tonight will be a long night; buckle up, cowboy." I ran my fingers over his arms, tracing the definition of his muscles before trailing them down his chest.

I washed him first, laughing as he growled at me for being a tease. I couldn't help it; his body was incredible. All sharp edges and fine lines, there is no softness to him, none. He is edged in steel and carved like a blade, and it wasn't often he let me take my time touching him.

We would get carried away, and I'd lose my focus. I watched his whiskey eyes lighten, and when they grew unfocused, I knelt in front of him. I took him into my mouth, then pulled back to trace the lines of his legs. I licked as I traced, worshipping his body in the manner it deserved. He may not be king of the fae, but he is definitely a God.

Burying his fingers in my wet hair, he held me to him, shuddering at the sensations I slowly drew out of him. I swirled my tongue, and he sighed as every muscle in his body went lax, well, almost every muscle. He released my head, and I pulled back to fill my lungs with air before taking him deeply again. Whether it was the cost of an emotional day or something else, after a few minutes of repeating the same movements, he spilled across my tongue, moaning my name.

I washed as he leaned against the wall to catch his breath. His eyes were closed, and he didn't see the soft smile I couldn't wipe off my face. I enjoy having him at my mercy; it's satisfying in unimaginable ways. There is so much power in that particular act, and few understand that. As the strongest man I know leaned against the wall, trying to recover, I did.

"Let's rest now," I said, pulling him from the shower and handing him a towel.

His eyes popped open, and he looked like he wanted to protest. "No," I started. "I like taking care of you. You always take care of me; it's my turn."

I pulled the covers down and tucked him into the big bed before walking around to the other side and sliding in behind him. He hadn't slept enough, and even though it was nighttime, which was usually his time, he was asleep before me. I snuggled into him and let the sound of waves crashing on rocks drag me under.

Chapter 15

When I awoke, Aedan was gone. He had wanted to get up and take the vampires to a safe place in Talamh na Sithe before the sun rose here. As time passes differently there, we weren't sure exactly what time of day we would be walking into. I showered one more time, knowing it may be my last hot shower for a while before dressing and going down to try to find coffee in the land of tea.

Turns out they have a tea in Ireland that's stronger than the average cup of coffee and almost as good. My mother handed me a cup as I walked into the kitchen. Knowing my penchant for violence before being properly caffeinated, she had it waiting. Irish Breakfast Tea is a deep red when appropriately brewed; she added a hint of cream to it. Even though I drank my coffee black, she insisted that Irish Tea must be had this way.

"Are you ready to go?" she asked, sipping her own cup.

"I think the bigger question is, are you? I don't really have a dog in this fight other than that Aramea is a bitch, and I'm going to enjoy smacking her down." I said, grinning her over the rim of my cup.

"I'm ready," she said. "Long past, actually, but the time away from Talamh na Sithe has made me stronger. Your grandmother is old, older than even Aedan. Though her magic may be weakened, it is still strong. It will take all of us to win this, but we will. I believe that," she finished.

"I do too. Speaking of Aedan seems like y'all are busting on him a little." I sat my coffee down and buttered a piece of leftover soda bread, groaning when it hit my taste buds.

She nodded her head steadily before saying, "It's true. We are. His mother says it will take strength, resolve, and preparedness to keep you from changing on us. We do not want to see you change in any way. If Aedan is the man you're choosing, then we are merely making sure he can handle the job. No disrespect intended." She moved beside me, pulling me into a hug. "I will be Queen of the Fae in Talamh na Sithe, or I will die trying; there is no middle ground. Like it or not, you are the Queen of the Fae who will come to America. You are betrothed to the Vampire King, and together you are beyond formidable. You will succeed me as Queen in Talamh na Sithe someday, and we need to make sure he can live up to that." Her grip on me was like iron, and I could feel the sincerity behind her words.

"Mom, I don't want to be the queen of anything," I said, pulling away from her.

"In this case, it matters not, Lara. You will be Queen of many things in many lifetimes. You will be more than a queen someday; we all know it. You've chosen him, and we must assure ourselves that he is what you need. That's what parents do, dear." She took another piece of bread and handed it to me, taking another for herself. "When this is over, I am reopening my bakery, and you will come. We will sit and drink tea and discuss how long-life works. You're still a child, like it or not. We are your parents, and while we still have a chance to parent you, we will."

I smiled inwardly, not daring to show it on the outside. Like I told Aedan, they were protective. They had missed a lot of their lives and mine. I had no doubt once their next baby came, they would back off a little. At least one can hope. "Maybe my little brother or sister will want to rule Talamh na Sithe," I said on a whim and watched as her face fell.

"I think there will be no more. I used all the magic I had to make you, not that I regret it one bit. Your brother was not well formed. I won't risk that again," she said, smiling sadly.

"That's not how it works; magic doesn't make babies. Do we need to have the talk, mom? Sometimes things go haywire, and that causes problems, but the chances of it happening again are slim. You're going to live a long time too, don't give up on a dozen more Lanns and ten more Saiges," I said.

"I know you're right in my head, but my heart is afraid. Plus, I don't think I could handle a dozen of any of them. They are incorrigible," she said with a small smile.

"Be that as it may, don't give up on babies unless you really don't want one. Plus, it might take some of the pressure off of me. Aedan could hold it all he wanted to, and I could give it back."

"They are not its," she scolded.

"Don't let Dani hold it, that Fae is shady with a baby," I murmured. "Then again, let her hold it. Maybe she'll leave me alone if she has another baby to play with."

"Lara Liann Hennessey, you stop that," she chuffed, making me smile.

Aedan found us hugging in the kitchen and gave us a wide berth and some serious side-eye as he walked to pour a cup of tea. "Is everything okay?" he asked, watching with one eyebrow raised.

"Quite," my mom answered, giving him one of her best smiles, and I watched his eyes narrow.

She did an excellent job keeping him on his toes. "Everyone is ready and awaiting your word," she said, giving him a slight bow.

His eyes crinkled at the edges as he turned to me for guidance. I shrugged my shoulders and took another sip of tea, watching them. It was better than Netflix. "Give us a few moments, and we will be ready, Airmed," he said. "I will meet you at the gates."

"You can call me Ari," my mom started. "Or you can call me mom," she finished, turning away with a smirk.

Aedan choked on his tea. "Thank you," was all he could say. He added neither moniker. "Lara, one moment, if you please," he said, stepping away from the kitchen.

I followed him upstairs. Our rooms had been tidied, and the bed was made. I wondered if Aedan had a brownie here or if that sneaky Cook had somehow traveled with us. He moved in ways I didn't understand, and his magic was impossible to comprehend.

Our packs lay on the bedroom bench, and the fire had been extinguished. Elizabeth's painting was gone.

"Last chance to change your mind." He picked up his pack and slung it over his shoulder. "I genuinely wish you would." He hugged me to him, placing his chin on the top of my head.

"Whither thou goest, go I," I said, holding back a chuckle.

"I do not believe that verse from the Christian Book of Laws applies to this particular situation. Ruth was actually speaking to her mother-in-law, not her husband," he said into my hair.

I stood stunned to silence for a minute. The vampire had read the Bible? Hell, maybe he had met Ruth; he was about that old. "You've read the Bible?" I asked.

"Hmmmm. Of course. I have looked for redemption in many places, only to find it lies with you." He kissed me and pulled away.

I grabbed his face, forcing it to mine. "You are redeemed, Coi. You have suffered enough. I know you've done horrible things, lots of things, but you don't have to search for redemption anymore. You've found it. You don't have to fight anymore either, not unless you want to." I let his face go but held his eyes with mine.

"I will see this through," he sighed.

"Then, so will I."

He closed his eyes for a heartbeat. When they opened again, all traces of softness were gone, and only the warrior remained. "Come, let us go."

As a group, we walked away from the castle. Aedan did not bar the gate; he said that staff would be by to make the place ready for our return.

At the edge of the moor, Galahad grazed. He wore T4's old western saddle, and it made my heart glad. A bridle hung from the horn, ready for me. Black armor covered almost the entirety of the horse. I knew for a fact that he was the only warhorse in history to go into combat wearing a Circle Y Park and Trail saddle along with his armor. I appreciated him endlessly.

I walked up to him, placing my hand on his outstretched nose.

"You moved right past Jesse James and went straight up Billy the Kid, Galahad, you look terrific." He preened at my words, arching his neck and striking the ground with his hoof.

"You should change, put on a dress or something. We need to look the part. I'm not sure jeans and a Gamecocks sweatshirt give off the vibe we are looking for," he said. Behind us were some snickers that let me know I wasn't the only one who could hear him.

"And what vibe are we trying to project?" I asked, finger combing his mane with my fingers.

"Wild. Dangerous. Mysterious," he answered. "Not college girl shabby for sure," he finished.

"What would you like me to wear then, Gally. It's only fair. I dressed you; you get to dress me." I winced as I said it, but I meant it. He put up with a lot from me; he deserved his day in the spotlight.

"How about a flowing white gown? It will make me look princely," he tried.

"It would make you look princely, but I'm not sure about mysterious," I countered. "You certainly wouldn't look dangerous.

"Yeah, you're right. How about a black dress? That's more mysterious."

"We might blend together, and the ladies would think you were deformed."

"Goddess, but you are smart. Oh, I know. Leather. You should wear leather, plus the arrows will have a more difficult time slicing through." He nodded his head up and down in affirmation that I would wear leather. I really didn't want to wear leather; it would chafe.

"Arrows? I don't plan on getting hit by any arrows."

"No one ever plans on getting hit by arrows; that's just silly," he said, side passing over to me. I took the bridle, sliding the bit into his mouth. He took it without complaint.

"Wait!" he snorted, nickering happily. "Buckskin. I want you to dress like a Native American Warrior woman. Feathers and all. That will definitely add to my mystic. The ladies will be so stunned by our appearance, they'll be speechless." He finished, pleased with himself.

Aedan stood behind me, his shoulders shaking from laughter. At some point, he'd had to turn away from us or laugh in our faces. My parents' eyes twinkled so brightly, I thought they might actually shed a tear.

"Speechless is an excellent word for what the ladies will be," I sighed, pulling off my favorite sweatshirt. I wove an outfit that might pass for what he requested and still be suitable.

Leather chaps with fringe wove down my legs, covering my jeans, while a buckskin vest with matching fringe covered my torso. I trimmed the outfit in turquoise and bone. I had no idea what a native American warrior woman would wear, so I winged it. I added a copy of the red feather Dani left on my vanity when she took Aedan's locket back, weaving it into the braids in my hair.

I stamped a red handprint on Galahad's rump because I knew that warring tribespeople would paint their ponies. When I was done, I felt ridiculous, but Galahad beamed with pleasure.

"That is much better than even I imagined, little Goddess," he said, blowing air through his nose. "Mount 'em up and move 'em out."

I shook my head, moving to his side. Aedan came up behind me, placing his hands on my hips and rubbing his hard length against me. "We must revisit this outfit at a later date, Liomsa," he growled before tossing me onto the tall Friesian's back."

I threw my head back and laughed into the morning Irish mists. I should have known Aedan would like the outfit too. I wouldn't be the first Native American Warrior Woman he ravaged when he got ahold of me wearing this getup.

His eyes twinkled with mischief. "Just like before, I will lead, and you will trail. We are walking into the back of the city center, and that is all we know." His face darkened at the thought of the coming danger. I could probably walk right beside him, and everyone makes it through the way just fine, but Aedan wasn't having it. This was his way of trying to keep me from danger; only war is dangerous by nature.

I nodded my head, letting him win this time. It's all about compromise.

"I will keep the link open and send you a picture," he said, looking up at me with intense focus.

"Aedan, I don't need the picture. I can follow you without it. Keep your focus on what's in front of you and not behind. I'll be there." I leaned down from the horse and placed a kiss on his head. "I'll see you on the other side."

I watched as they stepped through the sparse grass into the thicker brush and disappeared. I loped Galahad in a few lazy circles to warm his muscles while the others drew their swords, knives, and guns before walking into thin air. My parents did not smile or wave as they stepped through, their swords glowed with the veracity of their feelings, and together they disappeared from sight. With a Native American war cry that would make any raiding party proud, I kicked Galahad into a gallop and followed the link to Aedan.

We burst into chaos. Galahad's hooves clattered on the brick street. We were instantly assaulted by the sound of heavy fighting. I had a sword at my back but hadn't thought to draw it. I leveled the first fae to reach for Galahad's bridle with a bolt of fire. Heavy smoke blanketed the area, and the smell of death hung in the air. I could almost taste the blood that had been spilled in this place.

Around me, our contingent fought. Handily they sliced through ranks of ragtag fighters. These tattered men were not the Queen's ranks. I didn't know who they were, but their lack of organized structure and the wildness to their fighting meant they were something else. I sent a chord of power into the earth, using its waves to knock down an encroaching line of men. I didn't see my parents or Aedan in the mass of roiling bodies around me, but I felt him through our link and knew he was fine.

Using magic instead of the sword, I fought my way to a clearing with a babbling fountain.

"This is a diversion," Galahad said as I stopped to catch my breath. "Those fighters aren't wearing the Queen's colors. It may not be a trap, but it isn't a fight in which any ground can be made."

"Agreed. Maybe Aramea thought she could protect her best by sacrificing a few. Maybe she thought we would be beaten easily." I laughed and took my first good look around.

This place could've been anywhere, really. Well, anywhere in old-world Europe, it was quaint. Shops lined brick streets, and gas lanterns hung on carved wooden posts. The thing that made it different was the extent of destruction surrounding us.

When Dani had worried that there wouldn't be anything left to this place to save, she wasn't kidding. Aramea had destroyed her own capital. No house or shop was unscathed. Windows were broken, and fires had been set. To root out her daughter's sympathizers, she had destroyed the base of her power. There wasn't much left. It was heartbreaking for those of our group that called this place home.

One by one, the fae found me. The shock on their faces told the tale. This was not the home they left. I felt for them endlessly.

"We need to make a camp," Lann said. "Laith's forge is just there, and there are more weapons hidden inside," he said, pointing to a wide storefront. The windows had been boarded after being broken, but that was the only visible damage.

Laith stepped forward. "Once camp is set, I will get the weapons and sound the horns. "Our allies who stayed behind are waiting and will come. The palace and armory are too close; we should move to the crossroads so that we can control travel in and out. Also, it's defensible.

"Let's get the weapons now. We can be in and back out quickly. We need to get to the crossroads before Aramea realizes we are here. Come," Saige said, walking briskly to the old forge.

Most of the Fae moved away, packing trunks and bags with them. Aedan, my parents, and I waited while Saige, Lann, and Laith broke into Laith's forge, dashing out again with crates filled with swords and knives. Aedan pushed a cart laden with armor, bows, gauntlets, and the like. It was odd seeing such primitive weapons. Having grown up in the age of automatic firearms and smart bombs, it was startling.

We were out of the city center quickly and saw no others during our brief time there. At the crossroads, tents were raised, and supplies passed out. We had arrived in Talamh na Sithe sometime in the afternoon, judging by the sun. The people worked to get the camp ready. I rode Galahad around the edge of the crossroads, thinking of the stories I had been told about this place.

My mother had gone over a cliff here that was so high the bottom was shrouded in mists. According to my father, if you jumped off of the top, you would come out in the small town of Clifden. Kind of ironic, that. I wondered what kind of people had formed this particular way, and I wasn't planning on trying to find out the truth of his words.

I wondered if this was one of the ways the Goddess had made. After all, why would people jump off of the cliff enough times to create a path? Laith had almost died at these crossroads, and one of The Eight, Teagan, had been taken by trolls down these paths and never seen again.

There was so much history in this area that the air felt heavy. Talamh na Sithe had once been on the same plane as my own home, yet has existed here in perpetuity. It was hard to understand how all of this had happened, but there was no denying the truth of it.

For the first time, I noticed how cool it was. It was almost chilly, and the trees were just beginning to green up. At home, it was summer, but here it must have been spring. I knew time moved differently; it was just hard to wrap my head around.

I heard a whistle and turned to see my mother standing at the road to the right, two fingers in her mouth the way she had taught me. She whistled several times, my fathers and some of the other fae joined her, and I wondered what in the hell was happening.

I heard the hoofbeats before I saw them. Galahad started prancing and half-rearing as I fought to calm him. From the surrounding wild, brightly colored horses ran at us. They whirled and danced as the fae sorted through them, laughing with joy. The little horses whinnied and nipped playfully at one another as they went, their long thick manes and tails flashing. They looked like Irish Gypsy Cobs, and maybe they were. This place was still Ireland, just the original one.

I watched my mother's hand drop from her lips and her shoulders slump. "No," she said. "It can't be." She walked to a solid white horse with large, expressive, dark eyes and a dish-shaped face. "Solas?" she asked.

"No, Love," Saige walked to her, putting his arms around her shoulders. "We buried Solas years ago. This must be one of her daughters, as she had many and always bred true. No daughter of hers ever looked like its sire."

Tears ran unrestrained down her face as she reached her hand slowly to the horse's nose. Where the other horses were small and thick, this one was tall and refined. She looked like a cross between an Arabian and an Andalusian but was obviously something else entirely.

The big horse rubbed her head on my mom's belly, and Airmed, Queen of the Fae, the small but fierce warrior, broke down into sobs. She wrapped her arms around the mare's neck and held onto her like she was the last solid thing in the world.

My mother once told me that only good fae can call to the wild horses of Talamh na Sithe and get an answer. She said that fae horses lived wild but formed loving, long-term partnerships with those they liked. I had heard about her horse, Solas, many times.

Seeing her with a daughter of that horse was humbling. It reminded me of how much I loved T4, and I knew that she'd had to walk away from not only my fathers, but Solas too when she conceived me. I couldn't imagine what she lost during that time that she might never regain, but watching her hug that tall white mare made me think that maybe some of it she could.

"I bet I could make her have a spotted baby," Galahad said in a mock whisper, and my mother threw her head back laughing.

"You incorrigible stallion," she laughed, wiping her eyes. "You keep your teeth off this one unless she invites you to do otherwise. She leveled Galahad with a glare, and he ducked his head, turning away.

I slid off the stallion and walked to my mom, reaching my hand out to pet the white mare while Galahad walked off and took a deep drink from a stream that ran near the crossroads. He milled with the other horses, and squeals sounded as they greeted one another. I didn't worry about it; the mares would drive him away if he got too randy. They could take care of themselves.

Our tent city was up in no time, and colorful Emerald green and sun-yellow banners flapped in the breeze from spikes around our camp. I guessed they were my mother's colors.

Aedan hung his banner near our tent, and it seemed to serve as an introduction as well as a warning. It was black with a silver dragon emblazoned on it. In one front claw, the dragon held a sword, and in the other, a crown. The dragon had blood-red eyes and a wide-open maw.

I had stopped to stare at it when I felt his arms around me. "It was my banner, all those years ago. It is the banner I fought under for over a hundred years, and had I stayed and been king, I would have flown it over the palace. It is also the banner of my original House. The one here in Talamh na Sithe. It is the Goddess's dragon I fight for. I will fight for your mother's House, but under my own flag," he said softly, his voice full of emotions I couldn't put a name to.

This had to be hard for him. He was meant to rule this place and had everything, including his life, taken from him because of greed. He was back after being forced out by the magic that had once been his to call. He was made into an amalgamation of a vampire and Fae, leaving him belonging to neither group. Yet, here he was again, on his home soil, fighting a battle so someone else could rule.

"I'm sorry, Aedan, for everything. You would have been a good King of Talamh na Sithe, but you are a better King of the Vampires. They need you no less than the fae did all those years ago, maybe more." I kissed his cheek and moved past him into our tent, leaving him alone with his thoughts. I threw my pack down on the pile of furs and blankets spread out in one corner but kept my sword on my back and my Glock on my hip.

"Let's do this," I said, walking back to where Aedan waited.

A horn sounded. I turned to see Saige with a ram's horn to his lips. The sound echoed through the air, and there was no way we were concealing our arrival any longer. Galahad raced to me, and I jumped on his back. Aedan jumped on the back of another stallion trailing Galahad and pulled his sword. Together we raced to where my fathers waited.

Armed and armored fae lined up beside my mother, under her colorful banners. Before the echoes of the horn faded, the sound of approaching hoofbeats could be heard. The ground vibrated from the pounding of them. Dust shimmered on the horizon, and sunlight flickered off the backs of hundreds of horses galloping our way.

"Hold," Seal said, drawing his sword but not moving forward. "These are allies; Cory sent word to be ready." His horse danced underneath him as the riders approached. Even though these riders might be allies, unease still rippled down our ranks.

The approaching men and women stopped their horses under a cloud of dust in the chilly Faerie spring. There was absolute silence as the two groups looked across the distance between them, making me wonder if Seal was wrong. The leader of the group dropped from his horse, walking to us. Seal slid from his own horse and went to meet the other man.

"Gods, it has been too long, brother. I started to believe you were as dead as the rumors suggested." He reached his hand toward my dad, and they clasped forearms before pulling each other into a hug. Patting each other on the back, they talked for a few moments before coming back to us.

The moment of tension passed, and the fae gathered together, talking excitedly. More tents went up, and the smell of cooking meat filled the rapidly cooling late afternoon air. The newcomers explained that they had been hiding in the mountains beyond the river, waiting for the signal while continuing to gather support for Airmed.

When Aramea lost her mind and made traveling the old ways difficult, they hunkered down. They explained that the city center was deserted and that the soldiers loyal to Aramea had moved into the armory. They weren't sure what they were waiting for, but one of the men loyal to my mom was still with Aramea's soldiers and passing messages to the rebels.

Aramea was holed up in the palace. Waiting for what, no one knew, but she hadn't been seen in a while. Together, we numbered several hundred, and the new warriors swore our numbers were almost a match for my grandmother's. They were confident. Having spoken with Aramea not all that long ago, I felt they might be underestimating her.

Aedan left and came back with his vampires. After gathering supplies and weapons, they disappeared again. Aedan hadn't said more than two words before leaving, his thoughts so heavy I felt the weight of them through the bond we shared. I sat around a fire with my parents, talking with their friends long into the night before going to bed alone.

I awoke in the hour between true night and sunrise. A light mist fell as I walked from our tent, and an eerie half-light made the camp look haunted. Judging by the lack of a vampire-shaped impression in our covers, Aedan had not rested last night. I hated that he was so unsettled.

I pulled my long cloak around me as I walked through the cold Irish morning air, looking for something I didn't quite understand. Using almost no power, I called to the shadows around me, finding comfort in their depths.

I came across sentries as I walked. They didn't notice me, and I was glad; I didn't feel like having idle conversation. The feeling of anticipation was so thick that I knew these warriors would find action today. It was like reaching the top of the incline on the world's tallest coaster, you knew the climb was over, and there was nothing left but the ride itself. We were committed; now it was time to get on with it.

I found them huddled together: Laith, Lann, Saige, Seal, and Aedan, their heads so close they almost touched. I could feel their worry from yards away. I stood in the shadows trying to catch snippets of their conversation but could not. Aedan was shielding so tightly that I felt nothing from him. I pulled the darkness to me, hoping to hide in it a bit longer. Only Aedan cocked his head my way, and I knew that I'd been made.

Stepping from the mists and shadows, I walked to them. My father's faces snapped up, and I wondered how I looked to them. Aedan did not seem surprised.

"Daughter, you are ethereal in your beauty," Laith said as he rose to greet me.

"You're only saying that because I look the most like you," I whispered, adding no small amount of sarcasm.

"You are also a little too good at stealth," Seal grumbled.

"Which I got from you, Master Huntsman." I turned, nodding his way.

"It would seem she has you both dead to rights, gentlemen." Aedan rose from his seat, pulling me the rest of the way from the shadows still clinging to me. "I had hoped you might sleep a bit longer, Anamcara. It will be a long day."

"And I had hoped you would come to bed for a few moments for the same reason, Coi." I watched as the earth's shadows reached for me again. With a small wave of my hand, I dispersed them.

"We will lose her Coimeadai Lasair. If we do not watch, Gaia will take her." Lann came to me, gripping my small hands in his large ones.

"I'm fine, dad; stop worrying." I squeezed his hands back, smiling into his face.

"We will never stop worrying," he said, dropping a kiss to my cheek.

"We needed to finalize a few details away from the others, Lara. As with any war, there are plans within plans. Even though battle plans do not survive the first contact, we must plan for contingencies the best we can."

"I understand." And I did. Understanding didn't stop me from missing him, though.

The smell of cooking and coffee drifted to us on the breeze, and I knew that the camp was waking; the time for rest was over. I tried to let go of the dark anticipation roiling just under the surface of my mind, but it held on, unwilling to leave quietly.

I cycled the excess power sparking off my skin into the ground and felt the sigh of appreciation beneath my bare feet. My dads' faces went from concerned to downright scared as my skin began to glow a soft rose gold, creating a dim halo of light around me. I needed to get control of my emotions. Taking a deep breath, I pushed a little more excess power into the ground beneath me and watched the halo of light disappear.

I would get better at this; I knew that. I was just barely old enough by Fae standards to be considered a functioning adult. This Goddess magic would get better over time. I knew they worried, but I thought they were a tad overprotective. Gaia wasn't sucking me into the earth: Dani wouldn't let her. "I'm going to find the fae making coffee and kiss them on the mouth," I said lightly.

"Think twice about kissing any male fae, Anamcara. I am feeling a bit protective today," Aedan chuckled darkly. "And a tad hungry." He scowled at me.

"Well, then you better hope a female is making that coffee." I smiled up at him, feeling it reach all the way to my eyes.

"I am not sure the outcome of you kissing a female fae will be much better." He narrowed his eyes at me and pulled his lip up in a mock snarl.

"Then you should have come to bed last night. Maybe you would be in a better mood and not be quite as peckish." I popped him on his chest and turned to walk away.

"Lara." Laith stopped me with a firm hand on my arm. He looked down at me with such a look of love and concern that I melted a little.

"Yes, dad?"

"Be careful."

I nodded once and walked away. I knew what he meant. He didn't mean I wasn't safe here; he worried I wasn't safe anywhere.

"I will, dad. I love you." I walked away from them, feeling their eyes on me as I went.

I found coffee. Turns out, most of The Eight had developed a secret taste for it in my world. The women sat around a low burning fire with an honest to Goddess coffee pot hanging over it. I was handed a cup of the thick black stuff before I could take a seat.

"Thanks," I said, clutching the cup to me like it was the last solid thing in the world.

"Are you alright?" Ravena asked me as I settled onto a camp chair next to her.

"Yeah," I answered.

"Good," she said. "We felt your power leaking this morning, just making sure. Your mom's used to do that all the time."

I laughed out loud, probably waking up anyone else that may have been still asleep. That was the difference between men and women. A man will ask if you're okay and not believe the answer when you tell him because he is still looking for the dragon to slay. A woman will take you at your word, knowing that if you need help, you will ask.

I clutched the warm cup in my hands, sipping slowly as I listened to the excited chatter of the women around me. Most of them had homes here and were anxious to see if they still stood, my mother included. I drifted in my own thoughts as I listened to their quiet conversation. Everyone had different motivations for being here.

Some simply wanted to come home and live free, while others wanted to make their own choices and carve their own paths. All wanted to rid this world of the scourge of Aramea; my mother wanted to be Queen. Maybe wanted is a strong word; she felt she needed to be Queen to set things right. Aedan wanted to put the trauma of his past to rest and see wrongs righted. I just wanted to make sure everyone survived another day. Whatever our motivations, the time for talking had come and gone.

Chapter 16

The first cannon rounds landed in the center of our camp, interrupting my third cup of coffee, and I was none too happy about it, let me tell you. As chaos erupted, I stayed where I was, finishing it before it went cold. People scrambled around me in a mad dash for horses, weapons, and clothes. We should have known it was coming, but despite the restless anticipation that permeated the morning air, we had not.

Aedan shouted my name through our bond, and I knew the overprotective vampire would walk through live rounds to find me, so I rose, whistling for Galahad with a sigh. I could've used some bacon, but it was not to be.

I changed into my buckskin warrior woman outfit with a thought and jumped on the back of the giant warhorse.

"Anamcara!" Aedan shouted through the dust and smoke.

"Here!" I wheeled Galahad around and went to meet him.

He rode a horse that was nearly a match for my own, and I wondered if his old Guardian had joined us for the fray. Things like that happened here. I rode T4 the last time I was in Talamh na Sithe, and he had been dead for months by then.

"Your sword," he said, sidling up to me and handing me the sword and my Glock. "The first shot was just a warning; they are coming. I do not want you in the middle of these battles. Stay to the edges." I followed him through our camp, where already, people repaired the damage. We wouldn't be caught by surprise again.

"Last night, my vampires took out twenty of Aramea's guard. They are hiding in the shadows, doing what they can, but will not be at their best until the sun begins to go down. Your priority is to keep safe," He grabbed my reins, forcing me to stop and look at him.

"Right. Safe," I said, forcing my face into the perfect countenance of sincerity. What was he thinking? There is no safety in war. That's an oxymoron if I ever heard one.

He seemed satisfied with what he saw. Even someone as old as he was could be guilty of seeing what they want to.

"If you get separated or are in trouble, ride this road, and it will take you to your mother's old home. She thinks it still stands and is easily defensible. She said you will know it when you see it. If anyone needs your healing magic, I will call you through the bond." He let my reins go, watching me intently.

"Okay, sounds good," I said, trying to look like I meant it.

He narrowed his eyes at me, arching a brow. "I am serious, Lara."

"Me too, babe." I nodded my head once and skirted Galahad through the camp, leaving the thick knot of warriors behind.

Riders went out in groups separated into archers, swordsmen, and infantry. Horses pulled cannons and set them on the gentle swales surrounding our camp. Cannon fire sounded over and over as the back and forth testing between sides began. As the day wore on, clashing swords could be heard and muffled shouts as small groups engaged with one another.

I rode the outskirts of these skirmishes, looking for wounded. I healed minor lacerations and concussions caused by the nearness to heavy artillery, sending them on their way. I lost sight of my family but felt Aedan through our bond. None of the skirmishes happening around us were serious, and the surreal feeling continued to build. You knew that the three-hundred-foot drop was coming; you just couldn't be sure when.

The sun was high in the sky when the fighting began in earnest. I was sitting under a shade tree watching for casualties when a horde of riders dressed in dark armor crested the hill and descended on our forces en masse. Swords clashed, and arrows flew; the sound was deafening.

As a child of modern-day warfare, no preparation can ready you for what war looks and sounds like in the iron age. Cannons thundered, swords clashed, and the random sound of small arms fire rang out. Our side had brought a large variety of weapons, saying they preferred their swords to a gun but bringing them anyway. As the fighting intensified, more and more shots rang out, making me fear our people were desperate.

Men and women were dragged to the edge of the field and left for me like carrion. I rushed from one to the next, healing their injuries. It was dirty, ghastly work, and I felt my strength flagging from the complexity of it. Severed arms, legs, hands coupled with disembowelments and punctured lungs were the worst I saw. I fixed minor cuts and breaks, too, weaving the broken together with Goddess magic and intent. There were no smart bombs and no clean kills from planes far above the ground here. This was brutal and horrific.

I felt Aedan reach for me through our bond, his relief at finding me okay was palpable. I shut him out and kept working on getting a Fae warrior's insides back where they belonged. The injured piled around me, and I worried I couldn't keep up. I was elbow deep in blood and gore with no end in sight. Years of nursing had not prepared me for the scale of what real war brought. I was one; they were many. Still, I worked without a break, refusing to allow our allies to die.

Whether I healed those on the other side, I can't say. I wouldn't have refused them had they found me, but all people look the same when they are suffering and covered in blood. I am a Healer, and I would heal.

I didn't tend to anyone I knew. I saw faces I recognized but no one I knew personally, and that helped. I worked with precision and detachment as the smell of copper and iron filled my nostrils. Blood ran through my hands, leaving its mark all over me.

There were no gloves and no sinks or soap as I moved from one to the next. There were no instruments or sterile fields; it was all magic and very little medicine. I moved like in a dream; it was unreal.

Everything changed when Seal came in with an arrow through his neck. I screamed, sinking beside him to grip his hand tightly.

"Daddy!" I cried over and over again, forgetting everything I knew about medicine. "Daddy!" I cried until my mother slapped me hard across the face.

"Crying for your father will not fix him, Lara Liann Hennessey. Fix your father!" she shouted at me, shaking me with all the strength her small frame allowed.

My other fathers were not there, and I didn't know if they were safe or also injured. I stared at my mother over the body of my dying father. I let the steel in her spine infect mine. The whole point of coming to this Goddess-forsaken place was so that no one I loved would die. It was time to put my money where my mouth was. Nodding once, I met her eyes before placing my hands on him.

Wisely, no one had removed the arrow. It was through his middle cerebral artery at the base of his skull. It had been shot from behind him, and the arrowhead came out the front left side of his neck while the fletching, the back. He was unconscious. The arrow blocked most of the blood flow to the left side of his brain. In effect, he was having a stroke as well as being at risk for bleeding out within minutes. His brain was already showing signs of damage, and I sucked at neuro. Goddess, did I suck at neuro.

Closing my eyes and falling back on touch to compliment my inner sight, I got to work fixing the smaller vessels. Removing clots that had formed at the site of impact, I worked the intricacies of his brain. Slowly, I unmade the arrow, fixing the holes it caused and chasing small clots down, unmaking them before they could cause a stroke in another part of the brain. Once the arrow was gone, I worked feverishly to heal all the parts damaged by lack of blood flow before running through his other systems to make sure there was no damage there.

During this time, my mother kept silent. Seal did not wake up or so much as move. When I thought I was done, I went through him again, system by system, saving his brain for last. I found one more clot in a tiny artery in his midbrain that I unmade, fixing the small amount of damage it left behind. After what felt like hours, I pulled my hands from him, slumping where I sat.

"There's nothing else to fix," I said, exhaustion riding my voice hard. Months ago, this many complex healings piled up on one another would have been impossible for me. I would have passed out hours ago. Now, I just needed a minute.

"Why isn't he waking up?" she demanded, crossing her arms. "Look again."

"Mom. I looked a hundred times. He'll wake up."

And he did. He went from lying in peace to on his feet and yelling in two seconds flat. My mother jumped up next to him, squeezing him tight. He looked at the blood, covering himself, then over at me. He nodded once, kissed my head, and together they ran back into the fray without a backward glance.

I went limp where I sat, wishing I was anywhere else. My adrenaline faded, leaving me cold and shaky. Sweat dried the clothes to me, and the sticky feeling of blood, sweat and other things made me need to get clean. I whistled for Galahad, and he appeared out of nowhere. "I need to clean up," I said, shivering so hard I could barely mount the giant horse.

"There seems to be a lull in the fighting," he answered, trotting away from the edge of the battlefield. "There may be a few moments of calm while they regroup. Many would have died if you weren't here, Lara. Don't be discouraged. This is war, and you are doing great."

I said nothing as he maneuvered his way into a broad stream deep in the thick brush. Galahad stood guard as I unmade my outfit; it seemed silly now anyway. I laid my sword and gun on the ground before wading into the cold water, then watched as it ran red around me before eventually clearing.

The sound of distant cannons was intermittent, and overall, it was quiet. I dunked my head under the water, letting the flow of water clean the blood of others from me. When I surfaced, I heard voices and went still. Galahad's ears were pinned to his head, and every muscle in his body was rigid.

"She's here somewhere," a man said. I heard the cracking of sticks as he walked my way. "I watched her ride away from the others. If we take her, the rebels don't stand a chance."

"Aramea wants her alive," another man said.

"That doesn't mean we can't have a little fun with her first, does it?"

"Aramea says her magic is powerful. She's a true Healer; we won't be about to take her alive, regardless of what Aramea says."

The voices got closer, and there was no way they weren't going to see the massive black horse standing a few paces away from them. Closing my eyes, I focused on Galahad and felt myself sift from the cold water to his warm back. With a thought, I wove jeans and a sweatshirt to cover my wet skin. The movement toward me stopped.

"What was that?" the second man asked.

"You're paranoid," said the first. "She's just a lass. She can't be as strong as they say. Come on, let's get her."

Using magic, I pulled my gun and sword to me, holding them both as Galahad exploded through the thick brush. He surged forward, revealing our hiding spot, and nearly knocked the men off their feet. I swung my sword in a wide arc, slicing into the arm of the man in front of me. He let out a surprised yelp and fell forward into Galahad.

The other man drew his sword, and the fight was on. Galahad wheeled, kicking the injured man and sending him flying. I swing at the second man, missing him by a hair. He grabbed Galahad's reins, trying to force him to stand. I unmade the reins and watched the man fall back as his balance shifted. Another man ran through the brush toward us, and we were surrounded. Pulling my Glock, I shot a round into the leg of the man struggling to rise from the ground. I kicked Galahad into a run, and we bowled over the third man. I slid my Glock into my waistband and placed the sword behind my back.

Gripping the Guardian's mane, I held on as he plowed through the thorny brush with no concern for his skin, even though mine ripped and snagged with every step. In the clearing, we ran straight into an enemy garrison. Turning, Galahad raced back toward the crossroads with twenty men fast on his tail.

Shouts rang out as they closed in on us. Galahad took a sharp left, almost unseating me. I hang on with sheer will and determination as he dodged and wove through the terrain, heading back to our camp. I turned my head, lobbing a ball of fire behind me. It took out the first two riders, but in their place, two more appeared.

The path was narrow, and two by two, I picked them off with magic pulses and fireballs as the warhorse ran for our lives. One misstep, and we would be finished, but the giant horse moved with nimble grace around all obstacles. I had never been more grateful to Dani for gifting him to me.

We burst into the meadow where it all started; I was flat against his neck, and his black mane tangled with my auburn hair, sticking to the blood on my arms. We raced across the open space as arrows flew over our heads, magically striking the men behind me. I lobbed more fireballs as I raced to the line of men I knew to be on my side. We didn't stop. They parted for us, closing the line once we were through, and the fight was on anew.

Hands jerked me from the horse's back, pulling me around roughly.

"What happened?" Aedan growled, his eyes so yellow that I worried.

"I was rinsing the blood off in a stream and was ambushed. Galahad got us out of there; I'm fine," I shouted, pulling away from him. Jumping back on Galahad, I turned the horse with a thought and nothing more. We raced back to the front line, ignoring the shouts from an angry vampire.

I saw a break in the line ahead and threw a magical dart at the man advancing on my mother. She fought with two swords; they both glowed with her aura and righteous anger. She sliced through the man I hit with magic, and he fell at her feet. I used magic and anger to fuel my empty tank as the fight wore on.

Vampires joined the fray, and the screams of our dying enemies were short and sharp. They had not seen warriors like them before. Darkness settled over the landscape, and still, the sound of fighting could be heard. Fires sprang up, and the silhouettes of warriors danced with the flames.

I healed many more men and women before falling into my tent when the sound of fighting faded. I just needed an hour, no more. I could go again soon, just not yet. Galahad stood guard as I closed my eyes and was asleep before my lashes met my cheek.

Shrill crying woke me before the moon had moved more than an inch in the sky, and I was at it again. One of Ravena's men was dragged to my tent and dumped lifelessly at my feet. Instantly awake, I did mundane CPR on him while running through his injuries with my magical sight, finding the one that had killed him and fixing it. He had taken a bullet to his lung, and the internal bleeding had caused pressure around his heart, stopping it from beating. Within minutes, I had the lung fixed and returned the blood to circulation where it belonged. He walked out of my tent with a tear-soaked Ravena by his side.

I rose on shaky legs, joining the others under the light of the moon. I fixed the minor injuries that had piled up during my short nap before finding a warm fire to huddle near. A cup of hot soup was placed in my hands, and I drank it greedily, wishing it was coffee. I hadn't eaten all day, but I was also desperate for caffeine. I healed several more people and listened as the sounds of fighting slowed to silence. Even soldiers needed a break.

The call to retreat was made, and our fighters were left with no one to fight. Some slept where they dropped, and others crawled to their fires before closing their eyes. I rose from my fire and walked to my covers, and as Galahad stood guard, I slept again.

Aedan came in the night. I felt him run his hands over me, looking for injuries as he growled softly under his breath and breathed in my scent deeply. If I could have opened my eyes, I would have soothed him; I just didn't have it in me. He curled up to me for what seemed like minutes before rising again, leaving with the whisper of tent flaps closing. His scent was all blood; there was no honey or fall leaves left to him. But at least he had eaten.

The morning started before the first rays of dawn. Cannons sounded, and the vibration left from their impact on the earth woke me. I almost rolled back over and went to sleep, but I needed caffeine and something in my stomach before the bodies started piling up. I changed my clothes and checked my arms; they were healed from the encounter with the thorns.

Galahad stood outside the tent, keeping a watchful eye as he ate grain from a dish. Coffee and a metal plate covered with eggs and bacon were shoved into my hands before I closed the tent flaps. I grunted my thanks and sat on a log beside the low burning fire.

Keelin dropped beside me, the swell of the baby bump showing beneath the dress she wore. The six pregnant women had insisted on coming, even though they weren't fighters and had babies to protect. This was their fight, too, live or die, and they wouldn't shy away from it. They cooked for the fighters and kept the camp from falling apart. They were as safe as war allows, tucked in and surrounded by warriors determined to protect them.

This was war, I thought as I ate. Men fought harder if their females needed their protection, and the women cared for them as no one else could. Though this war had been brewing long before I came along, it was still humbling to be a part of it. If I'd learned one thing since I got here, it is that war should be avoided if possible, as there is nothing Civil about Civil war. These fae fought cousins or brothers, and that was difficult to swallow. On the other hand, these people had been through enough and deserved better. Aramea shouldn't inspire the loyalty she had in her fighters, and I hoped they would bend the knee to a new Queen instead of dying.

"How are you holding up?" she asked, passing me a biscuit and refilling my coffee.

"I'm okay, I guess. This definitely isn't what I expected," I answered between bites.

"War never is." She scooted closer, patting my knee. "You are doing amazing work. Our fight would have been over yesterday were it not for you."

"Oh, I don't know about that," I said, taking another gulp of coffee.

"I do. Our losses would have been heavy. We thank you."

"There's no need for that, Keelin. But you're welcome anyway."

"Your mate is a vicious thing," she added, looking at me over the rim of her tea.

"Thanks," I said, nodding my head in agreement, watching as her face split into a smile.

"He fights like nothing we've seen. He's here, there, and everywhere. He's making them pay for their sins."

"Good. They need to." We sat quietly, listening to the distant cannon rounds.

"And so they do," she said finally, standing and stretching her back to loosen the muscles. She was the furthest along of any of them, her babies nestled safe and growing stronger inside her every day. They needed a world to grow up in that was as safe as their mother's womb. They needed a world where sons weren't murdered and daughters were not sold like cattle. Isn't that why we do the things we do? For the future? For our children? Mostly anyway.

She left to see to the others who stirred from their tents. I pulled my hair into a ponytail and swung onto Galahad's back to make my battlefield rounds. The sounds of fighting intensified as I neared the main field. Trenches had been dug overnight, and short stone walls erected. Wire curled across places here and there, and no longer would there be wild sprints across the open space. I wondered which side had put them up.

Galahad and I stuck to the periphery, blending in with the shadows and supplementing them with magic to keep us hidden. I had learned a lesson yesterday. I was a lynchpin to the people on both sides. If I were captured, the fight would likely be short, bloody, and over before I could get free. As careful as I had been, I needed to be more so.

I watched in horror as flame-tipped arrows flew towards our camp, lighting fires where they fell. Fae Archers have strong magic. Their arrows fly far and accurately, and their quivers never go empty. The strengthening of their land had helped this. I heard the screams before the first fighter fell.

I raced on Galahad, but for the first time, my magic wasn't enough. By the time I wove through walls and wire, the man hit with the flaming arrow was dead, and there was nothing I could do about it. Wails sounded, and one of the women from camp sank at my side, gathering her mate to her chest. I kept my hands on him, looking for some spark of life, some sign that I could fix him, but there was none.

Another arrow flew, striking the woman's dress. It caught, and her screams changed from grief to pain. I pulled power from the earth, extinguishing the flames before jerking her from the reach of the archer. Galahad followed, providing a wall of black for cover until she was safe. We left the body of the man on the battlefield.

The archers continued to loose flaming arrows at us, effectively shutting the battle down. It was everything I could do to keep the flames from catching and spreading. I pulled so much power from the earth beneath my bare feet that the magic of the fae strengthened noticeably. As their power increased, so did their range.

Our archers set up and began firing back, helping slow the onslaught, but they did not have flame-tipped arrows. I ran from fire to fire and man to man doing the best I could, but it was a bandaid on a hemorrhage and not a solution.

Aedan found me as the afternoon sun blazed brightly onto the green grass. I was already exhausted and breathing hard when he pulled me to him, crushing me with his arms. His lips met mine, and I sank into him gratefully. All I wanted was our home and our bed. I was sleeping for a month and never using magic again once this was over.

"Anamcara, we are losing. You must cover the sun. The vampires can take the archers but not with the sun so high. We need help." He pulled away, watching my face.

Never, not once, had I heard Aedan talk like this. Gone was the easy confidence and slight swagger he carried. He looked haggard.

The angles of his body were wrong, and I knew that he was extending himself in ways he hadn't expected.

"Drink," I said, pulling him back to me.

"I've had my fill," he said with a smirk.

"Do it anyway, babe." I tilted my head, teasing him with the curve of my neck. He might be full, but I had more to offer him.

He struck the spot he loved so smoothly that I didn't feel his fangs until they were buried deep inside me. As he pulled blood, I opened myself up to the well of magic and let him pull that from me too. We had done this once before when he had to defend me from so many challenges that he'd nearly died. I'd only known him a few weeks then, and my magic was not what it is now. I felt his strength returning after a few sips. My magic had healed him then, and it healed him now.

Back then, I had fused the fracture between vampire and fae. Now? He pulled from me after one final sip, not taking enough blood to make a difference to me. He glowed faintly like I do when I get worked up magically. His eyes were whiskey-colored ringed in pale yellow, and I wondered what that meant and what new power I had given the old hybrid.

"My thanks, as always, Liomsa." He kissed me again, and my blood tasted like sugar on his tongue. I wanted him. Goddess, did I want him. As arrows flew and people screamed, my need for him was as great as it ever was. War is funny that way.

"The sun," he said before slipping away with a sigh.

I gave the sun a frustrated glare before pulling shadows from the base of trees and mists from far away bogs. I willed the weather to change. Thunder rumbled, and lightning flashed over distant mountains. In minutes the sun was blotted by thick, black clouds. Cloud to cloud lightning flashed while the thunder shook the ground. It didn't rain, though, not then.

My mom says it rarely rains in Talamh na Sithe and that it really is paradise lost. The grass stays green, and flowers bloom, despite the hot summers and bitterly cold winters. Once or twice a month, rain falls, yet lakes and rivers teem with life, and nothing ever dries up from draught. Around me, the Fae eyed the sky suspiciously, and the flame-tipped arrows slowed.

Perhaps I could end this now. Maybe I could reach down and use such a show of forceful magic that the other side would bow to me, but it didn't feel right. War is a battle for control, and control must be won, not forced. I didn't want to be in the position to force peace upon people who were not ready for it. If I did, I would be no better than Aramea. Maybe the bloodshed would be less, but the end result would not be peace; it would be fear. I didn't want that. They needed to win their freedom, not be handed it.

The sky got darker, and the thunder deeper. The ground vibrated with the strength of it. Mists rose on the battlefield, covering the ground and obscuring almost everything. The screaming from the opposition's front line started not long after, and those flame-tipped arrows stopped flying. Aedan and his small band of vampires worked to quiet the fighting temporarily.

Rain fell in droplets the size of walnuts, and I let it, maybe even encouraged it a little. It fit my mood. I was tired, these people were tired, and the feeling of loss was heavy upon the air. It wasn't just the loss of life but also of the commonality that once tied these people together. It was disheartening. And where was their Queen?

My Queen rode her stark white mare through the lines with a sword in her hand. She led the charge across the field and cried with her sister over a lost mate. She made fires and tended the injured. She led from the front, not from the rear. My mother would be a good Queen.

The weather kept the fighting to a minimum. That was the bonus to using medieval fighting tools. An airplane can drop smart bombs on the target the size of a pinhead from miles away, regardless of the weather.

For the fae magic to work and arrows to fly true, swords to cut deep, and infantry to fight well, they needed to see their enemies. Let the vampires fight in the shadows while the rest of us took a break. I walked back to camp under the deluge of giant raindrops, hoping the weather would hold long enough for them to make a dent in the forces beyond our lines. Otherwise, like Aedan, I wasn't sure we could win this.

Chapter 17

The inclement weather continued until dark when, as the moon tried to rise, the weather cleared. Fires dotted the meadow, and the masses of fae huddled around them. It was quiet. I sat with my parents, eating stew made from a stag, with potatoes and cabbage added to make it hearty. It was delicious and warmed my limbs as it hit my belly. Hot coffee sat on my right and my mother on my left.

"The weather provided us with a much needed break, Lara. Thank you. Aedan and the Huntsmen put a dent in Aramea's forces," she said hopefully. She looked tired but more rested than she had this morning.

"No problem, mom." I sipped my coffee, looking around for Aedan. Nighttime was vampire time, but I hoped he managed to find me for a little while.

I needed him.

Reading my thoughts, my mother added, "They are securing the field beyond this one, then they will rest. They are skilled mercenaries. The debt from us to them grows daily."

"There is no debt, Airmed. This is family business. All of it. Any debt is forgiven. Once this is over, I hope the relationship between our groups continues to thrive." Aedan moved my coffee and sat next to me. He looked better than he had this morning, too.

My blood went a long way with him, and I needed to make sure he had it often until we were home. Firelight danced on his molasses-colored hair, striking the red highlights and making them spark. He looked amazing; I ate faster. My mother smiled, turning away so I wouldn't see, but she wasn't fast enough.

Aedan talked quietly with my fathers as I finished my meal, soaking up the gravy with a fluffy biscuit. I rose, stretching my stiff muscles. When this was over, I was sitting in a hot tub for hours after a full body massage. I was used to riding for a few hours along the rocky trails at Union Mills. This was something else. Days on Galahad racing here and there while dodging arrows and healing others had taken a toll. Add the fact that I hadn't showered since we got here, and I was feeling like a wreck.

I sat my coffee into the waiting hands of Keelin, then Aedan and I walked to our tent. "You used strong magics today; you need to rest," he said. "How are you holding up?" He came to me, wrapping me in his strong arms.

"I'm fine," I said, snuggling into him until my face rested perfectly in his chest. "I want a shower and our bed."

"As do I," he answered simply as he held me.

"Do you think we can win?" I asked, pulling away from him to meet his eyes.

He sighed heavily. "We have no other choice now; we must win." He met my eyes, and I saw the uncertainty there.

I understood and agreed with him. Had we never come, we might have been able to stay home and ignore the troubles in

Talamh na Sithe. Now that we had shed blood on this soil, Aramea would never let us go. But I also believed that from the very beginning, this was always going to be the outcome. She'd wanted me for her breeding program or to strengthen her lands. For whatever reason, she had wanted me. Not to have a relationship with, but to control. She never would have let it go and being here, fighting this war. That was the only way to my freedom; I believed that. I knew the others did too.

"It will be hard-fought. More so than I initially believed, but we will prevail. The Goddess has said so, and I do not doubt her word."

I nodded once and turned from him, sinking onto our pile of furs without bothering to change. Aedan moved over me and, with tender hands, pulled my shirt over my head. He sank on top of me, kissing the line of my collar bone as he massaged my arms with strong hands.

"I smell like BO and a bloody battlefield," I moaned at the feel of his hands on me.

"You smell of the sun and the ocean, as you always do." He turned me over with a practiced motion and kneaded my sore muscles like bread dough.

Reaching around, he unbuttoned my jeans with deft fingers. "You could have made this easier on me by making the jeans disappear," he chuckled low, his voice growing thick.

"I could have, but I actually like these jeans."

With a move out of a magician's playbook, the jeans were off and on the floor. I lay unmoving on the bed, and the feel of his hands massaging my legs melted me. In between strokes, he unclasped my bra while I lay there and let him. My panties were next, but he took his time massaging my sore muscles and making me go limp. I heard the soft rustle of his clothing and the soft slide of his skin against mine.

His warm hands went to my feet, and it was like a string was cut. I sank so deep into the furs that I felt invisible. His tongue on the back of my thigh sent electricity straight to the core of me. I spread my legs for him and felt it catch the edge of my lips. I tried to turn over, but his hand on the small of my back kept me still. Arching my hips into him, he caught the edge of my hard nub, making me shiver.

"Aedan, I need you." I groaned.

"You always have me," he said as he edged his tongue deeper.

"No, like now. I need you now." I tilted my hips against him, asking for more. He rose over me, and with a knee, he spread my legs, then entered in one smooth thrust. I sighed at the feel of him inside me where he belonged. I needed this. Goddess, did I need to feel connected to him.

He stilled his hips, lowering his head to kiss along my shoulder. My eyes closed at the sensation, and every nerve ending tingled. With his hands braced on either side of me, he alternated between sliding into me and kissing my back, shoulders, and neck. Every time I tried to roll over, he pinned me down. I wanted to look at him and run my hands over his body, but he had other ideas.

Wetness poured from me as the friction from his weight behind me and the furs below me drove me wild. I came, bucking up into him and rising to my knees. As I tightened around him over and over, he stilled, letting himself feel my pleasure. Only when I was done did he let me turn and lie to face him. I was so slick that he met no resistance when he entered me again.

Trailing my fingers down the lines of his face, I watched his expression as he made love to me. His eyes were whiskey rimmed in yellow again, and his gaze intent on mine. I let my eyes drift closed, and my mind experience every sensation he gave. He tilted his hips to put pressure on my core, and within moments, I came again. Opening my eyes, I rose up to capture his lips with mine. He kissed me hard, holding himself up with one arm and gripping the back of my head with the other hand. His fingers tangled in my hair, pulling it lightly as he deepened the kiss. I knicked my tongue in the tip of his fangs in an old move I used to make him lose control.

He groaned into my mouth as my blood teased him with salty sweetness. Gripping me tighter, he increased his pace. Tracing my tongue down his neck, I opened his vein and latched on, sucking hard. I felt his blood renew my flagging strength and heal my sore muscles. Funny how he had that effect on me. His blood healed the Healer, making all the parts of me whole again. I could become addicted to this feeling and frankly didn't care.

He mirrored my pose, sinking his fangs into me with a sigh of relief. I came off the bed as another orgasm hit me hard. Deepening his bite, he pinned me to him, and I was helpless to do anything but feel. A muffled scream escaped my lips. I pulled from his neck and let my head fall back as he took me hard, increasing his pace until his hips stilled, and he emptied himself before crashing into me. A light shudder rolled through his body, and he sighed into my hair, not offering to move off of me.

Smiling into his neck, I traced my fingers down the muscles of his back until goosebumps rose on his flesh. A muffled "I love you" escaped his lips, and my smile grew.

Wrapping himself around me, he slid to my side and was asleep in seconds. I shimmied a blanket over us and joined him.

When I awoke, Aedan was gone as I knew he would be. The vampires were most active at night. As they were his men, he would work with them and rest when he could. I felt better, more sure we could win. At least until the camp was overrun with terrible creatures.

I had never seen anything like them. I stood stock-still, frozen as they rushed the camp. What seemed like a thousand medium height, vaguely human-looking things with dark leathery skin came from all directions. They had long, protruding lower fangs that overlapped their faces and bony ridges on their skulls. They grunted and growled as they sliced with their swords, swords that looked exactly the same as the one I carried. Although they did not glow with the aura of these things, I had no doubt my father had made them.

Aramea pulled the strings of many puppets from the safety of her towers. Whether by contract, design, or magic, she wielded the swords these things held. I raised my Glock and shot the one running toward me in the face, not feeling at all conflicted about it.

I dropped to the side and shot up at a second one. The bullet penetrated beneath its chin and went through the back of his brain, killing it. From the looks of it, their skulls were very hard. Before coming, I had reloaded my extended magazines with G2 RIP 9mm ammo. I had forgone bringing clothes so I could stuff my bag with a few boxes of them. It was viciously effective, and I had no doubt it would take these things down.

My dads wanted me to learn how to fight with a sword, and I had. But I was far deadlier with a Glock 19. I kept the sword on my back and crept around tents with my pistol in hand. I heard screams and the word 'Orc' as I went. I knew then what these things were and knew my mom had gone up against them from time to time.

Staying low, I rounded another tent as an Orc barreled towards me, chasing hard after Ravena. Gripping her elbow, I pulled her sharply behind me and fired the Glock into the Orc's face, watching as he dropped dead at my feet.

"Ravena, what the hell?" I heaved, checking her for injuries.

"I don't know," she answered. "They are everywhere! The fighting is worse in the center of the camp. You need to get to safety." She gripped my arm and tried pulling me away.

I threw my head back and laughed. She froze, and her fear-filled eyes met mine. "I'm not leaving, Ravena," I said, trying to sound less maniacal. "Go to safety if you can find it." I pushed her gently away and ran toward the sounds of clashing swords and shouts.

An Orc had Saige down and was about to take his head. I wrapped it in a rose gold net and pulled it off its feet. My father jumped up, but I had a bullet in its head before he could raise his sword. I kept running.

My mother had a pile of dead Orcs around her and a feral smile on her face as she tore apart another one with her deft skill. A group of Orcs had several women cornered and were advancing on them with fists raised high. Pulling power from the land, I used my inner sight and found the strings that held them together. I yanked them hard, and the things dissolved into nothing. Breathing hard, I stopped to heal a laceration on Arlie's arm. She would have bled to death otherwise.

"Ravena went that way!" I shouted, pushing them away.

"If it's all the same, we'll stay behind you," one of them answered.

Everywhere I looked, people fought. Smoke joined the mists, obscuring some of the details, and the smell of blood filled the air. I kept running. If I passed an injured fae, I healed them. If I passed an Orc, I shot it. I switched magazines when they emptied and began again. I passed more and more dead Orcs and knew we were gaining control.

I hadn't seen Aedan. Opening my link to him, I found him madder than a hornet but safe. He was some distance away, engaged in a fight with what felt like twenty guards, and probably was. He knew there was danger at the camp, and his fury at not being there was palpable. This was a setup. I wondered how many other fighters were otherwise engaged. I let him know I was okay, then shut the link and moved on.

I had kinda promised him I would stay to the outskirts of the fighting and just do my job as a Healer. In my defense, the fighting had come to me and not me to it. I stumbled, and an Orc grabbed me from behind. The thing I noticed first was how bad it smelled. It was like a putrid water hole, and a decomposing body had a baby, and a hundred pigs took a crap on it. I gagged.

It wrestled me forward, not trying to hurt me, but like it was trying to run, and I knew how that story ended. I tried to unmake it, and my magic fizzled. I felt the tingle of something on my arms where they were in contact with the Orcs. The tingle turned into a burn. Like some amphibians, these things must secrete substances designed to subdue prey. I tried again and failed to turn the Orc to slime.

Sometimes the best defense is to run. My feet were off the ground, cutting off my access to the extra power the earth gave me. I reared back with my head, striking the thing in what I thought was its nose. Its arms sagged, and one bare foot touched the ground. Pulling more power than I ever had, I threw myself from the Orc's arms, disappearing to a spot not ten feet away.

Then I saw the tree and became the tree.

Grania had told me a hundred times that this skill would come in handy, and I never believed her. I mean, come on. Right? As I watched the Orc bellow in frustration and look right through me, I knew she had saved my life. Not only my life but the lives of many others. By teaching me magic, she had ensured I would be there to help the next fae that dropped nearly dead in this terrible mess.

One of our fighters ran up to the confused Orc and took its head. I let myself coalesce. Aron's sword hand raised as he whirled on me. He was one of Keena's mates, and he knew me well enough not to accidentally take my head. Soon, I was surrounded by a mass of fae. My mom came up to me, gripping my arms tightly as she turned me from side to side.

"I'm fine, mom," I said.

She seemed not to believe me and continued checking me for injuries. Blood ran down her head from a small cut on her hairline, and she looked fearsome. Her chartreuse eyes narrowed up at me. "I'll be the judge of that," she said, her accent thickening. She ran a finger down my arm then popped it into her mouth. "Ack. It slimed you. It's a poison that will leash magic and lull you to sleep. You must wash it off because it lasts for hours."

"You would know, Ari. You have quite the history with Orcs," Lann said, scooping her up and hugging her tiny body to his large one. "They are gone or dead," he finished, and I let out the breath I was holding.

As the others set the camp to rights, I healed the damage Orcs had caused to our fighters. The hopeful feeling I had this morning, long gone. Aramea was a keen strategist. She had us on the ropes without lifting a finger. Aedan came, once again looking haggard and pale. He'd beaten the twenty-odd fighters, but he'd used all the extra strength my blood gave him. So, I gave him more.

He held me tenderly as he fed on my neck, pulling deep and hard. We stood behind our tent, and I felt like a teenager trying not to get caught doing something dirty. There wasn't anything sexy about it, and I couldn't remember if we'd ever done it in such a utilitarian way before. I didn't think so. It was weird, and I didn't like it. But necessity is the mother of invention, and for us, this was a new way. He kissed my lips and slipped away when he was done.

I knew he was doing a lot behind the scenes, and it was taking its toll. Rumor around the campfires is that he'd taken out over a hundred of Aramea's men on his own. No one knew how many fighters she had, but I knew he worked incessantly to end this. His sword was always bloody when I saw him.

A quick meal of biscuits, jerky, and strong coffee was shared while we put ourselves back together. After, I jumped on Galahad's back and patrolled the outskirts of the camp, looking for a way to give us an advantage. My mom joined me, and together we rode the shadows during a rare moment of quiet.

We stopped at the crossroads and looked over the cliff that seemed to be the start of all this. Galahad stayed close to the lovely white mare, so much so that my leg touched my mother's. We didn't say anything.

Above us, the sky changed. At first, it was slow and seemed natural. Fluffy pink clouds danced across the sun, casting a pink glow on everything around us. My mother stared transfixed. When the sky itself turned lavender, and the clouds went from fluffy to high cirrus, her eyes widened. Cirrus clouds are filled with ice crystals and often signal a change in the weather. Lavender is not the color of a natural sky but was Dani's signature color.

Change was coming, and I could only hope it meant the war was turning in our direction. We had made incursions here and there but gained no ground. After over a week, we had nothing to show. Aedan might have taken out a large number of their fighters, but each attack Aramea sent our way was more brutal. This was still the beginning, and it felt like we were losing. The only ground we had gained was a small battlefield; we'd made no inroads to the capital.

Over several minutes, the sky was transformed into a painting of lavender and pink hues. There was no white or blue, and the sun was absent altogether. Next to me, my mother closed her eyes and breathed in the scent of Lavender and Hyacinthe deeply. Her shoulders slumped, and I wondered what it all meant. I knew some of her histories, but not all. Isn't that how it goes with your parents? You never really know them, only what they show you.

The sound of hooves pounding the earth shattered the calm of the moment. Galahad wheeled and raced towards camp, the white mare hot on his heels. I drew my Glock and wondered what fresh hell awaited us. I crouched low on the neck of the stallion, keeping my eyes sharp for danger. The ram's horn sounded with short bursts, and I knew we were in trouble.

Hundreds of riders in black armor approached the camp through the brush on each side. The trenches, walls, and wire made sense now. There was nowhere to go. The crossroads were free, and we could run that way, but that was our only recourse. We were trapped. Our fighters scooped up women and jumped on horses as the Queen's Garrisons destroyed everything in their wake.

I didn't know where the crossroads went, but I knew we had to get back to them. My mother seeing the same thing, pulled her mare around and kicked her into a gallop. We had to hope our men would escape the wave of black-armored warriors, but to go back was suicide. I opened the link to Aedan and found he was fleeing as well. His anxiety vanished when I reached out to him, letting him know I was safe and running.

"Run," he said. I am the last in the line and will leave no one behind, but you must escape. There are too many." I felt his focus on each word and assured him with my own that I would go.

At the crossroads, my mother went left the opposite way I expected. I lost my balance as Galahad thundered after the white mare, scrambling to find my seat again. We headed North, leading the way to Goddess knew where. Behind us, hooves pounded the ground, and the vibration from it traveled up Galahad's legs into my soul.

We ran for miles. I had reloaded my magazines but only had one locked and loaded and three on my person. My sword hung from my back, and I was glad for it. We rounded a curve on the road, and an enormous expanse of grass opened before us. Free horses grazed with random stags, their heads popping up in alarm at our approach. Our riders caught up to us on the flat, and we slowed to stop. Pulling our horses around, we waited. It would end here, one way or another. Under the Goddess's sky, we would fight.

"Go!" my mother said, jerking my reins and smacking Galahad on the ass.

"Mom! No!" I yelled, pulling him around. "I'm not leaving you."

"You will do more from the shadows, Lara. Do as I say. We can hold them off without you; work your magic from safety." She insisted, continuing to smack Galahad, trying to force him to run.

"There is no safety here!" I shouted. "I'm not leaving."

"You can't heal the injured if you are dead," she screamed back at me. This is the front line, and I will fight on it. What if I fall? What of Aedan?"

She had me. If any of them fell after I took a flaming arrow, I couldn't help them. Could I die? Aedan said no, but I disagreed. Anything can die; you just have to find out how to kill it.

"Go. Please," she added. "You are the only thing standing between the other women and a sword. Ravena couldn't fight her way out of a bedsheet, and Keelin is pregnant with twins. Don't let them fall; they are all we have left.

I knew what she meant then. The future of these people rested in the bellies of six women; I couldn't leave them. I nodded my head once and rode to where the women huddled in the place they'd been dropped. They were on the backside of the meadow, under the shade of trees. I used the trees to weave more trees using Goddess magic and hid them from view. They would be safe; I would see to that.

But safety wasn't anywhere I was; I knew that too. I was a target in this conflict. I rode a giant, black warhorse, and my unmistakable appearance would draw fighters to me. I rode a few hundred feet away from the women so as not to draw attention to them and tried to lose myself in the shadows.

I saw Aedan and his vampires ride to the front line and stop. I rechecked the sky and saw that the sun was still missing. The soft pink and purple light must not have affected them; they pulled their horses around and raised their swords.

The approaching line of fighters was double what we had left, and I knew we had underestimated their numbers. They rode under Aramea's banner, and she, herself, brought up their rear. This was it. They meant to run us down and finish this. Beneath me, Galahad shifted nervously.

"I thought it would be easy," he said as his sides heaved. "I just. I just. I didn't know," he finished without his usual cocky demeanor.

"No one ever does, Gally," I whispered as a tear ran down my face. "We made a good go of it, and the fight isn't over yet." I pulled my Glock and chambered a round.

The ram's horn blew again, and our side raced to meet theirs.

We had armor, and we had swords. We had horses, and we had magic. Our shields were as good as theirs, and our swords glowed with conviction in the way theirs did not. But we were overrun anyway. At some point, I dropped from Galahad's back to heal those that fell. He kicked and fought to keep Aramea's soldiers off of me, and in the process, he took a sword through his shoulder.

"It will heal," he shouted at me and took another sword through the top of his neck, barely missing his spine.

Using magic, I covered him. To the soldier, getting ready to stab through his heart, he just disappeared. I shot the soldier in the face with the ammo designed to shred, killing my first fae. I tried not to regret it. Galahad was my Guardian, my friend, my savior; I would not let him die.

Aedan shot to my side, his sword dripping blood. We fought together like we never had, his back to mine. Somehow, I had ended up in the middle of the battle, or else the battle had come to me. Maybe that was the design all along. Aramea had wanted me from the beginning and had tried hard to get me at her side. Maybe this was always how this was going to end.

It was then that I remembered the dream I had all those months ago. When I first met Aedan and was conflicted about my feelings for him, I dreamed of us on a battlefield. I had ridden a giant black horse with sparks flying under his feet and fought back to back with Aedan in a battle we didn't seem able to win.

Tears streamed down my face as I shot another man and then another. Aedan's sword sang behind me, and his arm never paused. His back glued to mine, we fought. I emptied one magazine, only to change it out for a full one.

When the last one clicked dry, I grabbed my sword, but I was no match for these fighters. I used magic to augment my fighting, pulling hard and heavy on the resources of the earth.

I had no time to heal those that fell around me; my only thought was to somehow survive. I felt Aedan tire. We had been fighting for hours. He used magic he had kept hidden, and together we stacked up a pile of Aramea's warriors, but still, they came. I knew we couldn't last. Despite our best efforts, it was over. We had lost. We had lost everything.

I felt the first snowflake touch my eyelash and mistook it for something else. The second almost cost me my life because the distraction allowed the man I fought to land a solid strike on my sword arm. It healed immediately, without any thought on my part. Snow began to fall so heavily that around us that there was a pause.

When I looked up at the sky again, fat snowflakes obscured everything; it was a whiteout, pure and simple. The man slashed at me again, and I began my attack anew. Aedan took a moment longer, but then I heard the clash of his sword as he engaged.

The noise was muffled by the falling snow so that it sounded as if the fight was taking place in eerie silence. More bodies fell, either by magic or by sword. I ran through my magical options, trying to find some way to end this. Could I unmake them all? Should I want to? Could I use the earth to swallow them whole? Not without taking our warriors down with them. What could I do?

It was then that I heard a new sound, metal upon metal and deadly, silent hooves. It started in the distance and came closer rapidly. Drums pounded, echoing through the snow-covered hills and stilling my heart with fear. Through the snow came warriors, hundreds of them. The solid white of their horses and silver gleaming armor made it appear as if they came from nowhere and everywhere. They swarmed around us, taking the heads of the warriors we fought against. How they knew which was which, I don't know. More and more of these strange soldiers shimmered into existence as if made from the snow and air around us.

Then I saw they were mostly women. Oh, there were men, to be sure, but the majority of these new fighters were female. I stopped and stared. Aedan's movements slowed behind me as he noticed the new arrivals too. "Eruhini," he said to me, picking up fighting where he left off.

I had never heard the term Eruhini before. In my dealings with the fae, they had never mentioned them. I assumed they were friends, not foes, only because they seemed to be helping our side. We fought with renewed vigor.

With the addition of the new fighters, the focus was taken off of me as Aramea's troops had more to worry about. The Eruhini were good, very good. They moved with coordinated attacks, isolating and destroying Aramea's garrisons one by one. Our fighters had mostly lost their horses and were at a disadvantage because of it. They were also at the end of their strength. The Eruhini were one with their animals, and they fought in a way I'd never seen before. Lances flew with precision, and shields deflected strikes with ease.

Our fighters closed in, attacking Aramea's flanks, and for the first time, she was on her heels. Shouts in a strange language sounded over the din of swords clashing, and soon the snow was stained red.

I slid my sword back into its sheath and scanned the battlefield for Galahad. He stood where the women were hidden, unnoticed, and unbothered. His head hung low, and the ground beneath him was stained with blood, but he lived.

I moved from injury to injury, healing everyone that I could. Some were beyond fixing, and I let the lofty ideals when I joined this fight go. I'd sworn that our allies wouldn't fall. I'd meant it then, but you can't imagine what war is like unless you've seen it. The promise I made to myself was one I could not keep and would never make again.

Modern-day warfare hadn't prepared me for this. I'd seen skirmishes on TV from the safety of my living room, but in a real war, people die. There is no way around it. I was one Healer for a thousand men. I hadn't had a chance, and neither had some of them.

I fixed what I could, which was a lot. A hundred men would live because I was there for them; a handful would die because I hadn't been. It was all I could do.

I came across the strange warriors as well. They lay injured, and their blood ran just as red as mine. I didn't know them, and they didn't know me, but they fought on our side anyway. I approached one female slowly; my blood-red hands held up in the universal sign of peace. Her braided hair was silver, and her gray eyes dark. She growled at me but did not move to strike.

I whispered low like I would to a frightened animal. She didn't know my language, and I didn't know hers, but she understood my intent. She had taken a sword through the side. It had knicked her liver and tracked up to her kidney. She'd have been dead in minutes, but I found her before Death did and stole another one from his grasp. She was covered head to toe in armor, but where the top piece overlapped the bottom, the sword had skated through.

Slipping my hand between the same space, I used magic to weave her back together, her somber eyes never leaving my face as I worked. When I finished, she tested her strength, rising slowly. Then, sword in hand, she was gone to fight again.

I came across more of the Eruhini. They fell from their horses and were pummeled by Aramea's men the same way we had been. They were tall and lean. Most of them had silver or black hair; a few had white, but it was odd to see such uniformity in a people. I would have loved to have a minute to talk to them.

Around us, the fighting slowed. The snow stopped falling, and the lavender sky peeked through. I stood from healing the last warrior I found down. Glancing at the sky, I took in the beauty of it. Funny how beauty can be found anywhere, and where there is beauty, there is peace. The sky above me was one of the most beautiful and magical things I had ever seen; I just had to raise my eyes and look at it.

Though swords still clashed and blood still spilled, I gazed at the sky as I stretched sore back muscles. I let the sense of peace fill me, and at that moment, I understood that peace can be found in chaos.

I stared and gloried in the wonder of it. Dani was all around us. I felt her. I felt her in the faint brush of the snowflake that hit my eyelashes. I smelled her in the warm breeze that blew; she was here, she was there: she was everywhere. The Maker of All Things was all around us. She'd told us many times that she couldn't be directly involved in this conflict, but looking around, I knew she had fibbed a bit about that. She was assuredly here.

Dani had known this was coming; all of it. She couldn't avert the war, but she could stack the deck. Aedan was good at the long game, but a Goddess would be masterful at it. I saw the chess pieces scattered about the board and got it. I finally got it.

I was transfixed by the sky until a sword pierced my gut; I didn't take my eyes from the lavender clouds as I fell.

"I should have known it would take a woman to end this," Aramea said as she stood over me. "Never leave a man to do a job that needs doing. Had you come peacefully, I would have made room for you in my stable, but as it is, I just want you dead."

I blinked slowly at her, confused as to what had happened. She pushed the sword in further, and I couldn't hold back the scream. I heard Aedan roar from across the field and felt his attention snap to me. Around us, the fighting continued, but here in the circle of my own blood, all was still. Two men moved to stand around me, and I recognized her guards. The dark one was practically drooling on me.

With a thought, I unmade the sword in my gut and fixed the hole it had made, but I was on my knees and surrounded by the enemy.

Aramea shook her tightened fists and screamed at the sky. "That magic should be mine!" she shouted. "Give it to me, and I will let them live," she lied, and I felt it slide over me like oil on water.

"Aramea, you were never meant to be Queen," said the Goddess of Life and The Maker of All Things. She stood to the side, watching Aramea through sad eyes. "You were never meant to be anything. Through conniving and lies, you took what was never yours. Never.

"It is all mine!" Aramea shouted at the little Goddess, and I pursed my lips, thinking about the folly of her temper. Aramea was insane; that's all there is to it.

The dark guard grabbed me by the hair, wrenching my head around painfully. I sent a zap of electricity into him, and he jerked away with a vicious pull. Still on my knees, I disappeared, reappearing beside Dani. Beyond us, the fighting had stopped, and swords stilled. The hush of silence fell over everything the way snow had. I did not miss the fact that most of Aramea's soldiers looked relieved.

Aedan came to stand behind Aramea. He was joined by my mother, Lann, Laith, Saige, and Seal. Lochlann, Rory, and Finn circled around Aramea's henchmen, and a pregnant silence filled the air.

Dani reached for my hand, pulling me to my feet.

"You think you can end me?" Aramea cried out. "You think you can take my throne, Airmed? You cannot! I am…" The next word never left her mouth. Blood bubbled from it as she coughed, fighting to have the last say. She stared down in shock at the six swords that ended her life. They came from all angles, and each glowed with the conviction of the person wielding it. Laith's magic made those swords fatal, and they were.

My eyes snapped to my mother's. Her face was blank, and each of my fathers wore identical expressions of shock. Aedan's face glowed with ferocity, and his fangs gleamed in the dim lavender light. As one, they pulled out their swords and let her blood run freely onto the snow.

"Granddaughter. You must Heal me; you must. I love you; I am your grandmother," Aramea begged me as her hands moved to stop the flow of blood from too many wounds.

"No, Aramea," I said to her. "You are nothing to me. Nothing. How many times could you have changed the path you were on? How many? You could have fixed this many lifetimes ago, but you chose not to. You forgot who you were and where you came from if you ever knew."

"You're just like me!" she shouted, blood-stained spit flying my way. "The power will get you in the end. It will. Then it will be you who dies by the sword of the ones you loved."

"I am nothing like you, Aramea. You've never loved anyone in your long, hate-filled life, and I doubt anyone ever loved you. It's done." I turned my back to her, walking to where Aedan stood.

Aramea died shouting obscenities to the sky. She died cursing the Goddess standing three feet from her. In the end, she died alone and in a pool of her own cold blood because no one cared enough to end her suffering.

Rory killed the dark guard as he said it was owed to him. I didn't know that story, and I didn't want to. I'd seen enough. Ravena shed quiet tears as he sliced the man to pieces, ending him one bit of flesh at a time. I didn't care. Normally, I would have pled for compassion and a quick end, but I just didn't care. Not anymore.

Saige killed the light-haired guard. I'd once known their names, but they meant nothing to me. My part in this was done.

On a field slick with blood, my mother became Queen. Every Fae man and woman bent the knee to her while Aramea's body cooled in the faint chill of the Talamh na Sithe night. Fires were lit, and alcohol flowed.

Airmed, call me Ari; call me Queen cried, falling into the arms of her long-lost sister, Teagan. Teagan, who was now Queen of the Eruhini People. It was nice to see her with her Erhus mates. Her small stature, brown skin, and wild hair next to their starkness was beautiful. They loomed at her back, the picture of the land of ice and snow they spoke of, while she stood like a fire-breathing dragon below them. It was adorable, but I would never use that word out loud. Nope.

We gathered, feasted, and told tales into the night. Teagan had been taken by Trolls and landed in a foreign place she came to rule. She told her story with help from her husbands, who had once been slaves, slaves freed by the wild spitfire not much bigger than my mom. Stories were passed with ale and meade throughout the night, and the sisters caught up on their lives.

We met Teagan's son, Halan. He was tall like his fathers with long, wild reddish-blonde hair like his mother, except he had a streak of white through it. His eyes were the silver of dimes, and he was striking. He looked and acted so much like all his parents; it was hard to tell which man had fathered him. I knew that it didn't matter to them anyway. I saw the furtive looks between Teagan and her son, who kept glancing my way. We were about the same age. The third time it happened, I introduced Aedan as my fiancé. Thus scrapping any plans they had to join us in marriage.

It was a fantastic night. What sisters tore apart, sisters would rejoin. With both former Queens gone, nothing was stopping the two peoples from having a good relationship. Teagan had brought magic to the Eruhini, and both lands would benefit from a relationship. The women, once known as The Eight, loved each other like sisters, and anything was possible. As fires burned low and flagons of ale emptied, they talked about the future and what things they would share.

Teagan's People planned to stay and help repair the damage Aramea had done to homes and businesses. They would learn each other's languages and cultures. They were long-lost cousins, and bonds needed to reform. Winter Court and Summer needed to reunite. Plans were made long into the night, and high hopes were shared by all.

I had another hope. Eregion was a society once dominated by women, a lot of women. Some of whom stayed single once their society changed and power balanced. Many Fae males still looked for love, and I had a secret hope that together they would rebuild their populations. Fire and Ice can live in harmony; Teagan proved that. Her mates were as doting as any I had seen, and her face shone with love every time she glanced at them.

Aedan and I peeled off as the moon sank low. He took me to a wide stream so I could bathe the blood from my skin. Our camp barely stood, but we managed to pull the tent into a position that would allow us to sleep in it. I fell gracelessly onto my face, asleep before it hit the furs.

Chapter 18

I slept until the sun was high above the horizon. When I awoke, Aedan was by my side for the first time in ages. He was flat on his back, mouth slightly open. His chest rose and fell quietly, and once again, I wondered about him. So much had changed; yet, so much hadn't. My heart skipped a beat as I watched him, and my stomach did a little flip that not long ago, I had mistaken for indigestion. Now, I knew it for what it was- love.

I eased from the furs and stumbled into the clear Faerie air. A cup of coffee was placed in my hands. My mother stood next to me, her hair a mess and her clothes disheveled. She still wore the blood of her enemies, and I wondered if she had slept at all.

"Thanks, mom," I said, hugging the hot coffee to me gratefully.

"We couldn't have done it without you," she said without preamble.

"You could have. Between your warriors and Teagan's, you'd have done it."

"Do you know that every soldier has a story to tell about how you helped them?" she asked, smiling up at me.

"I did not know that," I said with a chuckle. "You know how war stories are. They're like fish stories; everyone has a doozie of one."

"Not like this, Lara. You touched every person here. You saved countless lives; I thank you." I wrapped her arm around me, and together we surveyed the scene around us. Already, the camp was being taken down, and the fae readied to return to their homes. I hoped they had homes to return to.

"Is the Queen thanking me, or is my mother?" I asked, giving her my biggest smile. I was so proud of her; she had finally achieved her goal. Once again, I saw the value in the long game.

"Both," she laughed. "And both are in your debt."

"There is no debt, mom. You know that."

"And someday you will take this place from my hands," she laughed. "But I'll get it all fixed up for you."

"Please do; it's a bit of a mess. Really though, it's all yours, mom. I don't want to be Queen." I hugged her to me as I finished my coffee.

"That's not how it works, honey. Good Queens don't want to rule; they simply know they must. Someday, you will take my place."

I had heard that a lot lately.

Dani said the same thing.

We walked the camp together, helping where we were needed. The plan for today was to go to the palace and sweep the grounds for stragglers. We needed to make sure that all the troops loyal to Aramea were now aligned with my mom or dead. I felt terrible for waking Aedan up, but ours was the last tent standing. I packed hurriedly while he dressed and sucked down a cup of coffee. He swore caffeine didn't affect him, but the way he chugged it, I wasn't so sure.

Galahad stood at the ready on the outskirts of town, looking only slightly worse for the wear. He'd done his job yesterday, and I had yet to thank him. Walking over to the warhorse, I pulled my sword and sank to one knee as I bent my head over it. "Brave Sir, I am in your debt. Thank you for your bravery on the battlefield, your strength of spirit, and your knowledge of the land. The mares will tell stories about you until the end of time," I said with a slight flourish of my arm. Galahad loved theatrics, and I knew my gesture would please him.

"It was my pleasure, Faerie Healer, Princess of Talamh na Sithe, Queen of the vampire nation, and Goddess in the Making. Your fierceness in battle will long be remembered, and I thank you for allowing me to serve you," he said with a deep bow of his head. His mane brushed the ground, and I started to feel like this was goodbye.

"Galahad, no," I whispered, raising my tear-filled eyes to him.

"You don't need me anymore. You never did." He rubbed his nose on my shoulder, and I jumped up, dropping my sword.

"Galahad, I will always need you. Who is going to keep me straight? You're the only one brave enough to buck me off into a snowdrift when I lose my focus." I wrapped my arms around his neck, standing on my tiptoes to hug the giant beast.

"And I will be there for that- I will. I am your Guardian until I die, but you don't need me every day, not anymore. But when you do, I will be there. Besides, I can't have you getting all uppity. I know my job." He preened, prancing away from me. "See that girl over there?" he asked in hushed tones.

"Which girl?" I asked, confused. I saw no girls.

"That brown and white one with blue eyes?" He waggled his eyes in the direction of a small mare grazing in the distance.

I whipped my head around and stared at her.

"Jeez, you aren't supposed to do that," he said, bumping me hard with his nose. "You have to be sneaky about it; now she'll know we were talking about her. Slick move there, Stealthy McStealtherton." He rolled his eyes at me so hard I thought he'd get a headache.

"Okay, okay, sorry. What about her?" I whispered, trying to play off my earlier faux pas.

"She's gonna have my babies," he said with a stomp of one foot.

"I thought the white mare was going to have your babies?" I asked, giving him the stink eye.

"She is."

"Damn, Galahad, good moves, buddy," I said, patting him on the neck.

"Thanks," he said. "I mean it, though; if you need me, I'll know. I'll always be there." He pulled me under his chin and gave me the best horse hug ever.

"What if I just want to go for a ride?" I asked, sniffling into his mane.

"I'll be there."

"Okay, Gally. Okay," I sighed, and feeling drained of emotion, I pulled from him.

With a swish of his tail, he trotted over to the brown and white mare, dropping his head to graze near her. Not near enough to be obvious, you know, but near enough to keep an eye on her. I laughed under my breath, picked up my sword, and walked back to Aedan.

"Ready?" I asked.

"More than," he said, dropping a kiss to my head. "I cannot blame the lad," he laughed. "She is a nice-looking mare."

I punched him in the arm, and together we went to where the others stood to wait.

Whistles sounded, and horses came; I jumped on Galahad's bare back, knowing it might be one of the last times I rode him. Regardless of what he said, he was right; he wasn't a horse and didn't belong in my barn. He could travel anywhere using magic, and he didn't deserve to be tied down to me. Like the Fae, he'd earned his freedom.

I hoped I would see him from time to time, and I believed him when he said he'd come if called; I would miss him. As my butt hit his back, he jigged sideways, promptly dumping me into a bush.

"And this is why I saddle you!" I growled up at him while everyone around us laughed.

"You had your head up your ass; I'm just reminding you to keep it out of there; it's a dark place." He side passed away from me with a laugh when I jumped to my feet.

I shook my fist at him. "Stand still, you big lug, or I'll weave that saddle you hate right onto your back."

"You wouldn't."

"I would."

He narrowed his eyes at me in mock anger but stood still. Aedan gave me a leg up, and, once again, I was astride the black stallion.

We rode under my mother's emerald and yellow banners through the center of town and to the palace beyond, where we found no stray fighters. Birds sang, and the fountain bubbled; it is a beautiful place. With my parents and the other good people in charge, it would flourish.

The palace was empty. Coldness had seeped into its stones overnight, and they held it, not wanting to relinquish the chill to the warm sun. I couldn't see my mother living here and wondered what she would do. After it was searched and no trouble found, Aramea's banners were dragged down and burned while my mother's were hung in their place.

I didn't feign to understand what my mom felt in those moments. Aramea was her mother; surely, her death meant something. I hadn't known her, but my mom had; I said nothing and let her deal in her way.

As the palace was tidied and my parents settled in, it finally began to warm. The feel of the place went from vacant to homey, making me wonder if it was sentient. Laughter filled the halls as The Eight explored and told more stories with Teagan and her friends. I heard my mom tell Ravena that they planned to live here but would vacation in their smaller first home when they needed a getaway. She had big plans, and I approved of them.

She spent hours talking with Teagan and her mates about how to bring electricity and other technologies to Talamh na Sithe. Technology that Eregion already enjoyed. She would be a good Queen.

The Warrior Queen, Teagan, revealed she was pregnant again, and I saw my mom's eyes sparkle. I wondered how long it would take her to have another baby; I wagered not long. She could have a hundred more babies in her lifetime, and I hoped she did. Maybe then she would get it out of her head that I was her replacement on the throne. I had enough to deal with. Her life would be long; there was no reason for her to plan on giving up her kingdom anytime soon.

Besides, I was to be the resource for any fae that chose to live in the so-called 'New World, ' adding a layer of responsibility to my already full plate. Adulting was hard. We talked, told stories, and planned long into the afternoon.

With all the chaos, I lost track of Aedan and wasn't sure how long he'd been gone. I drifted from my mother's throne room through the halls, looking for him. We had agreed to stay a few days up to a week and help with the transition and repairs. I opened my link to him and found him hurting; I didn't like it. I left the palace and followed the feel of him away from it.

I found him standing in front of an old building a short walk from the palace gates. He stared at the broken façade, his face blank. His eyes were pale yellow with warning and his emotions as wild as the Irish sea.

"This is where I was changed," he said, his voice raw with emotion while pain radiated from him in sharp waves. "The Eight are correct; I can still smell my blood. It is as if it seeped into the walls. Two-thousand years have passed, and it is as if it were yesterday; it has been harder to come back than I imagined," he finished, taking my hand and squeezing it tight. "Although I stand here, a part of me died that day. Perhaps even a large part, for I am not the same. This reckoning is more difficult than I anticipated," he finished.

"Burn it," I said.

"Anamcara," he started.

"No, Coi. Burn it. I can't imagine what you feel or what you've been through, but I promise that if you burn it down, Flame Keeper, you will feel better. Let the past burn with it. Let it go once and for all because it's done. Let them start over. They can build a new Great Hall, one deserving of the people here. We can share part of our lives in Talamh na Sithe, but only if the trace of the old one is gone." I leaned into him, lending him the support he needed.

A tear slipped from my eyes, and I felt the rightness of what I was asking him to do.

"Your mother," he started.

"Won't care," I interrupted. "She has said multiple times that this place is creepy; finish it, then we walk away." I tilted my face to his and watched as his eyes slowly darkened to their stunning whiskey depths.

"You are wise," he said, tucking a stray hair behind my ear.

"I had a good mentor, Aedan. You've told me many times that you can't mourn potential, only what you once held in your hands. It's time to let it go."

"And this is why I love you," he said, smiling down at me. A single pink tear slipped from the corner of one eye; I slipped my finger onto his face to catch it. I brought the tear to my lips, tasting the hint of sadness it held. I hated to see him this way and prayed to his mother that he took my advice.

Side by side, we stood, the silence surrounding us. Even the birds seemed to go quiet. I held his hand as he stared long and hard at the once beautiful Hall. Once upon a time, it had probably been filled with joy, dancing, and laughter. Aramea changed all that. Nothing would ever take the stain of blood and death from those walls now. Aedan likely wasn't the only person to lose his life there, but he was the only one left standing to rectify the problem.

I felt his magic coil within him. He'd shown me over the last several days just how much of it he had, and I had no doubt that he had more he kept to himself.

I heard the popping of burning wood before saw the white-blue flames climbing the walls. Old wood screamed like a thousand souls as it burned. Maybe it was souls, for all I knew. As horrible a person as Aramea was, maybe she trapped them in that awful place, and by setting it on fire, Aedan freed them.

I stood by his side as the air grew hot, and the flames spread higher; the white-hot flames burned or melted everything they touched. I wove a net around the structure so that the flames would not spread, but the sound of the burning building roared into the growing night.

People came.

My mother stood on Aedan's other side, gripping his hands. Tears fell down her face, and I knew she understood. So many had lost so much, whether it was the symbolic destruction of pure evil or an actual one, everyone understood.

When the massive crossbeams were embers, Aedan pulled the magical fire back to him, surprising those around us who did not know he was still The Flame Keeper in truth. With a wave of his hand, he cooled the burnt mass so that no possibility of the fire spreading remained.

And then he walked away.

In our rooms deep within the palace that my mother called home, we added a little more life to walls so desperate for it by making love. It was sweet and quiet. I met his need with mine, and together we celebrated the fact that it was over, truly over. The sword hanging over our necks was gone, and in no future did

Aramea threaten us, the Fae, or any children they might have. We were all free.

Talamh na Sithe was full of promise and choice, and if the death and strife they'd faced were worth it to them, then it was worth it to me. As the palace didn't have hot running water yet, Aedan heated water with his touch for me, and I sank into the giant, steaming porcelain bathtub with a sigh of pleasure. It was big enough for two, but Aedan let me have it to myself; I stretched my legs and luxuriated in the feel of hot water on sore muscles.

With a pitcher, he washed and rinsed my hair. The feel of his nimble fingers on my scalp could have sent me straight to sleep, but I didn't want to miss anything. When I was clean, Aedan wrapped me in a towel and carried me to the bed before changing the water and bathing himself. Together under the covers, with hearth fires burning, we shared blood, reconnecting in that other way we both enjoyed.

That led to more lovemaking, which led to another bath, and I warned Aedan against the endless cycle we spiraled toward. With a laugh, he tossed me over his shoulder, spanked my butt halfheartedly, and tossed me on the bed, and the cycle began anew.

We slept until the sun was near setting. Sometimes you don't realize how tired you are until you finally stop all motion. In the pace of stillness, I found myself exhausted. Drained of all reserves, my only option had been sleeping, and I took full advantage of the soft mattress and thick furs to do it.

When we awoke, we found a meal on the little table in our room, and I ate it, wondering if the damn Brownie had found us; it was impossible to hide from him. Aedan dressed in clothes that one of my dads had left for him. I wove myself a gauzy dress because it seemed to fit the medieval castle vibe the palace had going, and Aedan and I left our rooms in search of the others.

The throne room was filled with laughter and dancing couples, so it was a good thing I had dressed for a party. Fires burned bright, and the sound of conversations made actually talking impossible. It was wonderful. I danced with Aedan and anyone else that asked. The local dance was a cross between an American Square dance and some Irish thing I saw in a movie once. We drank and danced the night away before once again falling into bed exhausted.

Chapter 19

The next day I was up at dawn. As much as I liked spending time with my family and learning about Talamh na Sithe, I wanted to go home, so it was time to get to work. Crews moved through the capital, cleaning up and burning debris. Fires burned throughout the day and night, and in a few short days, the damage Aramea did was erased. New storefronts popped up, signs were repainted, and restaurants reopened. Things settled.

I stood with my mom in the shell of her old bakery. It had been empty over thirty-five years, and it showed. At some point, one of my fathers had covered the windows with boards and taken down her sign. This action alone may have saved the place from the bulk of Aramea's wrath. That, or she overlooked it entirely when she rampaged through the streets.

Every surface was covered with dust, but for the most part, it was intact. I could see that her last exit from the place had been a hasty one. Dishes still lay on the counter, and old, mice-eaten bags of flour sat in the storeroom.

Together we piled the trash in wagons that were taken away by horses. She lit lanterns and cleaned hearths while I swept and mopped floors. The first tray of cakes and muffins went into the ovens by mid-afternoon, and a deep sense of peace filled the air as the scent of vanilla spread. I helped where I could, but I am no baker. I can barely cook and am grateful every day that I have a Brownie to take care of that.

It doesn't hurt that my fiancé doesn't eat actual food, either.

People came and went. The Queen gave her fresh cakes and cookies away, bringing a new meaning to the phrase 'let them eat cake.' I left her in the bakery to settle her soul and moved on to the next place that needed my help. Store by store and block by block, Talamh na Sithe came to life. Once again, people walked the streets and enjoyed the warm, bright sun.

I found Aedan at the edge of the burnt hole that had once been the Great Fae Hall. Again. He stared at the site in contemplation, and I could see the wheels turning from twenty feet away.

"What are you thinking?" I asked as I walked up to him.

"I spoke with your mother, and she has no plans to rebuild the Hall," he said, scratching his chin and tilting his head as he took measurements with his eyes.

"Oh?" I asked, leaving the statement open so that he had room to tell me what was on his mind.

"I asked her if I could buy the property."

My eyebrows rose, but all I said was, "And?"

"I explained that she required gold and silver to begin her reign, and I needed a starting point in Talamh na Sithe. As I have gold and silver to spare, and she has this burned-out ruin, we came to a deal." I watched the slow smile spread across his face as he built plans upon plans in his mind.

"You made a deal with my mom?" I asked, grinning. I would have liked to have been there for that negotiation. The Fae can weave deals like mad, and these matters are often tricky. I can only imagine that both of them are intense; I was sorry I missed it.

"I did. She is a vicious negotiator for one so young," his smile grew, and I knew that he had enjoyed his battle with her immensely.

"This scrap of burned land is ours, Anamcara. It is ours for as long as we are married, should I divorce you, the land reverts to you, and should you divorce me, the land reverts to you," he laughed so hard a little pink tear slipped down his cheek. "I paid a fortune in gold and silver for a husk of a building and a cursed piece of land." I could feel his joy and wondered if he had finally lost his mind.

"Why would you do that?" I gasped.

"Because I have faith in us. Once again, I have a piece of my homeland, and I intend to make something here that will last for millennia to come. It is a good investment, and it will make us money."

"Ah. There it is," I laughed. I knew there was more to it. "We have money, babe."

"And this will make us more."

"I see. What are your grand plans?" I asked, taking his hand. He was so happy, burning that old Hall had done more for his soul than I imagined.

A piece of darkness I never noticed was missing. Now that it was gone, I could see the toll it had taken on him. His demeanor was light, and his spirit carefree. He practically danced in place as he told me about his plans for a grand hotel on the spot where he had been tortured and lost his life.

We would have a suite there and be able to come whenever we wanted. Still, more importantly, the high-end hotel would allow tourism to grow and the empty coffers of the land to refill.

Technology came at a price, and my mother wanted electricity, modern roads, and new infrastructure. Aedan told me she planned to guard the land carefully and not allow the character of the place to change, but some things needed updating. She wanted hot showers for all.

I laughed at that because I understood.

Their plan was a good one. Aedan would be taxed on the income of the hotel, and my mother would reap the benefits of added tourism dollars. The commodities, luxury, and history of the new hotel would attract the wealthy who could afford the high-end accommodations.

There would be other rooms too, maybe not as fancy, but affordable to those who wanted to learn the rich history of the place. It was a win-win. Only Aedan would take the ashes of his destruction and build something that would benefit all on top of them. Yes, he would make money, but that's how capitalism worked. I was proud of him.

"I am going to have Guy draw up the plans and supervise, but the work will be done by locals. They need to rebuild, and this will provide well-paying jobs for them."

"That's a great idea, Coi, it really is. How are these tourists going to get here, though? It's a long way for most of them. If they can't travel the ways, they won't be able to come," I asked.

"That is where you come in; I need your help."

I quirked up an eyebrow, waiting for him to continue.

"I would like you to build a stable route directly from here to Baltimore. The way would be guided by the Fae and monitored by Airmed's soldiers. In times of peace, they will need work. She does not want everyone to have free access to Talamh na Sithe, and I agree with her. The culture could be easily corrupted, and most modern armies would be stronger than Airmed's. Faerie needs to be protected."

"With the hub of the route in Baltimore, the vampires can assist with protecting it. We just need a stable way for them to protect."

"I see," I said, knowing I could make the way; Dani had already clued me in on that. "More jobs for the Fae and for the vampires. I'm sure these guided travels will come at a cost?" I asked while nodding my head at him.

"They will, with exceptions for school groups, historians, and the like. Humans will not be allowed to immigrate or purchase lands for some time. The Fae need to rebuild before that can be allowed, but there is much that can be learned without making a commercial nightmare of it."

"It's a good plan, love," I said. And it was. "Do you want me to bury this mess?" I asked, squeezing his hand.

"That would be helpful and allow construction to begin as soon as the way is open."

"I didn't say anything about doing the way," I said, laughing at the shocked look on his face. "Just kidding, babe. Of course, I will do what I can." I punched him in the arm for thinking I wouldn't help him make these dreams a reality.

Opening myself up to the unlimited power of the earth, I churned the dirt below the ruins of the fae hall, asking Gaia to accept them. She opened wide, pulling coals, ashes, and the remains of beams deep into her, covering them with clean level dirt. I continued cycling power through me, feeling her pleasure as I did so. Talamh na Sithe grew stronger each time I shared power with her, and for all I know, I did too.

I closed myself off the land below me, and my skin glowed softly with rose gold light as we stood looking at the clean slate on which Guy and the fae workers could build something beautiful.

Holding hands, we walked back to the palace to discuss plans for building the Way with my parents.

It turns out that planning way placement involves drinking lots of whiskey. I complained about the lack of vodka to the Queen, who took my complaints under advisement. At some point, we stumbled to bed with a vague plan for the ways in mind. I think, anyway.

The next morning, Aedan took me to a location on the outskirts of town behind the fountain in the square. The area was vacant and far enough from the city center to be a safer ending point for travelers.

"Do you want to go home?" he asked as we stood staring at the lush greenery and beautiful flowers surrounding us.

"Not right now; I'm good for a bit longer. This is kind of peaceful, no vampire politics, no clinic, no meetings; I like it," I answered, breathing in the strong floral scent of honeysuckle.

"That is not exactly what I mean, Liomsa," he chuckled.

"What do you mean then?"

"Did The Goddess tell you how to build a way?" he asked slower, like maybe the problem was that I didn't understand English.

I glared at him.

"She gave me the basics, I guess," I said, trying to decide if he needed another punch to the arm. I gave him a second to clarify.

"The reason the Old Ways in Ireland are stable is that they have been traveled over and over. Thousands of Fae have traveled them using memory and magic. As we do not have thousands of Fae able to independently travel the Old Ways, you must create the path using your ability to Weave."

"Okay. I get you," I said, bobbing my head.

He stared at me like I had three heads before continuing, "You have been to my office in Baltimore," he started, still talking slowly.

"Yes," I answered with confidence.

"In the lobby of that building, there is an empty storefront, do you remember?"

"Kinda," I started with less confidence now. "Wrought iron gate pulled down over the opening? Kinda looks like a shoe store behind that?"

"I would not say it looks like a footwear store," he said. "But the description of the gate is correct."

He projected a picture of the lobby and the storefront in question into my mind, then I remembered it well. Aedan's Baltimore office was in a swanky building with a doorman and everything. The vacant storefront used to be a high-end tailor shop that had gone under. We had commented on its continued vacancy whenever we passed it by.

"Ah, yes. Got it now, still looks like a shoe store."

Choosing to ignore me, he said, "One step at a time, you must weave a path from this place to that one. If you weave it from magic, it will be stable immediately and not require hundreds of trips to be reliable.

"But I don't have a map or know how to get from here to there," I said, looking confused.

I watched as he forcefully curled his lips under to hide his smile. "Anamcara," he said, the strain in his voice from holding back his laughter.

"Yeah?"

"You do not need a map. You simply need to want to go from here to there, and the memory will allow a path to be built; it will feel like swimming. I cannot weave in this manner anymore, I must build ways through repetition, but I remember it well. Keep your focus on where you are going, and you will end up there. Once the way to Baltimore is completed, you will make the return path as they are not the same."

"Okay, are you going to hold my hand or anything?" I asked.

His face fell, "I cannot go, not while you are weaving the way, it would be too easy to become lost. Weave the walls like a tunnel, and the way will be more durable than a roadway." He leaned down to give me a kiss.

This was big magic. It was big magic, and he asked me to do it knowing he couldn't go, which meant he had faith in me. It meant everything. I knew Aedan was worried. He was also protective, and sometimes that came across as controlling, but he only ever tried to keep me safe.

He was asking me to do something for him that he couldn't do himself, and in the process, I was spreading my magical wings in a way that would be challenging. And I was going to do it alone.

The smile broke from my face, and his matching smile let me know that he knew I had figured it out.

"Thank you," I said, resting my head on his chest.

"Don't get lost, and make sure you come back to me," he added, pulling me into a hug.

"I'll be right back."

"No driving home for a quick shower."

"Damn, good idea. I wouldn't have thought about that."

"Anamcara, time passes differently; do not forget."

"Right," I sighed. I would hurry back so that a half-day there wasn't a few days here or whatever. You never knew how time was going to react between worlds. Sometimes it seemed faster and sometimes slower. They would have to plan for that when touting their new tourist destination.

I stood in the spot Aedan pointed to and thought about the vacant storefront in Baltimore. Using the rose gold threads of my aura, I began weaving a path there. Aedan was right; it did feel like swimming. But it felt like swimming through an offshore rip current; it wasn't easy. In my mind, I began to see the Way like a wormhole in space, and maybe it was. In what felt like hours, I popped through right in the center of the empty room a world away.

The doorman jumped at my sudden appearance, and I thought he might faint. He was made of stronger stuff, though, and after his initial shock, he calmed down. He was used to Aedan, vampires, and fae now. He knew who and what I was, and I watched as he regained his stoic composure.

"Do you think you could throw me a bottle of water?" I asked, taking a seat on an empty bench.

"Of course, Mistress." He went behind the desk in the lobby and came back with an ice-cold bottle of SmartWater. It was one of the big ones, and I drank it down within a few minutes. Weaving Ways is hard work.

He pointedly ignored me, and I could only imagine his reaction when I disappeared as soon as the water was gone. Weaving the Way back was not as hard. I followed the tracers of rose gold and added structure to them going in the opposite direction. I could see that the path from Talamh na Sithe was stable, each thread acting like steel girders to keep it open. It was challenging but extremely satisfying work.

I stepped into the late afternoon sunshine to find Aedan waiting not so patiently. His vampire mercenaries were with him, and their fierce faces were focused on where I appeared out of thin air.

"Whew. That's work," I mumbled, sagging a little as I tied off the final thread.

"Are you okay?" Aedan asked, coming to stand by me.

"Of course. Why wouldn't I be?"

"You have been gone for over a day, Liomsa. I was getting worried and about to come through your path, whether it was stable or not."

That explained the narrow-eyed mercenaries.

"I guess it was harder work than I thought." It also explained why I was so tired. "Well, the Way is stable. Do you want to try it out?" I asked, beaming proudly up at him.

"You should rest," he said, his eyes concerned. "Your aura is thin."

"Stop being a worrywart. I used a ton of threads to make the path. I'll be fine. Come on." I pulled him to me, excited to give the Way a go.

"Harold will call the car service once we arrive in Baltimore," he said, turning to the waiting vampires. "You do exemplary work, The Queen has already thanked you, but I add my own thanks as well," he finished, then took my hand. "Lead the way."

We stepped through the path and appeared immediately behind the wrought iron gate. The poor doorman got another shock as now seven of us seemed to come out of thin air.

"Do you need another bottle of water, Mistress?" he asked, covering his surprise with a bland expression.

"No, thank you," I replied. "How long was I gone?" I asked.

"Just a few minutes, Madame."

"Excellent." I nodded my head proudly. Not only was the Way stable, but it was also direct. What had seemed like a wormhole was really just a door.

Aedan took a few minutes to ask Harold to call the car service. He wanted to go to his office and check on things, but if I couldn't get a shower, then his business stuff could wait, too. I grinned as he growled at me when I told him no checking his emails. We had left our cellphones and his tablet at his castle and would have to go back there to get them. He could check his emails then.

We stepped back through the Way and onto the same spot we left, and he declared the Way a success. Little time had passed between our departure and arrival, and that was a good thing too.

Back at the palace, we sat down to dinner with a large group of fae and the few visitors that had arrived to hail the new Queen while I was gone. I had planned on building another way from the castle to our home in Westminster, but Aedan was right. I was tired and could feel the patchiness of my aura. I needed to rest before making any more paths.

I ate the delicious meal laid out before me, struggling to keep my eyes open. Each bite required concentration to chew, and my eyes felt like they had bricks on them.

I awoke when strong arms carried me up the stairs. I must have fallen asleep with my face on my plate because I didn't remember finishing. I tried to wake up but was unable to even open my eyes. It was like gravity had conspired against me, weighing me down. The bed met my body, and that's all I knew. I was gone before I felt the mattress dip and Aedan settle next to me.

Chapter 20

We said our goodbyes at the palace gates. My parents came, hugging me tight to them. I know they wanted us to stay, but we had responsibilities at home, and we needed to get back. Now that Talamh na Sithe was just a trip to Baltimore away, I could visit when I wanted.

I loved having them back in my life, and the fact that they were in a different world didn't change anything. We'd all grown close again, and none of us were willing to give that up. I would go home and build ways to and from Pawleys Island, Westminster, Talamh na Sithe, and damn near anyplace else we wanted to go. Distance meant nothing.

But it was time to go back.

Our plan was to spend a few days in Béal an Mhuirthead before flying back to Baltimore. We had earned a vacation before jumping into real life, and I couldn't wait to explore the countryside around Aedan's so-called cottage.

In a quiet place near where we first entered Talamh na Sithe, I said goodbye to my Guardian. Galahad deserved a break, too, and he would get it. I knew he'd come if I needed him, but it was my plan not to need him. I was ready to be at peace for a while. For the last year of my life, I had spent more time running from disaster to disaster than breathing. I was ready to live a little and remember what it is like to just be still.

I grasped Aedan's hand, and we stepped through the way and out onto the sparse grasses of his estate in Béal an Mhuirthead, where we walked to the edge of the cliff to watch the sunrise.

Over the next few days, we explored the countryside, ate local foods, and made love on the edge of the cliff while waves crashed below. I even dressed like a Native American Warrior woman and let him chase me through the scrub and heather. I used magic and everything else at my disposal to keep him from catching me, but that old vampire is wile.

He caught me in the root cellar and enjoyed tearing off my buckskin pants immensely. He bent me over a barrel of whiskey and made me scream his name until I was hoarse; I loved every second of it.

We made small changes to the cottage and formed stronger relationships in the town beyond. They looked to Aedan the way serfs once looked upon their lord, and he took that seriously. He fixed problems with work or money, whichever was called for. Once things in Béal an Mhuirthead were settled again, we drove through the gorgeous Irish countryside like he promised.

I had never seen Ireland, and it truly is the Emerald Isle. Heavy mists hung over lush greenery, giving the country a certain mystique its history has earned. To the Tuatha de Danann, this was the home of their Origin Story. They had lost this place when they'd been forced out by the new gods, but it was theirs in the beginning; the sense of history is so deep that you can't help but feel it.

I was so glad to have a chance to spend the day on the way to the airport sightseeing with my fiancé. If something looked interesting, we stopped. Yes, we could have walked the Old Way to the airport. We could have saved days and walked the New Way into Baltimore, but life is lived during the moments in between, and I wanted to take full advantage of them. Once we got home, vampire politics, the clinic, and life would happen; I wanted to be in the moment as long as I could.

We boarded the plane after the sun had set, and I slept in the bed next to Aedan the entire way home. I could hear the clicking from his laptop as he returned emails, made appointments, and caught up on his myriad business dealings. His voice whispered during returned phone calls, and he calmed the empire antsy for his return. From start to finish, we had been gone for six weeks. To us, it wasn't that long, but to those we left behind, a month a half had passed.

The plane's landing gear descending woke me up. The sun was rising over the Inner Harbor, and its golden rays glimmered off the water as we made our final descent into BWI. The landing was smooth, and we gathered our things as the jet taxied to Aedan's hanger.

A brand new McLaren 720S that was the color of venous blood sat waiting for us, and I wondered where this particular midlife crisis mobile had come from. I didn't remember it being in Aedan's stable, but who knew? It very well could have been.

The attendant carried our stuff down to the car and placed it in what might be called a trunk before shaking Aedan's hand and walking away. Aedan took the T-tops out before we left, insisting that the hot, dry, Maryland air would remove the cool, Irish mist from our bones. On the way home, Aedan demonstrated that this particular McLaren would do zero to one hundred in under six seconds. I demonstrated how high I could scream when he darted through traffic like a hot knife through butter.

I wanted to drive it, but he said no. I was going to get my own McLaren one of these days since he spoiled all my fun.

We coasted down the paved driveway, and I saw another part of Aedan's long game come into place. Had the driveway been gravel, he never could have brought his midlife crisis collection to our house. Most of them had such low clearances that the garage had specific grading and angles to accommodate their entry. The McLaren purred as he eased it down the drive, and the warm morning air smelled like cut grass and home.

Our house stood out among the smaller country homes, but it wasn't an eyesore. Despite its size, it blended beautifully with the surroundings, looking like it had been there forever; something in my heart eased when I saw it. Its graceful beauty was an amalgamation between Aedan's style and mine, and I'd missed it.

The wide, wrap-around porches filled with people, and I knew they had missed us too. Grania and Paul stood at the top of the stairs, waiting patiently as we approached. Already, the gentle swell of her belly hinted at what lay within as her reed-thin frame hid nothing. Her hand rested lightly above the small bump, and her ponytailed smile was infectious. As much as I had missed my parents, I missed this family more.

She hopped down the stairs with Paul trailing behind her, dragging me from the car and into a choking hug before I got on my feet. I probably looked like a dolly swinging around her as she twirled me.

"I missed you!" she said, dropping me to my feet while Aedan parked.

"I missed you too," I said, smiling into her ice-blue, husky eyes.

"I know you won, but you have to tell me all about it." Grabbing my arms, she forcefully shoved me toward the stairs. I laughed the whole way up them, hugging the other people who stood to wait.

"I'll tell you everything," I laughed.

We walked into the house and had to stop while I wrestled my emotions under control. I was home. Everything. And I do mean everything we had fought so hard for was done. Would there be other turmoil? Undoubtedly, but for now? Now, there was peace, and I would enjoy it.

Jeremy ran by yelling hello and was gone. He'd almost grown out of running through the house, and it was nice to see him do it from time to time. Soon, he would be all sullen and emo the way teens seem to get, but for a little while longer, he was still the sweet skinny-armed boy who always seemed to find trouble.

Grania talked animatedly, following me from room to room as I soaked it all in. We hadn't spent a whole lot of time in the new house, and I looked forward to making it my own. Grania told me she and Paul had done some light remodeling and moved into the house next door, the one that used to be mine. They'd wanted more privacy to prepare for their baby and decided that the apartment inside Fangs in the city wasn't the right place to start a family. I agreed.

As I roamed the house, she filled me in. A lot can happen in six weeks, especially in the supernatural community. Word about the war had gotten out, and there had been some mention of it on the national news networks. With the disappearance of myself, Aedan, and the Fae, everyone knew something big had happened, but no one was sure what. I was amazed that our arrival at the airport had gone mostly unnoticed and wondered when the calls for interviews would start.

Word about Grania's pregnancy had gotten out too, and there had been some hushed whispers; we knew that was coming. Grania was Aedan's second and held a very high-profile position among the vampires in Baltimore. She claimed it was her Fae background that allowed the pregnancy and that she was just as surprised as anyone else. Still, she wasn't fooling everyone.

If they hadn't already figured out I was the key to that, they would. No one looking at Grania would mistake her for the vampire she was a year ago. The one difference in her life then and now was me. Enough people knew about our binding, that talk would spread, and my doorbell would be ringing with requests for babies. That would be a touchy one, but Grania, Aedan, and I would handle that together.

The vaccine for Vampire Infectious Disease had been released, and humans that lived with or fed vampires no longer had to worry about the fatal disease taking their lives. The spin from that had been excellent, and the Lycanthropes were enjoying the benefits good PR brings. The city had calmed in our absence, not boiled over.

Aedan came in, heading straight to his office. He had that look on his face he gets when something is spinning out of control, and I shook my head; it had started already. He was back in work mode, and I smiled as he walked away with the phone plastered to his ear.

The clinic had been quiet in my absence, and Noah hadn't been called upon to do much. Now that the truth about the paranormal was out, some people were returning to their prior doctors. I was okay with that. I liked being a Faerie Healer, but I liked my days off and personal life, too. There hadn't been much work-life balance in the months following the attack that revealed my true heritage. I was okay with not being continuously needed.

Grania and I settled on the couch in the living room to catch up while the house moved on around us, and I couldn't get over the change in her. Her face was losing some of the sharp angles it usually held, and her eyes danced with a life they had not before; pregnancy looked good on her.

We talked about wedding plans and the baby into the afternoon when Cook brought food, which we promptly devoured. Afterward, I walked the tunnel to the clinic and checked on things there. The smell of my old house hit me hard, making me step back. I was amazed at the number of changes that had taken place in such a short time. Life is funny that way. I had cruised along at the same speed doing the same things for a decade, then wham- change.

Change can be good, and change can be bad; I had been through both. Life was settling now to the point where I could see blue skies and calm seas on the horizon. I looked forward to them.

We still had one significant change left to come, and I dreaded facing it- Paul. Nothing had been said, but I could feel the unresolved tension of it hanging over our heads. To Aedan and me, it felt like we had just left. But to Grania and Paul? It felt like a lifetime, and she was over three months pregnant now. We didn't talk about it, but we all saw the elephant in the room.

Guy came over, and he, Aedan, and I started planning the Hotel in Talamh na Sithe. The Flame Keeper Inn would be the first hotel of its kind anywhere, at least that we knew of, and Aedan wanted it perfect.

We talked long into the night as the people in our house listened in. In the end, we decided on a low country South Carolina-style Inn. Its old-style grace would fit with the local landscape and add a bit of class to the land. That last part was my opinion, and it wasn't necessarily shared.

Plans were drawn, and deposits paid. Aedan and I held equal shares in this venture, and it had the potential to make us both a pile of cash, not that either of us needed it. Guy shook his head and our hands before leaving. He probably wondered how he ever landed in the position to be the first human tourist in Talamh na Sithe since the fall of the prior Queen. He also probably wondered how he was going to manage fae materials and workers on this scale, but Guy was a great contractor; he would do it.

He was going to meet Aedan in Baltimore at nine in the morning to travel the way to look at the site. He didn't seem at all worried about that part, and I hoped his faith in me was well placed. It wouldn't do for him to end up in the middle of the ocean, or anyplace else for that matter.

That night, Aedan and I opened the curtains on the floor-to-ceiling infinity windows in our room and let the starlight in. After the longest, hottest shower in the history of Lara Hennessey, we laid in bed and watched falling stars streak across the sky and talked about tomorrow.

And then we talked about a thousand tomorrows. I felt like a teenager making plans for an uncertain future, but in reality, our future looked pretty sure. I was certain I loved him and that our marriage, oops, handfasting, would be a success, and he was too. We talked until the stars shifted, and the moon sank low, then we made love.

In a quiet moment with the stars hanging over our heads, he slipped inside of me, and I welcomed him home.

"I cannot believe our lives have come so far," he whispered into my ear as he moved inside of me.

"You can't?" I chucked, rolling my hips into him and making him growl. "I figured it was part of your long game," I said, nuzzling into his neck and taking a sip of his blood for myself. I felt the patches of my aura close as, once again, Aedan healed the Healer.

He stilled above me, and my playful mood went serious.

"I loved you from the first moment I saw you," he said. "And I did plan on making you mine; I admit that, but that is all I will admit."

I smiled again. "So, you walked across that field on a windy December night, and the rest is history?"

"That windy December night was many, many months after the first time I saw you. I loved you from afar until I got the nerve to introduce myself," he said, kissing down my jaw to my neck and up the other side again.

It was my turn to go still. "So, it was all a long game for you?" I asked, slapping at his chest half-heartedly.

"Everything in our lives is a long game, Mo Chroi, and finding you and making you mine was the longest. How could I have known you would exist? How could I have known how perfect we would be together? It is as if you were made for me." His whiskey eyes filled with so much love found mine, and I wondered.

Maybe I had been made for him. Specifically, maybe Dani's games were the farthest-reaching of all. She had woven me together for many, many reasons. Some reasons I am sure we didn't even know yet. Perhaps, Aedan was just another one of them. But you know what? I didn't care. I loved him, and together we were whole, long game or not.

His lips met mine, and he kissed me like a man starving. His tongue caressed mine with electricity and velvet need until I was panting. Funny how a kiss can push you right to the razor's edge; with a roll of his hips, I fell over. Clawing at his back and whispering his name like a prayer, I came. And when his fangs sank into my neck, just where the shoulder meets the base, I came again. Only this time, I took him with me.

Chapter 21

"Are you sure?" I asked Paul one more time.

After being home for a few days and settling in, Aedan had decided to set a date for Paul's changing, and that date had come.

"I'm sure, Lara. I've never been more sure of anything," he said, his striking blue eyes meeting mine.

His hair had grayed even more these last few months, and fine wrinkles had developed at the corner of his eyes. His relationship with Grania had kept him young past his years, but that was changing now; time had caught up with him.

I took a big breath and squeezed Grania's hand in mine. "Okay. Okay, I'm done. No more objections; I just wanted to make sure you were sure."

"I am," he said, watching Grania and not me.

I knew he loved her. I had asked him once if he thought she loved him or was even able to love. He had told me then that she loved him as much as a vampire could. Grania was always so glib and flippant in her approach to life that I think he missed the truth of the matter then. He saw it now. Grania loved him with an infinite passion. The same way, I believed, that Aedan loved me.

You would think that something that can live lifetime after lifetime wouldn't love so deeply, or for long, when, in fact, it's probably the opposite. A nearly immortal creature can form bonds that last for literally ever. They form them well and wisely, for the most part, bad choices aside.

I watched Grania watch Paul, and I knew they would be okay.

The only problem is, Paul was aging. The transition from human to vampire is not an easy one; even the younger ones don't always wake up on the third day. I knew Grania worried that he wouldn't survive. Knowing the strength of Aedan's blood, I worried less about survival and more about the outcome. What kind of vampire would Paul be? Aedan and I shared blood so frequently that Paul would get a little piece of me, too.

We had abstained in sharing blood in the days leading up to this, but I doubted that mattered. The changes I brought about in Aedan all those months ago didn't fade anymore. Where once they would wear off, now every advantage my blood gave Aedan was permanent. At least we thought so. We didn't need to share blood often, but we did because the side effects were orgasmic for both of us.

Aedan sat on a chair in the corner of our living room and watched the back and forth. He looked like a snake ready to strike. Not long ago, he had sworn never to make another vampire. The outcome of the last one hadn't been positive, and he feared his blood and magic were too strong to pass along. Then Paul, his most loyal servant, had asked, making him rethink it all.

"Grania?" I asked.

"I'm ready, too. I'm scared. Goddess, am I scared, but I'm ready."

"Okay," I said, getting up from the couch where I sat next to my best friend. Going into the kitchen, I grabbed water from the fridge and downed it.

Aedan said nothing as he rose; his eyes were yellowed around the edges and whiskey in the middle. It was a new normal for him under emotional circumstances, though we didn't understand why. Dani thought it was because the fae and the vampire had finally melded into one being, and maybe she was right.

His dark red, button-down shirt was untucked from the pants of his suit. He'd only been home from work for a short period and hadn't changed his clothes yet. He walked to Paul, who rose from the couch. This moment would change everything, and there was no undoing it and no going back.

I slid around the couch and sat back down next to Grania, taking her in my arms. Silent tears rolled down her face, and I knew she understood that everything was changing, too. She buried her face in my neck and let out a strangled sob.

She had assured me that she and Paul had settled things between them last night in case he didn't come back from this, and I hoped they had. Sobs wracked her body as I held her. She couldn't watch, but I couldn't look away.

Paul knelt before Aedan, bowing his head. "I promise my service, my fealty, and my life; let the promise be binding," Paul said, and I felt the promise snap into place, more proof that Aedan's fae magic was strong.

"How long will you serve?" Aedan asked, his voice holding an edge better than a knife.

"I will serve all the days of my life," Paul answered.

"You will serve until released," Aedan corrected. I knew he didn't want to do this, but I was proud of him for taking the chance. He had lost his only daughter to me, but he would gain a son and a grandbaby.

"Yes, Master," Paul said.

Aedan offered his bloody wrist, and Paul drank from it. He drank long and deep, taking more blood from Aedan than anyone that I had seen, including myself.

When he could take no more, he stood facing Aedan.

"Blood of my blood," Aedan said, mirroring the words I once used to bind Grania to me.

"Blood of my blood," Paul repeated.

Then Aedan struck. Grania screamed, clawing at me to get to Paul as Aedan drank down his life. I held her with magic when my muscles failed. She cried and raged, but Paul's fate had been decided, and there was no going back.

Aedan drank until he was obscenely full. I watched as he drank the aura right off of Paul, and I watched as Paul's soul left his body. Where it went, I did not know. Paul died with Aedan's blood on his lips, and I watched while Grania railed against me for holding her back. We'd known she would react this way; she is very protective of him.

When it was done, Aedan carried Paul lovingly to our room, laying him in a coffin in our reading area. He crossed Paul's arms over his chest and arranged him so that he looked peaceful and comfortable.

All the while, Grania cried and tried to get to him. When Aedan was done, he walked to her and pulled her into his arms.

"Daughter of my heart, it will be okay," he said. "I promise."

I bristled at the words because how could he know? In three days, Paul might not rise, and we would be forced to bury him in the coffin he rested in now. It was a risk, and we all knew it. That's why I had been so insistent that they think this through.

"Daddy, I'm scared," she said, clutching at Aedan while he rocked her quietly.

"I know, sweet fae. I know. He will rise. He will rise and be strong. You will raise your children in a peaceful world, and when it is their time, we will decide this again. I promise you. I have promised you nothing and given you very little, but I promise you this. Hear me?" he soothed into her hair, continuing to rock her, and I felt calming magic seep from him.

Her eyes fluttered closed, and he carried her to the couch next to the coffin in our room. She would stay with us; we had known that. And should Paul rise, he would be attached to our hips like an infant. We had known that too. That's why we had taken a few days to get to this point. Aedan had needed to be available and have an open schedule.

I showered, slipping between the sheets while Aedan told Mavis to turn out the lights. I prayed to the Goddess in the darkness that Paul would be okay, then we slipped into sleep together.

The next three days passed in agony for all of us. I forced Grania to leave our rooms and eat. I dragged her outside into the sun so the baby would get some vitamin D, and I forced her to shower so that she didn't stink. She was a mess, but if I am honest, we all were. Each hour that passed where Paul didn't awaken, Aedan grew more grim.

The third day started, and still, Paul didn't rise. Aedan tried to console an inconsolable Grania, telling her that it wasn't unheard of for this to happen. She clutched at him and cried while I worried about her pregnancy. This stress couldn't be good for a growing fetus, but there was nothing we could do to calm her.

As the third day came to a close, I stood at the edge of Paul's coffin and used my other sight to look at him. I waited until Aedan physically dragged Grania to the kitchen to force feed her something because I didn't want them there to watch, in case I had bad news.

When I looked at him, I saw no life. The veins under his skin had turned black days ago, and the darkness of them against the pallor of his skin was striking. But I could feel him in there and knew he wasn't dead. I didn't dare interfere with Aedan's magic or the transition of a new vampire. My magic could be wonky, and my luck, he'd wake up a troll.

I left him and went to sit on the couch near the coffin. Aedan had told Grania this could happen, but if he didn't rise, I wasn't sure she would recover. I tucked my legs under me and pulled a new copy of poetry off of the end table. Turning it to The Road Not Taken by Robert Frost, I began to read.

This poem hits me straight to the core. There is something about it that speaks to my life, and isn't that what poetry is about? A lifetime ago, while sitting on a similar couch, I had been reading a much older version of the same Robert Frost book. I had fallen asleep only to wake up in the middle of a fire that took five lives. Grania, Aedan, and I had gotten through that; we would get through this.

'Two roads diverged in a wood, and I—
I took the one less traveled by,
And that has made all the difference.'

And it has. It would continue to make a difference for the rest of my days, but I regretted nothing. You must never regret the things you survive and never forget the things that make you stronger.

From the corner of my eyes, I saw Paul's fingers twitch. I yelled at Aedan through the bond we shared, telling him to come. Within seconds, Paul went from still corpse to raving mad.

Aedan barely made it to the room in time to keep me from having to incinerate Grania's baby daddy to keep him from attacking me. When Aedan stepped in front of me with a scowl, Paul stopped. Aedan arched his eyebrow, and Paul was under control again. I stood stunned, staring at the scene.

Paul stilled with one look from Aedan, dropping his head and falling to his knees. Aedan opened his wrist, holding it out for the other man. Their eyes never leaving one another's; Paul drank his fill. Grania clung to me, her wordless mouth wide open. She didn't act like this was unusual, but she didn't move either.

When Paul was done, Aedan helped him to his feet. There was still fog over Paul's blue eyes, an opacity that covered the usual bright iris. It was freaky, but again, no one said anything.

Aedan led Paul to the couch, and they sat side by side as Aedan began to speak. Aedan talked to Paul about Grania, his baby, and their new bond. He didn't talk to Paul like he was a child, and slowly the opacity in man's eyes cleared.

A few short hours later, I knew Aedan had spoken the truth about not letting Paul stay dependent long. Though he looked at him with deeper fondness, this child of Aedan's wouldn't be allowed to linger the way Grania had; we all saw that right from the beginning.

As the sun rose, Aedan fed Paul again before tucking him into the coffin in the corner of our room. Once Paul was out for the day and Grania sleeping peacefully beside him, Aedan and I went to the shower together. With a feral glint to his slightly pale eyes, he backed me into the corner.

Hiking one leg over his arm, he hauled me up and entered me slowly. Despite his urgency and obvious need, his kiss was tender. Licking the cleft of his lips, I nicked the tip of my tongue on the tip of his fang; his kiss changed in an instant. Pressing me hard against the wall, he rolled into me and finished his slow intrusion in one stroke.

I gripped onto his arms to steady myself against the storm that is Aedan, always Aedan. His emotions whirled through him and into me through the bond we shared. He felt so many things at once that I couldn't discern one emotion from the next. It was like being stuck in the eyewall of a hurricane, which is the deadliest part by far.

He plunged into me over and over as he pressed me against the wall until all I could do was fall apart around him. And I did, going limp in his arms. Spurred on, he kissed me harder, tracing the line of my jaw, down the curve of my neck to the spot he loved most.

He sank his long fangs over the marks he made in South Carolina, the one bite he demanded I not allow to heal. They were his marks, his claim on me. More than the ring on my left hand, more than the promise I'd made to bind with him a year and a day; those marks made me his. He took his fill of my blood while I took my fill of his, and the cycle began again.

There was no one I loved more, no one I had ever thought I would spend the rest of my life with. Aedan came when I was at my lowest; I just didn't understand that. He built me up, helping show me the road to becoming a better person. Together, with our friends around us, we would build something great.

He threw his head back and growled like a beast when he came deep inside of me. I felt the spasms of his orgasm, and I clenched so tightly around him that my own orgasm followed. He slumped with me against the shower wall, holding me loosely as we fought for breath.

His slow smile when he met my eyes was the most beautiful thing I had ever seen, and for the first time, I wasn't afraid of the wedding to come. I could see my forever in that smile, and I wasn't afraid anymore.

Chapter 22

Paul came to his senses faster than any vampire Aedan had sired. Word had gotten out in the vampire community that the old man had finally made another child. Vampires flocked to our home to meet him and bring their congratulations; it was an absolute zoo for a while.

Combine that with the fact that there was no way to hide the growing swell of Grania's baby, and the questions were endless. Aedan blamed Grania's pregnancy on his mother. I laughed so hard the first time he told the story that he had to glare at me to shut me up.

I suppose it was true in a way. The Goddess of Life and the Maker of All Things had made me; in turn, I had remade Grania. So indirectly, he did not tell a lie. Aedan suggested that if the vampires wanted children, they should pray to the Goddess.

Vampires praying to Dani would make her magic stronger, and the cycle would begin again, as cycles always do.

Within weeks Aedan was giving Paul lists and sending him on errands with Grania. They took a page out of my book, giving him something to do and someone to watch him. His leash was short until it wasn't anymore, and soon, Paul was helping Grania at Fangs, and the club was ready for the grand opening.

Everyone came.

And I do mean everyone.

Half of Eregion and all of Talamh na Sithe came to the biggest vampire party the east coast had seen. Grania sipped water from a champagne glass and basked in the glory of a job well done. Time passed quickly, and in between plans for The Flame Keeper Inn, Fangs, Grania's baby, and our handfasting, I didn't have time to worry about anything else.

The rush of the river carried us toward our fate, and I wasn't as worried about it as I once had been. In fact, I wasn't worried at all.

Chapter 23

I wore red. I mean, it's not like I can get away with white. I wove the gown myself, using my aura, my intent, and my love for Aedan.

It was a stunning gown.

Emily was upset that she hadn't gotten to make the dress, but I assured her that she could make the dress for our reception, as long as it was all red; that seemed to smooth her feathers.

I added the necklace and earrings Aedan had given me the night of the Dracula showing, then piled my hair in a complicated mess on top of my head. I followed Grania through the softly lit tunnel between my old home and our new one. The large swell of her belly in the creamy white dress she wore was glorious. The sister of my heart had never been more gorgeous.

We met in the courtyard, Grania by my side and Paul by Aedan's. It's not that we didn't want people to know; it wasn't that at all. It's just that this was personal. A binding between Aedan and me: no limos, no photographers, and no crowds. Just him. Just me. My parents stood to one side and Samuel, Kimani, Alisondro, Sarah, and Jeremy to the other.

We wanted it simple. Marriage isn't about one ridiculously expensive day to share with thousands; it's about the thousands of days that come after. It's about those victories and defeats a couple must traverse together.

Dani stood with Aedan in the courtyard, lightly holding his arm. Torches lit the space, and the koi ponds bubbled happily; it looked almost the same as it had the night Daniel died here. Except that tonight, this place was all about life and nothing about death. It had come full circle.

Aedan's eyes widened and paled when I walked through the door. His fangs dropped just enough that I caught a glimpse of them through his smile, and I knew he liked my dress.

Dani was resplendent in a gown of soft ivory, her silver hair loose at her sides, blowing in the soft breeze as she called us forward.

"My Children, come forward and kneel," she called.

Aedan and I knelt before the Goddess of Life and the Maker of All Things, bowing our heads deeply.

"Do you come into this binding with full understanding, free will, and good intent?" she asked without preamble.

"I do," Aedan and I said at the same time.

"Then rise and face each other. Lara, raise your right hand and Aedan, your left."

We stood, clasping our hands before us. Dani took a white ribbon and wound it around our arms, elbow to wrist. Clasping her hands over our joined fist. She wove her magic. It wasn't the words she spoke but the weaving that bound us; I could feel it settle like a blanket over my soul. It wasn't suffocating at all; it was comforting.

"For a year and a day, I bind you. During that time, you are one person, one heart, and one mind. As one lives, so does the other. As one dies, so does the other. You take this binding willingly and with full understanding." She continued to weave her spell over us, smiling as she did so. I could only hope she kept her word not to bind anything else into that spell.

"On the last day of this binding, you must separate and consider for one cycle of the sun; you may not contact one another in any manner. On this day, you must reflect, not only on the past but also on the future. The next day, should you choose to come together again, the binding is then permanent and cannot be undone. You will have one day to consider what this means. This does not mean that you cannot retain your identities and that you cannot disagree. It does not mean that one has the power and the other must submit. It means that you must, at the core of you, value the other as being greater than yourself. You must protect the other at the risk of yourself, and you must love the other with a greater love than you have for yourself. These are the terms of the binding you have agreed to."

We stood, our bodies touching, our hands bound, and our eyes locked together. The binding settled in and took hold; I could feel it in the pit of my stomach, a warm spot- a tiny flame. Dani unwound the ribbon from our arms and tucked it away in her gown.

"It is done, my children. May you prosper." She smiled, a soft look of affection on her face as she looked at Aedan, her son. The smile said everything; she loved him and was glad he'd found his peace. She left in a soft rustle of air and a shimmer of silver light.

"Wow," I said as a little tremor ran through me.

"Yes, wow." Aedan agreed.

Our friends and family stood speechless. They had known the Goddess would marry us, but most of them had not felt her power before, not like this. She meant this binding to last, and the thought made me chuckle.

Aedan and I walked into the house, leaving the rest behind. Their part in this was done, and ours was just beginning. He was mine for a year and a day. It's what I agreed to because I had been afraid to make it permanent, but at that moment, I knew a year and a day was never going to be long enough.

Forever isn't long enough to explore this wild, crazy, insatiable love I have for him. I love him with a ferocity that will outlast time itself. I know that. I don't even know why I was stubborn about it, but old habits die hard.

He completes me; he makes the pieces of me a whole thing. He is my Alpha and my Omega. The beginning has been written, and the end will come, but the middle bit? That is where life is lived. And we will live it together.

One man for all time doesn't scare me. Not one bit. Especially when that man is Aedan. Maddeningly infuriating, wickedly sexy, and unerringly strong: he is mine, and I am his for all time. I won't tell him that, though; it will make his big head bigger. Let him sweat it a little. Someone has to keep him in line. He was born of a Goddess and meant to be a King. He married a Faerie Princess. I'll use all my skills to keep him from getting uppity about any of that.

We walk to our room, closing the door behind us. At the end of the handfasting, we will celebrate our marriage with the biggest party the whole world has seen. But tonight? Just him. Just me. I unmake my gown with a thought, baring all that I have and all that I am to him. His eyes pale to the palest of golds, and his fangs descend. I pull the threads of his expensive tuxedo, and my personal God stands before me naked and growling in all his glory.

We fall into each other. For the first time as husband and wife, I know him, and that knowledge is power. The fact that he is my husband and I his wife for all time is freeing. Never before have we shared such pleasure.

The house shakes with our power, the land beneath it quaking, absorbing what we cannot contain.

There is nothing I will not do for him. For us. Does that make me dangerous? You bet it does. They say I am immortal, truly immortal. If I am, then so is Aedan because I will drag him kicking and screaming into eternity with me; I would unmake the world for him.

His lips crash to mine, and my dark thoughts fade to only him. He enters me again, and I can't tell where he ends, and I began. His fangs sink into his favorite spot, and I lean into him, making him take my neck deeper. He groans against my skin, and I come apart, pulling him into the core of me until he follows behind.

Beginnings and endings; both are beautiful.

Epilogue

Aedan

She stands at the edge of forever, the endless ocean spread before her. Soft waves crash, rolling to bow at her feet, as is her due. Shades of blue and white highlight her rare beauty, and her beauty sharpens the loveliness of everything around her. The sand beneath her feet is whiter, and the air she breathes into her lungs is cleaner upon exhalation.

She cycles the power of the mother Gaia through herself at all times now. I do not think it is conscious; I do not know if she realizes it is happening. She strengthens the land every time she steps onto it; that is what she is.

Goddess, how she has changed.

It is like watching a butterfly break free from its shell or a young dragon taking her first flight. She is stunning, hauntingly powerful, and achingly beautiful.

She is my wife.

I would burn the world for her.

The Goddess of Life and the Maker of All Things and I have talked at length about what is to come for Lara. When she was created, she was woven with the power of five and bound in Goddess magic. Infinity was infused into her soul before the zygote first split, and my mother worries it was perhaps a bit much that perhaps she overreached.

I was bound by the Goddess to the Goddess Rising. My existence, my trials, my wars, my enemies, my successes, my failures, my loves, losses, my everything brought me to this. She will need balance. She will need a tether to this plane, or she may transcend it. I will challenge her. I will fight her, fight for her, and fight beside her for all time.

I will be her anchor when the Goddess spirit at her core starts to sift away. She is blooming, growing into something even bigger than The Great Goddess. My mother kissed the first life onto the Earth, and she still walks it today, so I have faith in her council. But even she worries.

Our children will come, and they will ground her. Her friendships will grow, and they will ground her. The responsibility she feels towards those around her will ground her.

And I will ground her.

She went from Human to Faerie Healer; she will go from Faerie Healer to Goddess.

Someday.

Her story is not over and can never be as she is tomorrow into infinity, and I will walk at her side. With the very first gift of her blood, she saved me. She healed me. She healed all the broken parts of me, making me more than Fae and more than vampire. Just as Cerridwen did with her lover on the battlefield all those millennia ago, she created herself a counterbalance, and I take that responsibility seriously.

She is the horizon my sun rises upon, and no being is more loved.

She steps into the water's edge, letting the sea kiss her feet. The water curves toward her, desiring her soft caress.

As do I.

A year and a day have passed. We were to separate yesterday and find one another today. But my Goddess often needs more time to parse her thoughts, so she left our home four days ago to ponder forever. It is not that she does not love me, for I feel the strength and depth of her love, and it is as devastating as it is everlasting. It is not that she fears forever, for her faith in us is unshakable. She simply likes her space, and she shall have it.

Will forever be perfect? Not always. Will forever be without pain and sacrifice? Of course not. But forever will be ours- always ours. There will be great joys and many sorrows, but happiness will endure. For what The Goddess has joined together, no one shall tear asunder.

I step toward her, unwilling and unable to wait another moment. Feeling me, she turns, and the smile that lights her face would bring me to my knees, were I a lesser man, which I am not. I am hers; she is mine, and we are forever one.

Dear Reader,

Whew, what a ride. I hope you liked the end of the Healer Series. For me, it has been a roller coaster of joys, tears, and success. My life started in one headspace and ended in another. If the series touched you, made you smile, or pissed you off, please leave a review; I love reading them. Is this the end of Aedan and Lara? Like Aedan says, they can never end. The Healer Series is over, but Lara is a Goddess Rising, so it's hard to say that we won't hear from her again.

For me? Well, this book took a lot, so I'm going to finish the horse show season with a bang before I start the next one, at least I say that now. Thanks so much for following the series that started it all. I'll get busy on the next book soon, and the cycle begins again.

The Complete Healer Series:
Cerridwen's Tears
Healer
House of Fire
The Scarlet Heron
The Flame Keeper
Goddess Bound

The Eight Series:
Airmed
Ravena
Teagan

Omega Rule Series:
The Omega Rule
The Omega Challenge
An Alpha's Grace

Follow Sharilyn on Facebook, Instagram, Twitter, Goodreads, and her plain old website.

www.sharilynskye.com

www.ingramcontent.com/pod-product-compliance
Lightning Source LLC
Chambersburg PA
CBHW051954240626
47153CB00005B/1748